2¹⁰

THE JUDGMENT...
"A GRIPPING FIRST NOVEL"
—*Boston Globe*

STURDIVANT BACKED AWAY . . . *IF YOU PANIC,*
HE TOLD HIMSELF, *YOU LOSE IT ALL.* . . . *Erase
the fingerprints. Wipe everything.* Heart pounding, he
used his handkerchief to wipe every surface in the foyer
and the living room he might have touched. He put on
his coat, hat and gloves and let himself out.

He started walking toward the service elevator, heard it
open and ran to the stairway exit. He ducked into the
exit—before he saw a tall blond man emerge from the
elevator. . . . It seemed that Lady Luck had smiled on
Judge Sturdivant that night.

It did not smile on the young man who had thought he
was going to have a rendezvous with Andrea Blanchard.

"*THE JUDGMENT* IS PACKED WITH LEGAL
KNOWLEDGE ... ENDING IN A SCENE THAT IS
BOTH HORRIFYING AND FITTING."
—*Library Journal*

"ALL THE INGREDIENTS FOR SUCCESS
ARE HERE: A CRIME OF PASSION, MIXED
MOTIVES, AND FASCINATING CHARACTERS
...A BLOODY AND SHOCKING CONCLUSION."
—*South Bend Tribune*

D1557841

THE JUDGMENT

A NOVEL BY
HOWARD GOLDFLUSS

PUBLISHED BY POCKET BOOKS NEW YORK

This novel is a work of fiction. Names, characters, places and incidents are either the product of the author's imagination or are used fictitiously. Any resemblance to actual events or locales or persons, living or dead, is entirely coincidental.

POCKET BOOKS, a division of Simon & Schuster, Inc.
1230 Avenue of the Americas, New York, N.Y. 10020

Copyright © 1986 by Howard E. Goldfluss
Cover artwork copyright © 1987 Ron Lesser

Published by arrangement with Donald I. Fine, Inc.
Library of Congress Catalog Card Number : 85-81873

ISBN: 0-671-63194-2

First Pocket Books printing March 1987

10 9 8 7 6 5 4 3 2 1

POCKET and colophon are registered trademarks
of Simon & Schuster, Inc.

Printed in the U.S.A.

DEDICATION

To Laura, Lisa, Ellen,
and to David Michael,
who owns us all.

Acknowledgment

Writing a first novel is much like entering a dark tunnel without hope of a light at the end. One needs a lot of help and encouragement, and guidance.

To Frank Weissberg, Judy Shafran, Arnold Goodman, Bernard Geis, Donald Fine and his people, labor leaders Barry Feinstein and Victor Gotbaum, to B.F., to Doris Lilly and Hon. Owen McGivern, and to Al Miele whom I wish I knew longer, and to my colleagues who perform their duties without sacrificing their integrity, and to those I have inadvertently forgotten, I extend my sincere gratitude.

THE JUDGMENT

_____ CHAPTER 1 _____

WE HAVE A verdict."

The court officer made the statement with a sigh of relief, then handed the envelope to the clerk, who called the judge from his chambers.

The courtroom began to fill with those involved in the trial as well as with the curiosity seekers.

Marc Hammond smiled at his client, Ernesto Lopez, patted Lopez's hand. Hammond's smile hid his anxiety. From the time the jury had begun its deliberation fear had grabbed at him. He was frightened at the thought of what a guilty verdict would mean to Ernesto Lopez and to Lopez's family. He knew that if he tried a hundred cases, or a thousand, this moment would always be the bad time, the time when he would doubt himself. _What could I have said in summation that I didn't? What did I forget to ask in cross-examination? What strategies did I use that in retrospect were foolish?_

The "All rise" order was given by the court clerk as the judge entered. Everyone in the courtroom rose, waiting for the judge to be seated. Then the jurors, one by one, solemnly entered the jury box.

Marc Hammond gazed at the words printed in gold letters over the judge's bench: "In God We Trust." He stared at the oak-paneled walls, at the New York State seal prominently displayed and, finally, at his adversary, the assistant district attorney who, probably filled with his own self-doubts, was carefully examining a ballpoint pen.

When the jurors were seated the clerk asked the foreman of the jury to rise. To Marc Hammond, and to every lawyer before or after him, this declaration by the foreman would be not only a verdict of his client's innocence or guilt but a judgment on his own ability as a lawyer.

"Will the defendant please rise?" said the clerk.

Ernesto Lopez stood, visibly trembling. Hammond tried to steady him by holding his arm.

The foreman looked directly at the verdict sheet he held in his hand.

"Mr. Foreman, has the jury reached a verdict?"

"Yes, we have."

"In the one and only count of the indictment charging the defendant with the crime of manslaughter in the first degree, how do you find?"

"We find the defendant not guilty."

Lopez started to collapse, and Hammond held him to prevent him from falling. Lopez's family wailed in relief. The family of the deceased shouted in anger. The court officer saw trouble and moved quickly to usher the two groups out of the courtroom separately.

Marc Hammond felt the tension leave his body but there was an emotional residue. He tried to wipe it away before it could be detected. He walked now into the hall with Lopez. Hammond was tall and thin, in good shape for his thirty-four years. The Lopez family was uniformly short but that did not stop them from reaching up to embrace him.

This case had been assigned Hammond by the court, and while he would have liked to have been paid a sizable fee, he knew this moment of human contact with the Lopez family could not be bought or sold.

From the corner of his eye, Hammond saw a woman angrily staring at him while she waited for the elevator. Her name was Randy Spencer, and she had been a witness for the district attorney. Her testimony had been damaging, but as it turned out, not fatal. She had testified that she had seen Ernesto Lopez hit the deceased in the skull with a wrench, a blow that had been the cause of death. Hammond's brief cross-examination had established only that she had not seen what occurred before she arrived at the scene. While the jury accepted Lopez's plea of self-defense, it was obvious to Marc that Randy Spencer did not. Normally this would not bother him, but there was something about this woman . . . the way she challenged him . . . that made him want to convince her too of his client's innocence.

Of course he had recognized Randy Spencer as soon as she entered the courtroom. As one of the most successful models in New York, he'd seen her face on dozens of magazine covers and television commercials. Undoubtedly instructed by the D.A. to "dress down" so that her appearance would not detract from the importance of her testimony, she wore a dark blue suit over a man-tailored blouse, a simple enough outfit but one that also enhanced her clear blue eyes. Anyway, she couldn't have hidden her beauty if she was draped in a gunny sack.

The elevator door opened and closed. So much for Randy Spencer. Their paths were not likely to cross again. She was part of a young fast New York crowd. Hammond spent most of his time in his office or at social gatherings where the talk was more likely to be about current political events than of the latest fashions in *Vogue*.

Packed into an elevator with a dozen members of the

Lopez family, Hammond couldn't decide if he wanted to go to the office to catch up on the work that had piled up while he was in court or take the rest of the day off. After all, it was the twenty-fourth of December.

When he went outside he saw that what had been a manageable snowfall that morning had turned into a full-fledged storm, and that decided it for him. No more business, no more phone calls. He'd go home and rest up for the Christmas Eve party he was going to that night at the Sweeneys.

As he began walking toward the corner he saw Randy Spencer standing on Centre Street, trying to hail a cab.

I've got to talk to that woman, he thought. I can't let her walk out of my life without at least giving it a shot. I'll never have another chance like this. Besides, it's almost Christmas. Maybe there *will* be a Santa Claus for me . . . He walked toward her. She saw him and turned away.

"Hi," he said, instantly regretting his corniness.

She ignored him as she continued to wave in vain for a cab.

Well, corny or not, he wouldn't give it up. Not this time. He was still on a high from the verdict, feeling that somehow everything he tried would turn out okay.

"I'll be glad to take you wherever you want to go," he said. "You may have to wait here for hours."

She turned to him briefly, then looked away again.

"Oh, come on," he said. "I'm not a total ogre."

She still didn't acknowledge his existence, just stood there, making him feel foolish as he prayed no cab would stop. His luck, it seemed, was holding; the cabs that did pass were all occupied and the wind was really beginning to whip up, blowing fallen snow into deep drifts.

"Tell you what," he said, "I'll get my car. It's across the street in the lot. I'll have to circle the block to get back here. If you're here when I come back, please at least consider my offer. Besides, I'll only charge half-fare."

4

She still said nothing but at least the slight frown was gone. He ran to the lot, paid the attendant and pulled out into the stream of traffic, turning right on a red light, cursing the traffic. When he turned north again on Centre, he saw her. "All *right*." He hit the wheel in his elation. "It *is* my day." He pulled alongside the curb and jumped out on the driver's side, then before he could get to her slipped on the icy sidewalk and landed on his rear. She smiled, then laughed. Falling on his ass was a small price to pay for all that. He brushed himself off and solemnly held the door for her as she entered the car, barely restrained himself from skipping to the driver's side.

"Where to, ma'am?"

"The Plaza," she said, the smile lingering, he noted.

He moved his Honda slowly through the storm, said, "Now, let's get down to basics, Randy Spencer. Why don't you like me?"

"I don't dislike you, Mr. Hammond. You had your job to do and you did it well. What I didn't like was what happened to justice in that courtroom."

Obviously she was sincere. Marc couldn't remember the last time a witness had taken enough interest in a case to come back after testifying to hear the closing arguments and be on hand at the verdict.

"I saw what happened," she went on. "Your client *was* the aggressor."

"It appeared that way to you, I'm sure," he said. "But the law says you have the right to take the initiative when you fear for your life. All I did was prove to the jury's satisfaction that my client acted in justifiable self-defense."

"Is violence ever justified?"

He was not about to argue the merits with this lovely woman. "Well, philosophically you may be right, but the jury has spoken—"

"You manipulated that jury. You were very good, but I suspect the truth was lost somewhere along the way."

He remembered a law professor's advice. "One can never draw a completely accurate picture of the event. Truth is what appeals most logically to the jury. Aim for that." He thought better of repeating that wisdom to Randy Spencer.

"I'll tell you what *is* completely truthful," he said. "I'd like you to come with me to a Christmas Eve party tonight. And I know that asking you under these circumstances is *chutzpah* in the first degree."

"*Chutzpah?* As in unmitigated gall? I'm not a total rube, Mr. Hammond. And anybody in my business who doesn't know a little Yiddish is either an idiot or lying."

She laughed then, a soft laugh that broke the tension and caused Marc Hammond to float in the driver's seat. But not for long.

"I'm afraid, though, that I have other plans for tonight," she said as he pulled up in front of the Plaza Hotel. She got out of the car and stood at the open door, then bent down. "I let an empty cab go by while you were circling the block. I just wanted you to know that." And she shut the door and disappeared into the Plaza lobby.

Hammond couldn't help but feel hopeful as he drove to Seventh Avenue, then north into Central Park. He impulsively parked the car in a lot restricted to Parks Department personnel, got out of the Honda and began walking in the snow. This was a special twenty-four hours and he wanted to savor what was left of it. It was a day to win a case. It was a day to watch the wind and the snow and the ice carve a winter's scene on the trees in the heart of the city. It was a day to get his feet soaking wet and still not catch a cold. It was a day to meet a smart beautiful woman. It was a day when ridiculous dreams could happen, when everything went right. All in all a day to etch on his memory, because for sure they didn't come along that often.

───── CHAPTER 2 ─────

THE WEATHER FORECASTERS had predicted light snow flurries, and they were wrong, as usual, Benny Rabe was thinking. This was a *major* storm. Beginning with a few flakes just before midnight, three inches of snow had covered the ground by morning. Aided by the high winds, half a foot had fallen by five P.M. Benny Rabe left the Cadillac to wipe snow off the windshield, found that ice had frozen the wipers to the glass.

He looked across the sweeping lawn. Large oak trees surrounded the enormous house like sentinels painted white by the snow. The boss had been in there for over an hour. Benny hoped the conference would end soon. He didn't much like the sight of the patches of ice forming on the road.

For some reason, probably the direction of the wind, the sign in front of the car was not obscured by the snow. Benny squinted to read the words: "DELAFIELD AVENUE— FIELDSTON—NO TRESPASSING—PUBLIC PARKING PROHIBITED—AREA IS PATROLLED AND PARKED

VEHICLES WILL BE TOWED AT OWNER'S EX-
PENSE—VIOLATORS WILL BE PROSECUTED—
FIELDSTON PROPERTY OWNER'S ASSN., INC."

Benny had to laugh. The boss, Charlie Sweeney, would
never live in this fancy community, although God knew he
could afford it. Benny Rabe went back with Charlie Sweeney to the time when Charlie was district leader of the old
Comanche Club on the Lower East Side. Benny had been
hired then as Sweeney's driver and general gofer. As things
turned out, Benny had hitched his wagon to a superstar;
Charlie had eventually become state chairman of the party.
No question, Charlie Sweeney controlled the organization
in New York State.

Benny was sure that this exclusive section of Riverdale
would not appeal to Charlie. Charlie would still be living
in Queens if Peg hadn't insisted on moving into Manhattan
to an apartment on Park Avenue. Peg had all she could do
to see to it that her husband, courted by senators and presidents, lived in an appropriate neighborhood. Charlie didn't
care about where he lived. All he cared about was the party.

Benny saw the front door of the big house—mansion,
really—open. Sweeney, a bald overweight man of medium
height, shook hands with someone standing in the shadow
of the doorway, then walked briskly down the long twisting
path to the car and got in beside Benny. "Son-of-a-bitch,"
said the party chairman, "this blow looks like it's going to
go on forever. Some Christmas Eve. Let's get the hell out
of here."

Benny moved the car slowly toward the Henry Hudson
Parkway.

"Which way, Charlie?"

"Better get home. Peg will have my head if I'm not there
when the company comes."

Benny drove into the southbound entrance to the Parkway,
and after some minutes Sweeney broke the silence. "I just

8

offered the party backing for the gubernatorial nomination to Allen Sturdivant."

"I guessed that," Benny said.

"Did you also guess that I don't like that son of a bitch? I tell ya, it's not because he was born rich. I've known other old money guys, guys like Herbie Lehman, Ave Harriman. They would have had the same class if they'd been born poor."

"What about his uncle, the governor?"

"Wes Sturdivant used to walk around with his nose in the sky like he was smellin' manure, but he was a stand-up guy. He always did the right thing as far as the party was concerned, never broke his word. I was sorry to see Wes go. But this guy—I just don't know." Sweeney paused to light a cigarette, inhaled deeply. Forty years of chain-smoking had taken its toll on his voice, leaving it sounding as if it were being strained through gravel. He had tried to give up the cigarettes and the Irish whisky for Peg, but he just couldn't. They were too much a part of him.

He slowly inhaled, then went on, "Ya know, in the five terms Allen Sturdivant was a congressman all I ever got from our people in his district was complaints, but he still held the district for us. The s.o.b. could never be beaten at the polls. The voters love him. When he left for the state court we lost the district to a woman reformer."

"Well, that's why you want him, isn't it?" Benny said.

Sweeney nodded. "With all the money, and the family background, and the million dollar smile, we can take the election. The son-of-a-bitch was even an All-American—from Dartmouth. Jesus, the guy's got it all."

"Then what's bothering you, Charlie?"

Sweeney put his cigarette out in the ashtray with angry little jabs. "I don't know if we can trust him."

"Think he'll screw the party on patronage once he's in?"

"Maybe. But the county chairmen all went for him—all

9

except Jonny Klyk. And I can understand Jonny's position. Sturdivant isn't a team player now, and Jonny doesn't think he'll be any better if he's elected. And that's the problem. Maybe Jonny's right and *we're* wrong. Jonny's always been able to size up people. That's how he got to be mayor of the great city of Buffalo."

"What are you going to do, Charlie?"

"Go with Sturdivant. We've been on the outside for eight years. That's too damn long. Sturdivant's our best shot. And I'm betting he'll come to understand that he needs us to win—that officeholders aren't created through immaculate conception. He'll be obligated to us when he wins, just like everyone else."

They were silent until they reached the tollbooth, where Benny gave the toll collector a token and moved the car slowly onto the Parkway. The tires slid on the icy road, Benny straightened the wheel and the car crawled forward. "You know what worries me?" Benny said. "We've been together for over thirty years now. I've seen you wrong about elections, and wrong about issues. But you've never been wrong about people. If you've got doubts about this guy, then I got to worry."

Sweeney didn't reply. Each kept to his own thoughts as the big Cadillac crawled toward the city through the snow.

Justice Allen Sturdivant of the Supreme Court of the State of New York, and future gubernatorial candidate, placed a call to his wife at their home in Palm Beach. Loren was eager to learn if he was being given the party's endorsement. Sturdivant knew it was not because of mutual love, or even mutual regard; both had disappeared years ago. In truth, the fact that her husband was going to be governor of New York—and there was no doubt in Loren's mind that this was going to happen if the party tapped him—fulfilled her own ambitions. Loren Phillips Sturdivant wanted the pres-

10

tige and the power that would go to the wife of a man who held high office.

Their relations were always superficially pleasant, whether at their home in Riverdale, or if she was visiting him at their suite at the Carlyle Hotel in New York, or he with her when he flew down to Palm Beach in his private plane. The arrangement didn't upset Sturdivant. Loren, with her Grace Kelly good looks and impeccable family tree, was the model wife for a man with political aspirations. Their marriage of convenience suited him well. Especially since he had one of the most exciting women in the world as his mistress.

After speaking with Loren and the children, Sturdivant crossed the room to the bar and poured himself a Scotch. Continuing his relationship with Andrea Blanchard wasn't going to be possible now. It had to end, no matter how much he regretted it. Andrea wasn't going to be too happy about it either, but he couldn't let even Andrea compromise his chances of becoming governor. He'd worked too long for it, and he'd be a good governor . . . it was in the family blood . . .

Sturdivant thought of how offering him the party's backing must have stuck in Charlie Sweeney's craw, and felt better. Sweeney knew that he wouldn't take orders from him or any of the other party faithful after the election. Or at least ought to know.

Sturdivant knew his own value, and how desperate the party was, and that he was the only one in the state who could take the incumbent George Beale. He regretted, though, that Uncle Wes wasn't alive to see another Sturdivant in the governor's mansion.

Regret was compounded when he thought of Andrea. He walked to the window and listened to the staccato sound of sleet pelting the glass. He was jumpy. He poured himself another Scotch, drank it quickly and felt its effect almost immediately, having eaten almost nothing since morning.

He stopped in front of the mirror over the fireplace and addressed the tall, broad-shouldered image of himself, as if it were the most natural thing for him to do. "You damn fool," he said, "you should have ended it last year when you realized she was getting too involved. And maybe you too, to be honest . . . You just can't afford her."

He walked away from the mirror. Andrea had filled a deep void, and the very thought of cutting off the relationship had been painful—impossible—until today. He had to do it, and now.

Much as he was taken by Andrea, he also knew she could be bitchy. He'd seen that side of her when she thought she had been crossed in some way. His stomach churned. She *could* stop him from running. She knew every gossip columnist in town. She not only made news, she *was* news. Her two sensational divorces had been endlessly covered by the media. She had walked away from her first divorce with a title she never used, and from her second with two million of her Arab sheik's petrodollars that she did use.

Sturdivant felt suddenly weary. It had been a long day. He eased his six-foot frame into an overstuffed chair. The servants were away for the Christmas holiday and the big empty house was dark now. The only sound was the wind blowing the sleet outside, which lulled him into a fitful sleep . . .

He was at his induction ceremony. The judge was asking him to raise his hand to take the oath of office. Loren and the children were standing proudly at his side. ". . . And I will uphold the Constitution of the United States and of the State of New York . . ." He looked at Loren, but it was Andrea laughing. Loren was gone, his daughters were gone, everyone had gone. He was alone on the podium with Andrea . . .

It seemed that he had just nodded for a moment, but a glance at the radiated dial of his watch told him that he had

12

slept for several hours. It was late, almost eleven. Yet, he decided, before the news of the party's backing became public, he had better see Andrea. He felt panic. He had no plan, hadn't even the vaguest idea of how he was going to tell her . . .

He stood up and began pacing in front of the fireplace. Do it . . . there was no other way.

He reached for the phone and dialed her number. The familiar voice answered.

"Andrea?" Who else would it be. For some reason he was whispering. "It's Allen, I'd like to see you tonight . . ."

"Where are you, darling? Don't you know there's a blizzard out there?"

"I'm home but I can be there in an hour."

". . . Allen, I'm pretty beat. Tomorrow would be better. Why don't we meet at the—"

"No, I'm sorry, this can't wait. I'm leaving now."

He hung up and moved quickly to his upstairs study. Taking a key from his pocket, he opened the bottom drawer of his desk and removed a wide-brimmed gray fedora. He put it on, working it down and around to cover his thick black hair. He also took out of the drawer a pair of dark-tinted glasses with large black horn-rim frames. The hat and glasses were props and, as foolish as they always made him feel, they did serve as a disguise when he visited Andrea. In this get-up he doubted even his own wife would notice him if they passed on the street.

He slipped on a light-gray tweed raincoat, pulling the collar high up around his neck. He took the phone off the hook. The news of his selection had probably been released by now and the calls would come when the media had a chance to confirm it. The news could come from hundreds

13

of sources, not the least being Loren, who would waste no time in heralding what she would consider *her* latest achievement.

At least a busy signal would indicate he was at home. Otherwise he'd have one terrible time explaining why, on Christmas Eve, he was out in a raging storm past midnight.

CHAPTER 3

DELAFIELD AVENUE WAS a sheet of ice and the Parkway little better. The storm was full-blown now and Sturdivant realized that negotiating his Mercedes into Manhattan would be risky. He certainly couldn't afford to get stuck. He got off the Parkway at the Kappock Street exit and drove east to the Deegan. With low visibility he slowly proceeded to the Yankee Stadium exit, then parked his car behind the courthouse on Walton Avenue. As he headed for the subway a lone cruising cab turned the corner from 161st Street. He signaled the driver, who opened his window and yelled that he was calling it a night. Sturdivant showed him three ten-dollar bills and the driver showed a willingness to change his mind. Sturdivant handed the driver the money, told him to take him to Columbus Circle and sat back in the seat. He reached into his coat pocket for the two keys he had placed there—one opened the door to Andrea's apartment, the other a gate that guarded the rear entrance of the apartment building. The owners used this security measure because the house had been hit too often by burglars. Andrea

15

had managed to charm the key from the superintendent and had had a few copies made, one of which she had given to Sturdivant. The gate led into an alleyway, which in turn led directly to the service elevator. He had been visiting her this way for three years . . . well, at least this foolish cloak-and-dagger game would soon be over. He was, he realized, reaching for straws.

As they neared Columbus Circle Sturdivant directed the cabbie to drop him off at the corner of 59th Street. He waited until the cab drove off, crossed the nearly deserted circle and walked north on Central Park West to 63rd Street. The snow was sticking to the city streets but fortunately it was not nearly as deep as it had been in Riverdale.

The gate to Andrea's building stood fifty feet from the corner. Using his key, Sturdivant opened the gate, then locked it behind him and made his way through the darkness to the service elevator, pushed the button that opened it, then pushed the button marked eleven. The elevator moved directly to Andrea's floor. He walked to her apartment and, using the second key, opened the door.

The apartment was really a museum of the acquisitions of Andrea Blanchard—the spoils of victory, so to speak, of her matrimonial wars, as well as the treasures she had accumulated during years of jetting around the world. The walls were covered with originals by Cézanne, Matisse, Renoir. A prized impressionist work by Edouard Manet that had been purchased ten years before by her second husband for $350,000 was easily worth a million now. The sculptured pieces included classic Greek marble, Aztec stone and contemporary limestone.

Andrea entered the foyer from the living room. Even now, when he knew that he had to break with her, he felt mesmerized by her. It was difficult to ignore those literally sky-blue eyes set in an exquisitely shaped face, or her raven-colored hair, or her near-perfect yet piquant body. The overall impact was only slightly diminished by the fact that she was, obviously, drunk.

She saw him now and steadied herself, took a long drag on her cigarette, then slowly released the smoke in a strong smooth stream. "Well, the Honorable Allen Sturdivant, Justice of the Supreme Court. In God we trust. Aren't those the words over the bench? In Sturdivant we trust. Except Justice Sturdivant wears a hat pulled down over his face and phony glasses, so how trustworthy can he be?"

Clearly she was going to be even more difficult to deal with than he'd expected. He put his hat and coat in the hall closet and followed her into the living room, then guided her onto the couch and sat down beside her.

"Andrea, please listen. I have to talk to you . . ."

She looked at him with glazed eyes, said nothing, only ground out her cigarette in a crystal ashtray on the coffee table.

"What I've to say is difficult. Very difficult. We've had so much together. The past few years have been a part of my life that I'll never forget—that I don't ever want to forget . . ." He paused to gauge the effect of his words. She didn't give him the opportunity; she stood up, turned her back to him and poured herself a drink. When she faced him her eyes glinted with anger. "Look, Allen, I have a problem, which you should be familiar with. I'm allergic to bullshit. You want to deep-six me because Charlie Sweeney told you that you've got the party's nod. Correct, darling?"

He froze.

"Surprised?" Her voice ascended two octaves. "Allen, do you really imagine I don't know what's going on in this town?" She took a long pull on her drink. "I can't say I care much for your timing—giving me the gate on Christmas Eve, and all. You really are a son-of-a-bitch . . ." There were tears, which she quickly tried to wipe away.

17

"Let me give you, as they say in the boardrooms, the bottom line, Allen. I'm not going to *let* you run for governor. For all this time I've played by your rules. I've been totally discreet. No one knows about us, not even my friends. Not a peep from Andrea. Well, no more. I've decided I'm not ready to give you up. *Nor* do I intend to stay in the background. No more backstreet for Andrea. All clear, Allen?"

Allen Sturdivant saw the governorship, the service he genuinely felt he had prepped all his life to provide, going down the drain. Yes, he felt rotten about this, but what was it Kennedy had said . . . life *is* unfair. And wasn't he being too hard on himself? After all, the relationship hadn't been all one-sided. And Andrea wasn't exactly an innocent, yet here she was living out the old saw about hell hath no fury like a woman scorned . . . He moved toward her, wondering if there was any way to reason with her. "Andrea, please, you can't do this—"

"Can't I? One phone call to Sweeney and, my man, you're dead. As you know, I'm a collector, Allen, and you happen to be an item that I'm not ready to discard. So just stand by, lover, and *I'll* tell *you* when it's over." She wondered how she could sound so tough and feel so weak.

Hell hath no fury . . . he had never seen her like this.

She took another swallow of her drink and put the empty glass on the table. "You know, Allen, as long as I can remember nobody ever *gave* me a damn thing. Everything I have in this world I've had to scratch and claw for—with one natural resource, my body beautiful. I've been used and abused by men since I was fifteen. Women's lib can't wipe *that* out. I thought maybe I had finally found a man who was different. But it seems, Your Honor, you're not different at all. I really should have known better." She took a deep breath. "Well, Allen, it's like this . . . I'm going to make one New Year's resolution. I'm going to do the people of the great State of New York a huge favor—I'm going to save them from *you*." She crossed the room to a mahogany end table and picked up the telephone receiver. "And now, Your Honor, kindly get the fuck out of here—"

It came in a rush, as if he was propelled by a force detached and outside himself. An irresistible force . . . He took a step forward, grabbed at the receiver. She broke free of him, started dialing. He saw what was written on the piece of paper she was holding—*Charlie Sweeney EN 9-4411*. His hands encircled her neck. She stopped dialing, tried to scream. He didn't hear. He didn't see the fear that had replaced the anger in her eyes. He wasn't familiar with the cold fury that took him over, his hands were a stranger's, operating on their own, forming a stronger and tighter noose around her neck—tighter even after her body became limp and could no longer offer resistance. His mind said stop but those hands held the still body in a viselike grip, until, finally, his consciousness did take over, the hands released her, she dropped to the floor.

As she did she knocked into the coffee table. The ashtray and whisky glass slid to the floor beside her body.

Sturdivant backed away and sat on the end of the couch, looking down at her. Minutes passed before he moved. *If you panic,* he told himself, some part of his brain functioning clearly on its own, *you lose it all, you gain nothing. Erase the fingerprints. Wipe everything.* Heart pounding, he used his handkerchief to wipe every surface in the foyer and the living room that he might have touched. He began to reach for the ashtray and glass, changed his mind. He hadn't touched either of them. He searched the floor for any evidence of his presence, carefully inspected the couch. Using the handkerchief as a guard against prints, he opened the closet, put on his coat, hat and gloves and let himself out.

He started walking toward the service elevator, heard it open and ran to the stairway exit. He ducked into the exit—

but not before he saw a tall blond man emerge from the service elevator. He wasn't sure if the man had seen him, but no matter, he assured himself, the brim of his hat was pulled down low over his face. What was there to see? He ran down the eleven flights of stairs to the basement and, breathing heavily now, proceeded to the outer gate that guarded the service entrance. He was surprised to find the gate open. He must have forgotten to lock it. He would be sure to lock it behind him now.

Once on Central Park West he walked south to the Independent Subway station at Columbus Circle. With the exception of the blond man who had gotten out of the elevator on the eleventh floor, no one else had seen him. He checked his watch: twelve-fifteen A.M. Christmas Day. He boarded the D train, and in less than an hour had picked up his car at the Bronx County Court House and was on the way home to Riverdale.

It seemed that Lady Luck had smiled on Justice Allen Sturdivant that night.

She did not smile on the young man who had thought he was going to have a rendezvous with Andrea Blanchard.

CHAPTER 4

IT WAS NOT just the sex that Peter Jorgensen enjoyed in his late night encounters with Andrea Blanchard. She also offered him good liquor, the best Mexican gold he had ever smoked, and even some laughs. When she had called him at eleven-thirty he had been asleep. She said she was calling to wish him a merry Christmas. She had sounded drunk—and lonely. The storm was still bad but he decided to pay her a surprise visit.

Peter had showered and dressed quickly, and once in his '71 Chevy was alert and eager, anticipating the evening ahead.

The snow had not hardened enough to block him in and so he had managed to pull out of the parking lot. The light from the street lamp shining on the fresh snow had given Sullivan Street the look of a Currier & Ives print. It was one of the few times that Peter had seen the street look pretty.

It had begun between Peter Jorgensen and Andrea Blanchard when Peter's mother, who did domestic work for

Andrea, asked him one rainy night to come to Andrea's apartment to pick her up. When his mother introduced Peter to Andrea, he thought that he had never seen a woman as beautiful. The attraction, on a physical level, had been mutual. Peter was a classic Scandinavian—tall, blond, blue-eyed.

The following day Andrea had called him. She told him that she had a few electrical appliances that needed fixing. Peter suspected that Miss Blanchard had other fixings in mind, but nothing happened then or on another occasion when she needed repairs. It was not until the night of one of her parties when she called him to fill in for a bartender that a sexual relationship began, and after that night she called him at least twice a month. She swore him to secrecy, and no one, not even his mother, ever knew about them. Peter knew it for what it was. A good time in bed for them both. Good time? It was perfect.

This would be the first time he had visited her without an invitation, but it would be okay, he could tell by her voice that she needed him. As young and unsophisticated as he was, Peter instinctively knew that one of the reasons Andrea was attracted to him was the need to hold back the clock, or at least deny it. She used his attraction to her to reaffirm her own still potent attractiveness. Actually, it didn't really matter to Peter what her reasons were . . . The lady knew more things to do in bed than any female of any age he'd ever dated.

Peter was whistling as he parked his car on Central Park West and walked to the service entrance. This was going to be one *great* Christmas Eve . . . He grinned in anticipation of leaving the cold night and entering a warm bed and an even warmer body as he used the key Andrea had given him to open the gate and enter the building.

When the elevator reached the eleventh floor, he was startled to see a blurred figure in a tweed coat and a wide-brimmed hat turn and rush toward the stairway exit. At first Peter was merely surprised, then suspicious. He walked toward the exit door and opened it. He saw nothing but heard the sound of footsteps down the metal staircase. He felt uneasy, his anticipation of a moment ago abruptly gone. He turned toward Andrea's apartment, rang the bell. Rang once, waited, rang again. No response.

He used the key she had given him to open the door, took a few steps into the apartment—and saw Andrea Blanchard lying face up on the floor of the living room. Her neck was twisted, her eyes were open, staring straight ahead. He ran to her and kneeled, putting his ear to her chest. No heartbeat. No pulse.

Dead? He could not accept it at first. This incredibly warm and passionate woman? He half-expected her to open her eyes, to laugh at the gruesome joke she was playing on him. He touched her face. He held her, still hoping for a response. Only then did the realization of her death hit him with all its impact. Yes, this was Andrea Blanchard, and she was dead.

He felt a real sorrow, and sudden fear. He picked up the phone, dialed 911. The danger in *that* hit him before the connection was made and he slammed the phone back onto its cradle. Who did he think he was calling? The police. But how was he going to convince the police that he and a woman like Andrea Blanchard had an affair going? No one had ever seen them together. Were the police going to believe that he had come here in a snowstorm to surprise her after midnight on Christmas Eve? Or that he had seen someone run from Andrea's door, someone he couldn't identify except to say that he wore a tweed coat and a hat pulled over his face? How was he going to convince them that he hadn't killed her—that he had found her dead?

They wouldn't believe him. He panicked. He had to get out—out of the apartment and out of the building. He left her as he'd found her, ran out the front door to the service elevator, which was still at the floor, pressed the button for the basement. He ran to the gate, to his horror found it locked. He had opened it and left it open just minutes before. Someone had closed it since then. That someone knew he was there, could be watching him even now.

He fumbled for the key to the gate but his key ring, with all his keys, was gone. Where? He leaped onto the gate, pulling himself to the top by the pointed bars. He tried to let himself down slowly but his hand could not grip the cold metal surface, which was iced over. He lost his hold and tumbled to the pavement, the full weight of his body coming down on his left foot. A hot, searing pain instantly ripped through his ankle, so severe that he had to cry out. He made a frenzied attempt to get up and run but his ankle gave way and he collapsed, paralyzed, in the snow.

Dave Darby, born and raised in Corn Hill, Alabama, and Joe Lawrence, a product of the Harlem ghetto, were New York City cops, partners who, as a result of being cooped up together eight hours daily in a patrol car, had formed a strong bond of mutual friendship and respect.

That Christmas Eve—actually Christmas Day—they had started their patrol shortly after midnight. They were perhaps the only two people that night who welcomed the storm. Any collars made during the midnight tour could mean a court appearance the following day. Since they both had the next two days off, they weren't looking for any problems. A nice stormy night like this kept the bad guys off the streets, not to mention their victims.

Joe Lawrence brushed the snow from the sideview mirror as the car inched down Central Park West and turned into 63rd Street, where Darby stopped it. Reflected in the lamp light they saw the body of a young man falling to the ground from the top of the fence of a luxury high-rise. They had a collar on their hands for Christmas, whether they liked it or not.

"Son-of-a-bitch." They said it almost in unison. One of them had to take this collar, which meant one of them would have to go through the arrest procedure well into Christmas morning.

Lawrence cursed again. He left the car and grabbed the young man by the scruff of the neck while he was trying to run off, then pushed him over to the patrol car. The sudden pressure on the young man's ankle radiated a pain through his leg and he cried out. Joe Lawrence was not impressed.

"Stand up, you son-of-a-bitch. Put your hands on the hood of the car."

Peter gingerly let his foot touch the ground. Lawrence frisked him, then pushed him into the back of the patrol car.

Darby remained behind the wheel. Lawrence sat in the back and flashed his light into Peter Jorgensen's face. Lawrence could see that the kid was hurting—he was pale, and in spite of the cold his face was covered with perspiration.

"What's the matter with you?"

"I think I broke my ankle. Jesus, it *hurts*."

"Tough shit," Lawrence said. "You get hurt trying to rip off a building and you want us to feel sorry for you? Now listen up. You have the right to remain silent. You have the right to a lawyer. If you can't afford a lawyer you will be provided one free of charge. You have the right to consult with a lawyer before you say anything. Anything you say to me can be used against you at your trial. Do you understand?"

Peter did not hear him, much less understand him. His ankle was now swollen to double its normal size. "Please, take me to a hospital. *Please*, I can't stand the pain—"

"What were you doing in that building?" Lawrence pressed.

"If I answer your questions will you take me to the hospital?"

"Let's put it this way, the longer it takes you to tell me the truth, the longer it'll take to get you to the hospital."

Peter told his story through teeth clenched against the pain. "I'm a mechanic. I was looking for some tools or spare parts or anything I could cop in that basement. Once I got in there I realized how stupid I was so I tried to get out by climbing over the fence. The metal was covered with ice and I couldn't hold onto it and I fell . . ."

"How'd you get in?"

"The same way, climbed over the fence."

Joe Lawrence had made too many arrests to buy it. The kid was hurt real bad, no question, but his story rang phony.

"All right, we'll take you to the precinct. After we book you and you sign a statement of what you just told us we'll take you to Bellevue."

Peter nodded.

"Are you a junkie?"

"No. A little grass, never the hard stuff. Never."

"Where do you work?"

"At the Venner Garage, West 72nd Street. They're open twenty-four hours. Nick Venner's my boss—he'll be there at eight in the morning or you can check by calling there now."

"You sure you weren't going to hit an apartment?"

Peter remembered with some relief that he now had neither of the keys that Andrea had given him. "How could I do that?" he asked. "I have no passkey—no tools—nothing."

"Ever been busted before?"

"No."

Lawrence shook his head. The kid didn't make sense. A

mechanic would know that expensive tools would be locked away or hidden. Something else bothered Lawrence. How the hell could the kid see anything without a searchlight or a lamp? He turned to his partner.

"Dave, ask the superintendent to look around the basement and then bring him back to look at our friend."

Darby left the car while Lawrence stayed in the rear seat with Peter. Lawrence knew full well the pain of a busted ankle. He remembered when he was fourteen years old and he tripped over first base trying to run out a scratch hit. His ankle turned and fractured, and he still remembered the sound as the bone broke—like a pistol shot. He never forgot that sound, and he never forgot that pain.

"What's your name?" Lawrence asked.

"Peter Jorgensen."

"Address?"

"One hundred twenty Sullivan Street."

"Any ID?"

"In my wallet. Can you reach over? It's in my rear pocket. I can't move my leg."

Lawrence removed the wallet and flashed his light on its contents: driver's license, registration card, union card and seventy-seven dollars. He replaced the wallet. "Look, Jorgensen, as soon as my partner comes back I'm taking you to the precinct where I'll book and print you and then I'll take you to Bellevue like I promised. I know you haven't told me the whole story but I can't prove it. If you don't tell me the truth now, it might be tougher for you later."

"I told you the truth," Peter said weakly.

Joe Lawrence shrugged. They sat in silence until Darby returned with the superintendent, who told them that nothing had been taken or disturbed. The superintendent took a good look at Peter and told them that he had never seen him before. Lawrence advised the superintendent that he would have to sign a complaint at the Criminal Court later that

27

day, then he and Darby drove Peter Jorgensen to the precinct, where he was charged with burglary.

Lawrence typed the police report and a statement that he had Peter sign. The statement was a full and complete confession, but Peter did not even look at it. He scratched his name on the line. Lawrence asked him if he wanted to make a phone call.

"No, officer, I don't want to make a phone call. I don't want anything but to get to a hospital. *Please . . .*"

Lawrence moved quickly through the remaining formalities of the arrest, then took Peter to Bellevue, where X-rays of his ankle revealed multiple fractures. The attending physician set the ankle in a plaster cast that extended to Peter's left knee. Peter was supplied with crutches, brought back to the precinct and put in a detention cell until he could be taken to the Criminal Court.

"According to the prints this *is* your first bust," Lawrence told him. "You'll probably be released on your own recognizance. It's a burglary charge now, but unless I miss my guess, they'll plea bargain it down to a trespass. You'll get a fine and time to pay it, and you'll be out for what's left of Christmas." He looked hard at Peter for a minute. "You were up to no good tonight. I don't believe your story, but with that broken ankle and all, I guess you got more than you bargained for. I won't be seeing you again unless you plead not guilty and go to trial. Officer Darby will take you to court as soon as the transport arrives. Good-by, Jorgensen."

Joe Lawrence walked out of the precinct and pulled the collar of his coat around his neck. Dave Darby, like the good friend and partner he was, took the collar. Still, Lawrence resented the inconvenience that his partner was being put through. *Screw this Jorgensen,* he thought. *He got what he deserved. I'm not going to feel sorry for him. He loused us both up.* He checked his watch. Eight-thirty A.M., thirty minutes into his time. It was bitter cold, but it *was* Christmas weather. The snow was still falling lightly and the sky was lead gray. He eased his car out of the alley and began humming "White Christmas," smiling now as he thought of his own particular joy in spending this holiday with his wife and the kids.

_____ CHAPTER 5 _____

AT 8:30 A.M. ON December 25th, as she did every weekday, Helen Jorgensen opened the door to Andrea Blanchard's apartment. She had intended to use her key but did not have to; the door was open. She shook her head in exasperation. She had often warned Miss Andrea about the danger of not locking the door.

Helen hung her coat in the large hall closet and placed her galoshes and umbrella in the rack, carefully seeing to it that no water fell on the lush cream-colored carpeting. She was about to enter a small room off the foyer where she kept her uniform when her attention was drawn to an object on the rug in front of the couch in the living room. Her eyesight was failing, and she walked closer to the couch. When she realized she was looking at Andrea Blanchard's body, she indulged her first impulse: she screamed.

Then she knelt to the floor and took Andrea's head onto her lap. She rubbed Andrea's arms. The skin was cold. When the fact that Andrea was dead penetrated her mind, Helen screamed again—not out of fear but anguish. Andrea

Blanchard had been a kind and generous employer. Their relationship had existed for many years. Helen sobbed, rocking back and forth, holding Andrea's head to her bosom as if that movement could bring her back to life. Finally she placed Andrea's head on a pillow she pulled down from the couch. She closed Andrea's eyes.

Helen reached for the phone and dialed 911.

"Police Operator two-thirty-two. Where is the emergency?"

Helen tried to speak but words wouldn't come.

"Police Operator two-thirty-two. Where is the emergency?" the voice repeated.

"I . . . want to report a—" she could not finish.

"Look, madam, I can't help you unless you talk to me."

"An accident—no, not an accident. My employer. I think she's dead. It looks like she was strangled. There are red marks around her neck."

"What's your name?"

"Helen Jorgensen."

"What's the address you're calling from?"

"Monte Carlo Apartments, Sixty-third Street and Central Park West."

"What's the name of the victim?"

"Andrea Blanchard."

The operator paused. *"The* Andrea Blanchard?"

"Yes."

The operator picked up the tempo of the conversation. "What time did you discover her?"

"A few minutes ago."

"What apartment?"

"Eleven-G."

"Stay where you are. Don't touch anything. Police officers will be there in five minutes."

Helen hung up the phone. While she waited for the police

31

she prayed for the soul of Andrea Blanchard. And she prayed for the Lord to punish whoever it was who had killed her.

Operator 232 in the communications room at police head-quarters notified the 20th precinct and the Manhattan North Homicide of Helen Jorgensen's call. Then she asked her supervisor for an early coffee break, quickly grabbed her coat, left the building, and crossed Police Plaza. She stepped into a public telephone booth in the Municipal Building and dialed a number she had dialed many times before. She heard the phone ring at the other end but there was no response.

"Pick it up, damn you, pick it up, I only have five minutes—" In her frustration she hit the phone booth with her palm.

Finally a voice answered. "All World Media."

"I'd like to talk to Tom McPartland, very important."

"Hold it."

She heard the background noise of a busy newsroom. "Hello, hello? What did you do, forget me?" Finally she heard him.

"McPartland."

"Tom," she said. "This is Gabby Gertie."

Tom McPartland's interest picked up at hearing the code name of one of his "reliable sources." Christmas did not bode well for earth-shattering news, he badly needed something for the evening broadcast. "Hi, Gabby Gertie. Good to hear you. What do you have?"

"Dynamite, and I'm giving you an exclusive. But we gotta agree on terms first."

McPartland shook his head. Damned informants were getting more expensive all the time. But Gertie was one of his best. You couldn't do much better than a 911 operator.

"If I use it, fifty," he said.

"If you use it, one hundred."

"Hey, Gertie, you're holding me up. That's not nice."

"Bullshit. Every time I do this I put my job on the line. For all I know I'm committing a misdemeanor. I tell you, this is worth a hundred. Don't mess with me, I've got three mouths to feed and it's Christmas."

"Okay, Gertie. Shoot."

"Andrea Blanchard was found dead by her maid. Could be homicide. Just came in, not five minutes ago. I took the call. The maid says possible strangulation."

McPartland tried to tamp down his excitement. "What's the address?"

"Monte Carlo Apartments. Central Park West and Sixty-third."

"What's the maid's name?"

"Helen Jorgensen."

"Good-by, Gabby Gertie, I'll see you tonight after the six o'clock news. Same place. We'll have a drink on Christmas."

Gertie laughed for the first time since she took the 911 call. "As long as you're buyin'."

Less than a minute after Gertie's call, regular programming of radio and television outlets of All World Media was interrupted by a bulletin in which Tom McPartland delivered the news that Andrea Blanchard, "The Playgirl of the Western World," had been found dead. Apparently strangled.

At 9 A.M. Peter Jorgensen was helped into the police van, then started on the long journey to 100 Centre Street. The storm had moderated, but because over a foot of snow had accumulated the van didn't reach the Criminal Court building until 11 A.M.

Using his crutches, and with some help from the officers, Peter was herded into the detention cells behind the AR-1 Courtroom. AR-1 was the arraignment part, located on the Baxter Street side of the massive building that housed the

Criminal Term of the Supreme Court and the Criminal Court. The detention pens being behind the AR-1 courtroom made it convenient for the correction officers and police officers to deliver the bodies to the court. Otherwise, since the arraignment parts were located on the first floor of the building, they would have had to cross the lobby, which was constantly filled with people who had an interest in the proceedings. Pimps, prostitutes, defendants—as well as their families, friends and bondsmen—police officers, and retirees who had nothing else to do made up the knot of humanity that was in constant movement, ebbing and flowing along the corridors.

Not all of the lobby's habitués ever entered the courtroom. The drunks, for example, were left undisturbed to sleep it off on the imported marble floors of the lobby at 100 Centre Street. No one approached them; the custodial staff wouldn't get involved with them; they were too occupied with working on water leaks and falling plaster and faulty boilers and halfhearted attempts to keep the building clean. The police wouldn't soil their hands with them, and the court officers would be "working out of title" if they were called on to remove these eyesores from the sacred halls of justice. So the drunks, unless they got obstreperous, were left alone to become part of the mosaic.

The outstanding hangers-on were the pimps. They dressed like peacocks, with their multicolored spacesuits, four-inch-heeled shoes, white fur collars and wide-brimmed Stetsons. The corridors of the lobby were their domain. A pimp wouldn't let the fact that he was fifty feet from a courtroom deter him from cuffing a girl in punishment for getting herself caught. He enjoyed immunity, because even if he hit her in the presence of a police officer the cop would only be wasting his time in making the arrest. There was no chance that the girl would sign a complaint or testify against her pimp. A bizarre scene.

Peter Jorgensen had been placed in a detention cell with twenty prostitutes, transvestites, burglars and dope-sellers—part of the sum total of the police department's Christmas Eve productivity. He saw that in the other cells there were as many as fifty "holdovers" who had not made night court. Could be worse, he told himself. Could have twice as many dirty bodies crammed into the cell.

Peter had received medication when his ankle was put in the cast, but the effect of the drug was beginning to wear off and he was finding it difficult to stand. The aroma of the unwashed humanity around him, plus the spasms of pain, were making him nauseous. He held onto the bars now, letting his crutches fall to the floor, and felt a loss of reality. He stood that way, holding onto the bars, not moving, until a very thin girl with long black hair approached the cell. In spite of his misery Peter couldn't avoid noticing the over-large ill-fitted glasses that she wore over the bridge of her nose and that even with them on she held her clipboard close up to her face. She called his name, he mumbled an acknowledgment.

"Mr. Jorgensen," she said, "I'm not a lawyer. I represent the pre-trial service. My job is to interview you and make a recommendation to the judge about bail in your case. What's the matter with your foot?"

"Fractured ankle."

"That's good," she said, making a fast note on the clipboard. "With that kind of injury you have a good chance of being released on your own recognizance—if the charge isn't too serious. An injured prisoner is a pain in the ass to the Department of Correction. They'd just as soon not have the responsibility for your medical treatment. Now, let me get all the information right. That's Jorgensen, with an 'E'?"

"Right."

"You live at one-twenty Sullivan Street. That's in the Village, isn't it?"

"Yes."

She went down the checklist, employment, earnings, closest relative, prior record. When she finished she smiled at him. "Of course, you never know what a judge will do, but I can't see any reason for bail in your case and I'm recommending that you be released on your own recognizance. Let's hope the D.A. doesn't oppose my recommendation." She went on to the next prisoner on her list.

A short time later a tall, bushy-haired and bearded man called out Peter's name. He had a file in his hand and he identified himself as Peter's Legal Aid Society lawyer. "I've got the pre-trial services report here and a copy of the complaint," the attorney said. "You're charged with the felony of burglary. They claim you broke into the Monte Carlo Apartments with the intent to commit a larceny. Want to tell me about it?"

Peter repeated the story he told to the police.

The lawyer wrote in his file.

"Do you want to plead guilty to a reduced charge?"

"Well, I *am* guilty," Peter said.

The lawyer shuffled his papers and made another note on the front of his folder. "Technically you committed a burglary when you entered that basement unlawfully with the intent to steal. But this judge is a realist, and I think he'll go along with the reduction. If you plead guilty to Section 140.05 you're admitting that you committed a trespass, that you entered the basement unlawfully—period. You don't have to admit that you had the intent to steal. Maximum penalty is fifteen days or a two hundred and fifty dollar fine or both. This being your first arrest, you'll probably get a small fine, maybe not even that. It's cases like yours that make me thank the Lord for Uncle Herman."

"Who's Uncle Herman?"

"You can't miss him, he's the one in the black robe."

Uncle Herman was Herman Podnick, a judge of the Criminal Court of the City of New York and czar over all the proceedings in AR-1. He was *the* expert in the art of conducting plea negotiations leading to the disposition of cases. He "mediated" pleas of guilty to reduced charges. He knew the real value of a case and this adeptness in applying common sense to divide a truly serious charge from a "meatball" or a "schmeer" resulted in the disposition of almost eighty percent of the cases on his calendar. The D.A.'s liked him, the defense bar liked him. Even the defendants appreciated his common sense. Uncle Herman, more than any of his colleagues, seemed to know how to fit the punishment to the crime.

Uncle Herman was a gruff-looking man, short, heavyset with a small mouth drawn in a fierce line. Sitting behind the bench he looked like a vengeful Buddha, ready to impose terrible justice on all transgressors. But his eyes gave him away . . . he was a kind man, and his eyes reflected this, as well as an inner humor. All in all Judge Herman Podnick was as ideal a judge as one could hope for: a compassionate man who revered justice. The City of New York was damn lucky to have him.

A few minutes after one in the afternoon Peter's name was finally called by a correction officer. The cell was opened, and using his crutches that he retrieved from the floor, Peter hobbled out. He saw Officer Darby enter from the door leading to the courtroom.

"Ya'll better move along, Jorgensen," Darby said. "Can't afford to keep ol' Uncle Herman waitin'."

Darby helped Peter with his crutches, and Peter saw the legal aid lawyer waiting for him at the counsel table.

"Your Honor," Peter's lawyer said, "my client fractured his ankle last evening. May he be seated?"

Judge Podnick nodded. A court officer brought a chair. Peter let himself down slowly and the clerk went through the ritual of the arraignment.

"Peter Jorgensen, Docket #237654, charge is burglary. 140.20 of the Penal Law. Do you waive the rights and charges, counsel?"

"Yes . . . Your Honor, may I approach the bench with the district attorney?"

Uncle Herman nodded again. When they approached, Peter's lawyer spoke first. "Judge," he said, "this guy's never been arrested before. He had a few. I think he went in there to take a leak."

The old judge didn't buy it. "You know, counselor, I've been noticing that all your burglars break into buildings to take a leak."

The lawyer laughed, the assistant D.A. did not. "What bothers me," the D.A. said, "is that he admitted that he went in there to steal tools. And, Judge, it *was* at night."

Uncle Herman peered at Peter over his bifocals and saw a handsome, clean-cut looking youth, obviously in a great deal of discomfort.

"What are you looking for?"

"140.05," said the lawyer.

The D.A. stiffened. "I don't know whether I want to go that far down, Judge. This wasn't a trespass. From his own admission it's a burglary. And I don't buy the story that he went in there for tools."

"He was drunk," countered Peter's lawyer. "I really don't think he knew what he was doing. People do drink on Christmas Eve."

The judge peered down at Peter again, then perused the complaint. "Well, let's give him one bite of the apple. I don't entirely believe him either, but the pre-trial services report shows no previous, and a good work record. I think this experience scared him enough for future deterrence. Besides, that busted ankle is a punishment."

"Okay, Judge," the D.A. said. He knew from experience

that once the judge had made his decision it would be foolish to fight it. "He can have the 140.05."

Peter's lawyer nodded. "What are you going to sentence him to?"

Uncle Herman didn't like the question. "You'll find that out when I give it to him. You got your 140.05. What else do you want, a testimonial dinner?"

The lawyer quickly returned to Peter. "You're pleading guilty to the violation of trespass, okay?"

Peter, by this time numb with pain, nodded.

The lawyer resumed his place behind the counsel table and went through the ritual. "Your Honor, the defendant informs me that he offers to plead guilty to the reduced charge of 140.05 of the Penal Law, trespass as a violation."

"The People consent to the reduction, Your Honor," added the D.A.

Judge Podnick glanced at Peter. "Do you want to say anything before this court imposes sentence?"

"No, sir."

"All right, I'll give you one run around the track. Fifty dollars or five days. Can you pay the fine now?"

"Yes, sir."

"Okay, pay the clerk."

Officer Dave Darby accompanied Peter to the clerk's desk, where Peter paid the fine. The clerk handed him the receipt, Darby patted him on the back, wished him luck and left.

Peter was still clumsy with the crutches as he moved unevenly out of the courtroom and into the lobby, then turned toward the south entrance at 100 Centre. A tall prostitute in red hot-pants and a blonde wig approached him in the lobby.

"Looking for a little fun on a cold day?"

Peter pointed to his crutches. "What would I do with these?"

"Kinky sex don't scare me, sweetie."

"Maybe some other time."

"That's the trouble with people today," she sighed. "No imagination."

Peter laughed and hobbled away, his only thought to get something for the pain. It had been one rough night. Well, he figured, at least it was over. Right?

He managed to move slowly out of the building and down the courthouse steps onto a nearly deserted Centre Street. Now how the hell was he going to find a cruising cab on Christmas day?

CHAPTER 6

GROUND CONTROL, THIS is Twin Comanche two-three-three-six Whiskey. Request permission to taxi."

"Taxi via Bravo to number thirty-four," the controller said. "Proceed to the yellow line and hold."

As directed, Allen Sturdivant taxied his plane slowly to the yellow line. Although still bitter cold, the storm had passed and the plows had managed to clear the runways. The skies were now blue and the fresh white snow mirrored the blinding rays of the winter sun.

Allen Sturdivant's flight plan was filed for Palm Beach, and he sat at the controls waiting for clearance. He reached for the transmitter. "Tower, request permission to take active thirty-four."

"Taxi on to active and hold," the tower ordered.

Sturdivant moved the Comanche onto Runway 34. Suddenly his hands were shaking. He began to sweat. Great timing for a delayed reaction, he thought. Up to this moment he had somehow managed to push Andrea Blanchard and the events of the previous night out of his mind. Well, almost . . .

"You're cleared for takeoff, two-three-three-six Whiskey."

Sturdivant heard the voice but did not respond. His hands were still shaking, he felt nausea. The more he tried not to think of Andrea, the more, of course, he did.

"Take off, Twin Comanche two-three-three-six Whiskey."

It was as if he had just strangled her. He still didn't move.

The voice from the tower broke through: "You have sixty seconds to take off, two-three-three-six Whiskey. Clear the runway or we'll do it for you."

Sturdivant breathed heavily, steadied himself. He pushed the throttle, the prop pitch, and the fuel mixture levers forward. He moved the flaps one notch. After a short run, he was airborne. He brought up the landing gear.

"Request right hand departure, Control."

"Go ahead, two-three-three-six Whiskey."

"Departing two thousand feet—northwest on Tappan Zee Bridge."

Sturdivant adjusted his frequency. "Twin Comanche two-three-three-six Whiskey using Vector two hundred ten. Request clearance your zone. Destination Palm Beach."

"Okay, you're clear of New York Departure Control. Maintain present altitude."

Once off the Jersey Coast, heading south-southwest, Sturdivant maintained 7000 feet.

The panic had come, and gone. What was left was the cold reality that he had killed a human being the night before. Someone he had shared a major part of his life with, someone that he thought he had loved. He was no operator, no one-night-stand type. No, Andrea had been important . . .

He remembered when it began. He had just gone on the

42

Supreme Court Bench and had been chosen as a delegate to the Fifth International Conference of the World Judiciary in Milan. There were some judges who weren't happy with that plum being given to a newcomer on the bench, but the designation went unchallenged, at least publicly. The Sturdivant name carried considerable clout.

After the first three days he wished that the "plum" had been given to someone else. Bored by the endless and arid talk and panels, he was about to return home before the session ended. Loren, who had originally planned to accompany him, had used their youngest daughter's chicken pox as an excuse to stay in New York.

Sturdivant, though, stuck it out as a matter of personal obligation. After the last lecture on the closing day of the conference Sturdivant joined some other delegates escaping to the bar of the Milano Hilton. Glad to be done with the conference, he was listening to Gershwin music played, amazingly, by a good pianist and drinking good Scotch. Over the din of the babel of languages, he heard a woman's voice calling to *him* . . . "Allen Sturdivant—my God, what are *you* doing here?"

He turned and saw Andrea Blanchard. She was as beautiful as she had been when years before his cousin Freddie had brought her to a garden party in Southampton. He had never before, nor since, seen anyone as beautiful.

"This . . . this . . . is a most pleasant surprise."

Was it the alcohol that was making him stammer? No, it was distinctly Andrea. She had that effect on most men, including the most sophisticated and experienced. But it was more than just her beauty. Her smile was sensuous, her body language spoke an invitation.

"Judge"—she laughed—"you look lost." She touched his arm and pointed to an attractive couple who had walked up behind her. "I'd like you to meet Count and Contessa Leone.

43

Rudy and Maria, this is Judge Allen Sturdivant. He's a Very Important man back home."

The count and contessa smiled graciously, Sturdivant regained his composure, and, blessedly, after half an hour of making conversation over the din Their Highnesses offered their excuses and left. Andrea stayed. Sturdivant steered her to an empty table.

"I really should have left with them," she said. "After all, I'm their guest here in Milan. But of course they ought to know me well enough to know I never do what's expected of me." Followed by a dazzling smile.

"I'm glad you don't," he said. And saying it, Sturdivant knew he was beginning to sound like an inane schoolboy.

"What are you doing here?" she said.

He told her and that he was supposed to leave that night on Pan Am.

"That's too bad," she said.

As it turned out, it wasn't so bad. By the end of the evening Sturdivant knew he wasn't going to make that Pan Am flight.

The next morning he called Andrea and arranged to spend the day with her. He rented a car at his hotel and picked her up early at the count and contessa's villa, then drove along the Via Pizani, the wide and beautiful avenue the Milanese take such pride in.

They tried to decipher a city street map and after numerous wrong turns found the Saint Maria Della Grazia, a modest, inconspicuous church and monastery. History gave it its significance when in 1494 the good Dominicans prevailed on the Duke of Milan to order a Florentian by the name of Leonardo Da Vinci to paint an appropriate visual inspiration on the wall of the refectory. Da Vinci had other things in mind—he was more interested in his inventions and his proposed architectural projects—but in those days you didn't say no to the Duke of Milan. So he worked on that mural for three years, and he called it "The Last Supper."

They found the glass-roofed arcade, Galleria Vittorio Emmanuèle, which might have been the first pedestrian mall. And they found a café that served an unspeakably delicious canneloni. The proprietor insisted that they at least try the local wine, which went down easy. It wasn't long before the wine had done its work. Andrea then insisted that they look for Giannino's, which reputedly served the best risotto and pasta in Milan. They found Giannino's and they found more local wine.

The late July sun was beginning its descent when Andrea broke into their idyll with the remembrance that she had somehow misplaced her passport and felt a bit naked without it. She had, in fact, intended to go to the U.S. consulate that day, she told him, but had run into a slight distraction. He said he hoped she was glad that she had, and also suggested that they go right away and take care of it so it wouldn't be on her mind. Nothing ought to intrude on the perfection of this day. She agreed, and they managed to find their way to the consulate, where after a half dozen tortured inquiries and exchanges in Italian–English they got to the passport division, where an accommodating young man, Italian but reasonably fluent in English, and very friendly, took over and accelerated the process of getting the duplicate passport made out and stamped with a minimum of bureaucratic red tape. Andrea, in appreciation, visited her dazzling smile upon him, and out of politeness asked him his name, which he said was Vito Mondo and he was most happy to have been of service . . . His words trailed the couple as they turned and left the division, not really catching his name. But Vito Mondo doubted if he would ever forget the smile of easily the most beautiful lady he had ever seen in all his young years. He wondered if the man with her appreciated his good fortune. That smile and that lady in many ways symbolized the United States to him, a place he hoped one day to visit after he became a lawyer.

Driving back to the count's home, Allen Sturdivant behaved in a distinctly unjudicial fashion. The entire day had been a blessed escape from that boring conference, and from the reality of who he was and what his real life was like. He put it out of his mind. It had, indeed, been a perfect day. The attraction between himself and Andrea Blanchard was obvious. The next day, he informed her, they would take the Rapido to Lake Como.

In the context of his relationship with his wife, Sturdivant did not consider his occasional liaisons dishonest. Loren, in fact, never questioned him. He more than suspected she simply didn't care, that those occasions when she didn't have to share her bed with him were actually a relief to her. If anything in his life was dishonest, he often thought, it was his marriage, not his mistresses.

Sturdivant and Andrea decided against staying at the Villa D'Este. Too many people knew Andrea Blanchard in Europe; she was almost certain to be recognized. Instead they found a small hotel high on a slope that had an incredible view of Lake Como as it curved northward. Their room was enormous, and their terrace gave them a panoramic view of the long narrow lake winding between the mountains.

They hired a boat in the afternoon and traveled north, surrounded by magnificent forests of myrtle, bay and laurel, all growing profusely from the tips of the highest slopes to the crevices of the rocks at the shoreline. They passed ranges in the lower hills between the mountains and the lake covered by plantations of orange, olive and lemon trees heavy with fruit. As the lake zigzagged northward they passed picture-postcard villages: Cernobbio, Bellagio, Colicio.

Coming back they sailed toward the sun, and they arrived at the hotel dock just as the soft dusk was descending. They dined on the terrace, saying little; the beauty stretching before and around them said it all. After the sun disappeared and a full moon took its place they went inside and made love. At dawn they returned to the terrace and watched the sun begin its day's work, burning through the thick morning mist. Holding Andrea, Sturdivant could not remember a happier moment . . .

And now the woman who had given such pleasure was gone, her life ended by his hands. That his act, looking back, seemed uncontrollable changed nothing. He had committed the ultimate criminal act, the ultimate transgression. How could he now live his life with the stigma of that guilt?

Of course, he reminded himself, the stigma was self-imposed. The world knew nothing of his act. And fortune, luck, had arranged matters so that the world was not likely to know. What he had to do now was somehow get control of his guilt. He at least did not try to rationalize his act with her behavior . . . at least not consciously. But of course the thought was there . . .

The cloudless sky was the cold blue that only winter provides. Lost in his thoughts, he found himself bringing the Comanche up to 8000 feet in spite of the limit imposed by New York Air Control.

He thought of the overused line from Hamlet's soliloquy: "To sleep: perchance to dream; ay, there's the rub." How do you control the guilt? How do you sleep with it? How do you face the dawn with it? How do you pursue your still important goals with it?

Especially if you were Allen Sturdivant, who was, in fact, an idealist. He really believed what others considered cant—that justice was what distinguished a civilized society. Justice, up to now, had always been an uncomplicated notion for him. A code of conduct where right prevailed, without variations on the theme. It certainly did not permit

47

murder, no matter the reasons or circumstances. Up to now . . .

He thought of his daughters and his love for them that he had never fully shown, because try as he might he could not show love easily. What he had given them was a poor substitute, but he hoped something of value, nevertheless; a standard for living that could maintain them through the peaks and valleys. They were Sturdivants, and in the history and tradition of the family the name itself stood for strength and honor. Up to now . . .

At that moment, alone in his aircraft above the ocean, Allen Sturdivant could see no way to set things right.

He cut his power back to fifteen inches manifold pressure. The nose of the Comanche dipped and the plane went into a shallow glide, quickly building speed as it dropped.

He held the wheel steady, not pulling back. The sun-reflected water came toward him. Three thousand feet now—2500—1500—1000—500—

The ocean was waiting for him.

Not yet. Some primordial instinct snapped him out of his trance just before he reached the point of no return. He pulled back hard on the wheel—at only one hundred feet, only one hundred feet from peace and escape.

Whatever else he'd become, the judge thought, he had a little taste left. The cheap out of such melodrama offended him. At least he had that much left.

CHAPTER 7

JOE LAWRENCE CROSSED the Brooklyn Bridge on his way home from the precinct. The snow had stopped falling earlier in the morning, and the white accumulation on the streets made for a kind of quiet beauty. It would be a while before the natural rhythm of the city would change the virgin snow to a sickly gray slush.

Lawrence switched on his car radio just as a bulletin interrupted the traditional Christmas music. He concentrated on the news broadcast.

"Ladies and gentlemen, this is Tom McPartland for All World Media. It has been confirmed that Andrea Blanchard, whose body was found in her Manhattan apartment this morning, was murdered. Her death was caused by strangulation. Detectives from the Fourth Homicide zone are now at the Monte Carlo apartments—"

Joe Lawrence swore softly, activated his siren, set the portable flashing light on the roof of his red Buick, made a U-turn and sped back over the bridge. He traveled much too fast for the street conditions, but despite some close calls when he nearly skidded out of control, he was back at his precinct at 82nd Street within fifteen minutes.

He double parked, charged into the station house and up the stairs, found the fingerprint card he had placed in the files early that day and rushed down the stairs again and into the street. The desk officer was beginning to think that Joe Lawrence was losing his marbles.

Far from it.

Eighteen years on the street as a cop, and all his life before that as a ghetto kid on those same streets, had taught him that coincidences didn't happen. In the movies and television you saw them, not in the real world. Now his gut was being tugged real good. It started when the announcement came over the car radio . . . now what he needed was confirmation of what his gut told him—that Peter Jorgensen had indeed been lying, that he was involved in the Blanchard case. And if he was right, this was the break that he was looking for—his ticket to a gold shield. Jorgensen had been, after all, his collar—his case—his baby. No detective from Manhattan North Homicide was going to grab the glory on *this* one. He drove around the corner from the precinct and stopped in front of a phonebooth. He made two calls, the first to his wife, explaining his delay in getting home, the second to a former classmate at the Police Academy, Sergeant Jeremiah Rome.

Most everyone who knew Jerry Rome said he was wasted in the police department—most everybody, that is, except Jerry Rome. Sure, he'd had offers from private industry that could have tripled his income, but he stayed in the department because he liked and respected the work he was doing. One of the three forensic psychologists in the department, Sergeant Rome held a Ph.D. in psychology, and, among other duties, instructed police personnel, including the brass, in hostage negotiations. Primarily, though, he was a scientist, an expert on all phases of the forensic unit. It was Jerry Rome who was called on to testify by the district attorneys of all five boroughs when scientific evidence was crucial to a case.

After Joe Lawrence and Jerry Rome made it through the academy they were assigned to the thirty-third precinct in Harlem. One hot summer night a punk high on heroin bought a gun on Lenox Avenue and vowed to shoot the first cop he saw. That cop happened to be Rome. Joe Lawrence put a bullet in the addict's leg as he fired his piece and the bullet whizzed by Jerry Rome's head with less than an inch to spare. If Lawrence hadn't reacted as he did, Jerry Rome would have been another statistic. Whenever they met after that night, long after they had gone their separate ways, Jerry Rome always reminded Joe Lawrence that there was still a debt Lawrence could call in whenever and however he chose.

Lawrence had never called it in—had never intended to—until now . . . He heard the familiar voice answer the phone.

"Forensic, Sergeant Rome speaking."

"Jerry Rome," said Lawrence. "I need to see you, Jerry. Now."

"I'll be waiting."

Lawrence activated his siren again and sped to the Police Academy. Rome was waiting for him at the door of his office.

Jerry Rome even looked like a Ph.D. The potbelly, the glasses, the shape of the head, the bookish look, somehow didn't fit the .38 he carried holstered on his hip. Looks, in this case, were deceiving. Rome was a marksman with that weapon and a skilled cop in every other way.

Joe came right to the point. "Jerry, have you heard about Andrea Blanchard?"

"Are you kidding? That's all I *have* been hearing about. The commissioner's aide called me just before you. He wants me to supervise. I'm waiting to hear from the print man. I may have to go there in a few minutes."

"It's homicide, isn't it?"

"Yes, I spoke to the M.E." The phone rang. "That's probably the print man now."

Lawrence attended every word of Rome's conversation, his excitement building.

"I'm about to give you classified information, buddy," Rome said to Lawrence after he finished the call. "He's got three definable prints in the living room where they found the body. He suspects that two of them belong to Andrea and the maid because they're all over the apartment. The third one is a solo. Question: who left the third print?"

Lawrence shook his head. "Jerry, does your print man know his business?"

"Dixon is careful, one of the best. What's this all about, Joe?"

"I think I have the third print on this card." Lawrence proceeded to tell Rome about the arrest he'd made at the Monte Carlo Apartments, then showed him the print card.

"Joe," Rome said cautiously, "you're shooting in the dark. You have no evidence that the kid was in her apartment. That print they found could be anybody's."

"Only one way to find out . . . Look, Jerry, I can't prove it yet, but his story smelled. Would you have bought it?"

"No . . . but that doesn't mean—"

"I'm not saying he killed her. Maybe yes, maybe no. But I'm betting he was there—in that apartment—last night."

"You have to turn that print card over to homicide. I've got the names of the detectives assigned."

"Stuff homicide, Jerry. This is mine. You wait a career for a break like this. I'm turning this over to nobody. When Dixon comes back I want to compare his prints with these."

"Are you nuts? I can get Dixon to compare them, but if

I turn that information over to you instead of the detectives assigned to the case we can both get our asses—"

"I know—"

"Especially in this case."

"I know that too."

Rome glared at Joe Lawrence. "And of course you also know that I won't turn you down."

"Right, old buddy."

Rome dialed a number. "Hello, Dixon still there? . . . Hello, Al. Look, I've got to see the Blanchard prints before you go anywhere else. I know you have to go up to the Bronx but come back here first. Something may be breaking." He hung up and turned to Lawrence. "Joe," he said, "if this backfires I'm a dead man. The whole city knows about this case."

"Sure, and if the prints check out there'll be enough for an indictment, and no one will be pissed at *that*. You can turn these prints over to homicide *after* I bust this guy, which will be ten minutes after I find out that the prints are his. If the prints don't check out, all we lost is an hour of your friend's time."

Dixon arrived twenty minutes later, Lawrence gave him the card and Dixon took it to the lab.

When he came back he said, "Twelve plus on this one. Naturally I need more time, but twelve definite similarities that match the print taken from the phone."

Rome sat back in his desk chair. "I'd say that's good enough, Joe. Your man was there."

Only one cab had passed Peter as he stood in front of the courthouse, and it was occupied. He set himself for a long wait, wondering how he was going to explain his broken ankle to his mother . . . he was having Christmas dinner with her. She could be a problem, he thought, if she knew he had got himself in trouble. Any trouble. He'd tell her he slid on the ice in front of his apartment. Yeah, she'd go for that—

Suddenly a snow-splattered Buick pulled up to the curb in front of Peter and he heard a familiar voice call out his name.

"Get in, Jorgensen."

Peter bent down and peered through the open window, and recognized the cop who had arrested him the night before. "Hello, Officer—"

"The name is Lawrence, and I said get in."

The cop showing up like this frightened Peter, but he could hardly walk with his crutches, much less run. Awkwardly he slid into the front seat of the car.

Joe Lawrence drove north on Centre Street, eyes straight ahead, not looking at Peter. "You should have told me the truth, Peter. If you're wondering where we're going, let me fill you in. It's the twentieth precinct—again. Only this time, my man, the charge is murder. I'm going to give you your rights now—"

"Oh, God . . . no . . . I didn't kill anyone, I don't need any rights—"

"Peter, boy, believe me, you do. From now on we do everything by the book. Peter Jorgensen, you are under arrest in connection with the murder of Andrea Blanchard. The charge is homicide. You have a right to remain silent, anything you say may be used against you in court. You have the right to consult with counsel, and if you tell me now that you want to exercise that right there will be no further questioning by me. If you can't afford counsel, one will be provided to you free of charge. Did you understand what I just said?"

"Yes."

"Any questions about what I've just said to you?"

"No."

Joe Lawrence took a card from his pocket and gave it to

Peter. "I've just informed you of your rights. I've done it orally. The rights are in fancier language on this card. I want you to read it and sign the card at the bottom. Your signature means that you confirm that the rights were given to you and that you understood them."

Peter took the pen that Lawrence handed him and without glancing at the card signed it and returned the pen and the card to Lawrence. They drove in silence several minutes before Peter spoke. *"I didn't kill Andrea Blanchard."*

Lawrence said nothing, kept his eyes fixed on the road.

"Will you at least listen to what really happened?"

"I'll listen," Joe said. "If you want to talk, I won't stop you. But I tell you now, I may testify to what you're telling me, so think it over before you say anything."

"I haven't committed any crime, and I'm not afraid to talk." And Peter proceeded to tell Lawrence everything— from day one. He detailed the sex, and the drugs, and the good times. He told Lawrence about the man in the raincoat and hat running to the stairway exit, about how he found Andrea dead, about how he had jumped the fence when he realized he had lost his keys . . . "I had to lie to you before, I knew no one would believe the truth. But what I'm telling you now *is* the truth. Do I have a chance?"

Lawrence looked at him briefly, turned again to face the road. "You want my honest opinion?"

"Yes."

"With that bullshit story you haven't even got a prayer."

CHAPTER 8

Hershel Himmelfarb left Germany in time to escape the Holocaust. He was only twenty years old when he found himself on Ellis Island, alone and friendless, unable to speak the language and without the price of a loaf of bread.

Hershel had never lived in a country that did not discriminate against Jews, and once he adjusted to relative freedom his success was nearly inevitable. From the time he picked up his first tin can off the gutter of Cherry Street in the Lower East Side to the time he resigned as Chairman of the Board of Himmelfarb Metal Works nothing and nobody deterred him from succeeding—so he did what came naturally. He succeeded.

But the very drive that insured his business success made him a failure elsewhere in his life. His wife Sophie lived with him for thirty years, tolerating his indifference for the sake of her four children. When they became self-sufficient she intended to demand a divorce. Unfortunately, she died of a cerebral hemorrhage before she could taste her share of freedom.

Hershel's daughters hardly spoke to him. He sustained this rejection with a limited sadness, since he could not in good conscience blame them. He had, after all, deprived them of a father when they needed him most.

The one bright star on Hershel's horizon was Moshe, his youngest and only son. Moshe grew up knowing there was friction in the family but, unlike his mother and sisters, Moshe managed not to miss his father's attention. At least not seriously.

Moshe, like Hershel, seemed destined to be a success. Valedictorian of his class at Yale, salutarian of his class at Harvard Law, he could be remarkably objective about himself. He knew he was smart, well spoken, well schooled in the law. He knew that, as one of his dates had told him, he looked like a sexy Ichabod Crane—tall and ramrod thin, with strong features and prominent ears. He also knew his only major drawback was his name. So, with some reluctance, he changed it to Marc Hammond.

Marc had hoped to get out to Riker's Island by noon and to be back in his office by two. The Department of Corrections of the City of New York did nothing to help him keep to his timetable. Marc sat in a cubicle in the interview room for over an hour until, finally, Peter Jorgensen was brought in. By that time he was not exactly in the best of moods.

Marc motioned for Jorgensen to sit down. "Peter Jorgensen, my name is Marc Hammond. I've been asked by Father Brin to represent you."

"I don't understand. How can my mother—"

"Afford a lawyer? Let's say my compensation will be in heaven, if I make it there." Marc took out a legal pad and pencil. "I'm going to ask you some straight questions and I'd appreciate some straight answers."

Jorgensen seemed both frightened and depressed. He

57

fidgeted in his seat. Marc had seen the same lost look on other clients who had found themselves suddenly removed from the world they knew and thrown into the brutal, impersonal world of the penal system. But it wasn't his job to fix the system, his job was to get his client out of it.

Marc then took Peter through the events of Christmas Eve, Peter repeating the story just as he had to the police officer, just as he had to the legal aid attorney. This interview, however, was more detailed. Marc pushed Peter to be even more specific. He had Peter repeat his conversation with Joe Lawrence, repeat it again and again. He also had Peter repeat his description of the pain of his broken ankle.

Marc wanted to know all the details of Peter's relationship with Andrea Blanchard, asking Peter to pinpoint with as much accuracy as possible the number of times he had had sex with her and the kind of sex it was.

"Is all this really necessary?" Peter asked.

"Listen," Marc said, annoyance edging his voice, "do you think I get my kicks out of hearing how you made it with Andrea Blanchard? Just understand that I have a reason for any questions I ask you, and the questions only go one way—from me to you. Okay? Understood?"

Peter nodded his acknowledgment and didn't interrupt again as Marc continued to question him.

"What did you touch when you found her dead?"

Peter frowned, trying to remember. "I touched the table, maybe something else. I was excited, I don't remember."

Marc shook his head. "Chances are they've got your prints, which means that even if the court strikes out your confession as having been involuntarily obtained they've got independent evidence putting you there."

Marc tended to have a well-honed sixth sense that signaled a lie from his viscera to his brain. Physiologically that signal was supposed to travel in the opposite direction, but good trial lawyers sometimes developed the two-way after a while, which helped in evaluating a client's story, and more important, in judging how it would sound to a jury. In this case Marc's gut was not reacting to Peter's story. He just couldn't get a fix on Peter.

Marc knew the bromide that the guilt or innocence of a client was supposed to be irrelevant, that a lawyer should not even consider that factor because it would only add to the pressures of a trial. But Marc often did find himself caught up emotionally in a case, his adrenaline flowing because he *did* care about the injustice of someone being wrongly convicted.

But as for Peter Jorgensen . . . well, perhaps it was too early to get a reading on him. The fact that Jorgensen's story was the same each time he repeated it didn't, of course, prove his innocence. It could simply be a complete and consistent lie. And if Marc came to perceive it as such, so might a jury. After all, Peter had lied to the police in his first statement given after his arrest. Why should the jury believe that his second story was any closer to the truth?

It was going to be a rough row. Marc made it clear to Peter that if they went to trial on Peter's story alone, he was a dead man. Peter was not surprised. He had figured that out for himself.

As Marc now began to gather his papers, he was thinking that it might all hang on the question of whether the judge assigned to the case would agree to suppress Peter's first statement. But even if he did, Marc knew he had the problem of explaining why Peter hadn't called the police when he got to Andrea's apartment, why he had run off instead.

Looking across the table at Peter, Marc felt sorry for the kid. "You've done a lot of talking to a lot of people in this case. From now on, Peter, you're to talk to *no one* except me, and that includes your mother, your priest, anyone. Clear?"

Peter nodded.

"Before I leave, is there anything you'd like cleared up?"

"Mr. Hammond . . . There's one question that you didn't ask me that I thought you would."

Marc waited.

"You didn't ask me if I was guilty."

Marc suppressed a smile. He said, "Have you ever seen the movie, 'Gone With the Wind?'"

Peter nodded.

"Well, if I wanted to be a smartass, I could say, Frankly, Peter, I don't give a damn. Actually, I do. But for my job, it's irrelevant right now. I'm your lawyer, and that means I'm on your side, all the way. And *that's* what matters."

He picked up his briefcase and moved toward the gate. He felt for this kid, even though he had no idea yet whether he was guilty or innocent. Marc hoped he was a compassionate man, in fact worried it could be a courtroom flaw and so often played the tough guy to cover the supposed "weakness" in a supposedly hardboiled trial attorney. He walked back to Peter and put a hand on his shoulder.

"Like I said, Peter. I do give a damn." He paused, his eyes on his client's. "You had something to say and I cut it off. All right, Peter, did you kill Andrea Blanchard?"

Tears formed in Peter's eyes. "As God is my witness, Mr. Hammond, she was dead before I got there. But I guess what I say the truth is doesn't matter."

"No—it *does* matter. That's what our system is supposed to be about—a search for the truth. If the truth is out there, we'll find it."

He hoped he sounded more convincing than he felt. And the sign of hope on Peter's face didn't make Marc feel any better. He was beginning to believe that Jorgensen might well be innocent, but he'd hate to have to estimate the odds against his acquittal.

CHAPTER 9

CHARLIE SWEENEY'S FATHER, James Aloysius Sweeney, landed in America luckier than most of his fellow immigrants. He had the address of a bar on Third Avenue named Connerty's, and a letter of introduction from Connerty's mother in which she told her son about this fine broth of a lad who needed a job. Connerty welcomed James with open arms.

When James had saved enough he returned to the Old Country for the purpose of taking another look at Maureen O'Hanlon, about whom he had had serious thoughts before he left. The second look convinced him. He married her in the local church and they returned to live in Hoboken, New Jersey. Six children were born in the first eight years of their marriage.

Charlie was the firstborn. By the time he reached the age of ten his father had prospered and owned his own bar in the Village.

It was a great place, that bar. It had the longest and largest mirror in New York, and over the mirror James Sweeney had hung portraits of the Irish champions: Sullivan, Corbett and Fitzsimmons, and an adopted Irish champion, Joe Louis. James insisted that his saloon be antiseptically clean. The antique oak wood was polished daily, as was the mirror. The floors and the surroundings were spotless. James's aim was to make the place a second home for his patrons, and it was at least that.

James also was a cunning man, and so he invited political leaders to be his guests from time to time. Eventually his saloon became a meeting place for powers and would-be powers. The mayor was a frequent visitor, which led naturally to the attendance of his coterie. The word soon got around that it would not be a bad idea for aspiring office-holders or job-seekers to wind up at Sweeney's after political club meeting nights. Some Fridays they stood five deep at the bar.

Young Charlie learned the art of politics from his father, who as a saloon keeper was the best possible instructor. Because he was tough and strong, Charlie from time to time was called on to help out the bouncer. Charlie bore the black-and-blue souvenirs of these encounters as a badge of honor. His physical toughness seemed to lead to a mental toughness and a belief in himself—not the least of the attributes that eventually led to his election as district leader before he was thirty and Democratic county leader of New York County ten years later.

And Charlie's political muscles extended beyond the boundaries of Manhattan. At the New York County Democratic Dinner in 1959 Charlie Sweeney made it clear to those who packed the ballroom at a thousand per that the Eisenhower era was coming to a close and the Democrats had a mandate to retake the White House. Charlie Sweeney's candidate for the following year would be the featured speaker of the evening—John F. Kennedy. Charlie, in fact, was the first national political figure officially to support the junior senator from Massachusetts.

Sweeney became a trusted friend of Joe Kennedy and soon headed the Kennedy brain trust on strategy. He did his job well, and insiders said he was as much responsible as any other single individual for Jack Kennedy's nomination. When an assassin's bullet ended the days of Camelot, Sweeney survived because he had vested his power by collecting IOUs during those three memorable years. While he retained his New York County chairmanship, he became the New York State Democratic chairman as well.

Charlie was a plain-spoken man who rarely raised his voice; a private man, a family man. He was also the man to call when a union leader was indicted for embezzlement, a congressman was tried for perjury, or an oil tycoon's son was arrested for the sale of cocaine.

On the day before the New Year Charlie Sweeney stood at the large window of his office at Democratic headquarters, gazing down at the city still white from the Christmas Eve blizzard.

He was not happy. A week had passed since he had met with Allen Sturdivant and he was still bothered by a nagging guilt, or at least uncharacteristic unease. Call it what you will, he had abandoned Jon Klyk. To be sure, his reasoning was politically correct. Coach Vince Lombardi's credo applied to politics as well as to football: winning is not everything—it is the only thing.

Yet this rationalization did not offset what he felt about casting aside his friend for an outsider with little understanding of party loyalty. Sweeney could not dismiss the probability that Jon Klyk would rightfully perceive his support of Sturdivant as a stab in the back from a friend. Sweeney sighed heavily. He needed the ten days at the Keys, ten days that he and Peg had planned all year. He looked at the plane tickets he was holding and tried to feel better. They were scheduled to escape tonight on American Airlines—away from the party, the phone calls, the crises, the tensions and all worries except for whether the big Spanish mackerel might get away.

As he planted the tickets in his jacket pocket and took a step toward the door the intercom buzzed. He flicked the switch: "No more calls, Rosie, I'm through for the year."

"I'll tell that to Judge Sturdivant," Rosie said.

She knew damn well that he would take the call.

Charlie sat down at his desk, lit a cigarette, cursed softly. Sturdivant was the last man he wanted to talk to at this particular moment. Maybe an hour later, maybe the next day, but not now. He sighed and picked up the phone. "Rubbing it in, Judge? Basking in the Florida sun while I'm still freezing my ass in New York?"

"I'm calling from the Carlyle on Madison Avenue, and it's just as cold here."

"I thought you'd gone to Palm Beach."

"I had enough of the social life . . . Charlie, I have to discuss something with you."

Sweeney swore under his breath. There went his ten days in the Keys. What the hell could be on Sturdivant's mind? But Allen Sturdivant wouldn't have called unless it was important, and important problems weren't usually solved in a day.

"Okay," Sweeney said. "Where and when?"

They arranged to meet that evening at Sturdivant's suite at the Carlyle Hotel.

Poor Peg, he thought, replacing the phone. He knew that she would not go on vacation without him. He dreaded the phone call he would have to make to her.

Actually, he *had* been feeling concerned about going away. This was going to be a busy time. Sturdivant probably wouldn't announce officially until March, but there was much to be done before the September primary. It would be up to Sweeney to get Klyk in line, and that wasn't going to be easy. Klyk could, if he wanted, become a real spoiler.

Charlie broke out of his reverie and slapped his forehead as he realized that he still hadn't called Peg. He flicked the switch on the intercom. "Rosie, call my wife. Tell her to hold up on the packing."

"Oh, no, you don't. She's going to be heartbroken. You're going to do your own dirty work." Rosie had long ago earned the right to talk back.

"Insubordination, plain insubordination," he grunted. "If you could be replaced, I'd fire you."

"You'd be doing me a favor," she said.

Charlie grunted again and began dialing his home number. Peg wouldn't be happy. But Peg was a politician's wife. At least she wouldn't be surprised.

Sweeney arrived at the Carlyle suite promptly at 7 P.M., and Sturdivant met him at the door. The rooms were furnished with Louis XIV furniture. The carpets were white. Sweeney grinned to himself. Only the *very* rich would dare to have white carpets. If it were his house he could imagine Peg's face the first time someone spilled a drink on it.

The suite consisted of three bedrooms, three baths, an enormous living room and small study. There was also a full dining room and a kitchen with a stocked bar and a food pantry. The suite was used by Allen Sturdivant for business purposes and by his wife Loren and the girls when they were in the city shopping or going to the theater.

As Sturdivant led him to the study, Sweeney noticed that every surface seemed to be covered with a priceless antique. "You have a nice place here, Judge," he said. "Good enough for the president."

"The president *has* stayed here, Charlie," Sturdivant said, with scarcely a hint of his famous smile.

Matter of fact, Sweeney had been struck by the change in Sturdivant's appearance from the moment he opened the door. Just a week ago the judge had appeared confident, robust, even aggressive. Now his eyes were rimmed by dark circles and he was speaking deliberately, in a slow tired voice. Pre-campaign jitters? Sweeney had seen it before but hadn't expected it from Allen Sturdivant. He hoped for a quick recovery. There were tough days ahead.

Sturdivant waved Sweeney to a couch, sat across from him in a chair that looked to Sweeney like a throne and indicated with a nod of his head a tray of hors d'oeuvres set on the coffee table. When Sweeney declined he came to the point.

"Charlie, when I returned from Palm Beach the first message I received was that Jon Klyk had called. We met here last night. Before the campaign goes any further I think you'd better know what was said." Sturdivant stopped, waiting for a reaction from Sweeney, who lit a cigarette but said nothing.

Sturdivant went on, "It must have been difficult for Jon Klyk to come to see me. He did it because he was motivated partly by party unity and partly by his loyalty to you. I'm afraid when he left we weren't on the best of terms. He made it clear that I wasn't his cup of tea."

"One thing I learned in politics," Sweeney said, "not everybody can love everybody. But that doesn't mean we can't work together—"

"To Klyk's credit, he said that in the interest of unity he would step aside and fully support me—*if* I made certain commitments."

Sweeney puffed on his cigarette and shook his head. That sweet old son-of-a-bitch. What it must have taken for Klyk even to contact Sturdivant, much less make that statement. His affection for his old friend intensified, as did his guilt.

"We discussed what was expected of me should I win.

66

He told me about his concern for the thousands of state positions that a governor can fill through personal appointment or influence."

"He *should* be concerned," Sweeney said. "Hundreds of millions of dollars are involved in salaries and fringe benefits. I'm not talking about civil service, of course—but the exempt jobs are all over the lot."

"And I fully understand how important patronage is to you—"

"No, Allen, not to me—to you. When you're elected governor you'll be titular head of the party. As we sit here, neither of us can appreciate the power you'll have over people's lives and futures."

"I understand that and—"

"All right, but let me give you something else to think about. This election process is going to require the active help of hundreds of party workers throughout the state. A lot of them are office holders themselves, from county committeemen to legislators to mayors. All of them are gonna be working their asses off for *you*. Some of these people will go door-to-door in the sweaty heat of the summer, some will stuff envelopes all night, some will man the phones until they're croaking, some will work like hell to see to it that decent crowds show up for your campaign stops. No candidate—not even you—can win without them, Allen. Media promotion is great, but it's not enough. You need living breathing bodies to go into the streets and pull them out on election day, because you'll never know if a few thousand of those votes that weren't pulled out could have made the difference. Ask Ave Harriman."

"Yes," Sturdivant said, "I remember Governor Harriman telling my father that the efforts of the Democratic party *did* make the difference in his election."

"Well, if you know that, then you can understand the fact of life that people work for a reason. A good number of the people who will be breaking their backs for you out there are expecting you to remember them. I don't see how they can be blamed for expecting compensation. Political organizations don't survive on principle alone. Patronage is the grease that makes political wheels roll. If you've got no support, your principles aren't even going to get a chance to be tested."

Sturdivant reached down over the coffee table, took up a canape, put it back. "Charlie," he said, "I heard pretty much the same from Jon Klyk—and I don't completely disagree with you or him. But government also deserves people who are the best-qualified. I acknowledge my debt to the party loyalists who will work for my election. And if I'm elected I tell you now they'll get first preference for the positions they seek *if* they're qualified. I told Klyk and I tell you—I want to give the people of New York the best. If you can't accept that, then you'd better not endorse me." (And maybe you'd better not anyway—the thought poked through, and in near-panic he pushed it back.)

Sweeney looked at Sturdivant. He wasn't happy with the tone or attitude, but he did feel a grudging respect. It seemed Sturdivant had guts enough to give up something he wanted so badly he could taste it—if in the getting his principles got violated. And, after all, he had guaranteed preference for party people who were qualified. It wasn't the whole loaf, but Sweeney could accept it, even if Klyk couldn't. Sturdivant would be Sweeney's man, because Sturdivant had the best chance of winning. But the battle lines were drawn, and Jon Klyk was not going to be in their camp. Somehow Sweeney would have to live with that, and cope with it.

___ CHAPTER 10 ___

Loren Phillips Sturdivant was, as the columnists said, a classic beauty. Although in her early forties she had an unlined face and the body of a young girl. That she had unlimited funds to spend on herself to hold back the clock did not diminish the overall picture.

Warmth, however, was not one of Loren's qualities. Dedication was, dedication to her own personal power even if it could only be achieved through the accomplishment of her husband.

The quality of dedication came naturally to Loren. The Phillipses, like the Sturdivants, had made their fortunes during the nation's industrial expansion. They were an aggressive lot who let nothing stand in the way of financial success. And because of their dedication to their diversified interests—shipping, mining and finally retail chains—the Phillipses' fortune grew to enormous sums that even the Sturdivants could accept as adequate.

The Sturdivants and the Phillipses had not actually entered into a written or oral contract for the marriage of their offspring, but the marriage was inevitable. The two families, neighbors on Park Avenue, in Southampton and in Palm Beach, were as close-knit as possible without being related by blood. They did business with each other, served on the same boards of directors, belonged to the same clubs, moved in the same tight circles. They were a part of the American monied and social aristocracy, the Four Hundred, the beautiful people.

Loren Phillips and Allen Sturdivant . . . at Loren's coming out Allen was her escort; at his graduation ball at Choate Loren was his date. It was expected by the families that each would be the partner of the other on those and all similar social occasions, and the young people themselves raised few objections to their lack of freedom of choice. They seemed to understand the rules. So if it wasn't literally a marriage contract it was in effect. Without any formal expression of intent, it was nonetheless assumed by everyone in their circle that they would be wed. Indeed, the scenario could have been written in advance . . . Allen graduated Dartmouth; Loren, Radcliffe. He was an All-Ivy League running back, she a Cliffie brain and beauty. Naturally, inevitably, they married when he graduated Harvard Law.

They had, it seemed, everything going for them. They were strikingly handsome; they fulfilled the picture of the American dream. They shared the power and influence of their combined dynasties. The world was before them, for the taking.

They also acknowledged early on that theirs was a partnership, an arrangement, not a love match. On the rare occasion when Loren had allowed tears and said to her husband that she could not remember when he had told her he loved her, he not unreasonably responded that he had the same difficulty recalling when she had last directed those words to him. During the period of twenty years, while

70

producing two daughters, they never had occasion to address the subject again.

While they apparently could not share love, they did share other powerful emotions. Allen Sturdivant, bright, dedicated to the notion of service and achieving the position of highest potential for it, saw himself one day becoming the president of the United States; Loren lived a little girl fantasy of being First Lady—except there was nothing girlish about her determination that her fantasy come true. They were, then, equal partners in this joint venture. Her resolve was no less than his—if anything, even greater. Allen had enormous respect for her innate shrewdness, her ability to analyze a situation and line out the appropriate moves. They were both ready to utilize her beauty, her charm and her intelligence whenever and however the occasion required.

Not being stupid or unaware, she suspected his romantic dalliances, but she never reproached him. Nothing was said. They adopted the French code of conduct: "If the husband is discreet, the wife does not make a fuss." Allen did respect Loren, and that respect would not permit him to demean her publicly. He was discreet, and they both were comfortable with that. . . .

When Loren returned from Palm Beach at the end of January she was alarmed by her husband's uncharacteristic listlessness. This was hardly the time for such behavior. When she confronted him he dismissed her with a wave of the hand, insisted that everything was fine, that there were no problems he could not handle.

Loren was not reassured, but felt there was little she could do about it now. Besides, she was confident that the excitement of the forthcoming campaign would seduce him away from whatever might be bothering him. It had better, or she would not make it even as far as Albany.

* * *

Loren Sturdivant met with Charlie Sweeney at the beginning of February, the appointment having been arranged with Allen's full approval.

As for Sweeney, he was happy to meet with her. It was known in political circles that she was brilliant, and it was even more impressive to Sweeney that her background had not prepared her for the hardball of politics. Loren, it seemed, came by it naturally.

They sat facing each other now across his desk, discussing details of the upcoming primary. When he got to the problem of Jon Klyk she became especially curious. "Are you telling me that Mr. Klyk is the major obstacle we face?"

"That's about right," Sweeney said, lighting the inevitable cigarette.

"Why does he oppose Allen?"

"Well, Klyk represents the old political establishment. He was raised in the tradition of a favor for a favor. Allen won't go along. The other leaders see Allen as a winner so they'll overlook his maverick approach. Klyk, on the other hand, thinks Allen's a threat to the structure of the party. That's the way he sees it, and he's willing to sacrifice the election to save the party as he knows it."

Loren shook her head. "That's incredible."

Not so incredible, Sweeney thought, and privately shared some of Klyk's misgivings. The difference between them was that he believed the party was best served by winning. "His plan is to run in the primary and after he loses—he's sure to lose—to run on the third party line in the election."

"But then he splits our vote and elects Beale."

Sweeney shrugged.

"Can he be stopped?"

"My polls show he'll get a sizable vote in the primary. He's got his natural constituency. With his good looks and outgoing personality he'll carry a lot of other people over to the third party line."

"Well, what are you going to do about it?"

"I'll pull out all the stops to back Allen, but I can't drum Klyk out of the party. We go back too many years."

Loren stood up and began pacing on Sweeney's thread-bare office rug. It occurred to Sweeney, watching her move, that she had the beauty and grace of a panther, and likely was just as dangerous.

Finally she stopped pacing and returned to her chair. "He must be . . . neutralized."

Sweeney was startled. An odd choice of word, he thought. He could see the intensity in her eyes, a palpable force. Loren Sturdivant was no one to fool with.

An hour later, when she left his office, Sweeney had little doubt that Loren Sturdivant was going to find a way to deal with the problem of Jon Klyk. How she was going to accomplish this was unclear, but she left him with no doubt that some way—any way—she would.

Jimmy Powell had joined the New York City Police Department in 1950. After a few years he made up his mind that he was going to surpass his father and grandfather, who had chosen the same career. They had risen to the rank of captain, but it wasn't enough for Jimmy Powell. Ultimately he reached the rank of deputy commissioner, and for seven years was attached to the police commissioner himself.

When after thirty years he called it quits with the department, it was inevitable that he would open his own private investigation agency. He had, after all, made many powerful friends and moved in high circles. He decided, though, to give his agency a special cachet that would set it apart from the common private-eye type of operation he scorned. First, he parted his name in the middle. From Jimmy Powell, the cop of thirty years, he became J. Franklin Powell, Confidential Investigations. He invested in richly appointed offices and hired knowledgeable and competent operatives. The high crime rate created such demand for his security services that he had difficulty in keeping up with it. An even larger source of income came from the private investigations sought by clients whose bank accounts seemed bottomless pits. He also worked closely with the Wall Street firms, and they found him reliable. Powell knew his job, he had an excellent batting average, and he cheerfully overcharged everyone who came to him.

One of the secrets of his success was his ability to turn the tawdry into the acceptable. He told his clients what they wanted to hear, and he heard more of their personal confidences than their analysts did. He got the blackmailers off their backs, or obtained the information that gave his clients the ammunition to play a little blackmail themselves. He indulged himself in such conspiracies without any twinge of conscience, rationalizing that almost any conduct in the service of a client was acceptable and comfortably within the code of ethics of his profession—a code unwritten and infinitely flexible . . .

Accustomed as he was to serving the great and the near great, he did not find it extraordinary now to have Loren Phillips Sturdivant sitting across the desk from him. Still, the attributes of wealth and power and beauty combined in this lady gave J. Franklin Powell the right to say to himself that he had, indeed, made it. If there had been any doubts, her presence erased them.

"Will you have some tea, Mrs. Sturdivant?" His voice had just a touch of British intonation that he had picked up somewhere between Hell's Kitchen and Centre Street. It was lost on Loren Sturdivant.

"No, Mr. Powell, thank you, but I have a good deal to do today. If you don't mind I'll come directly to the point."

He waited.

"Are you acquainted with a Mr. Jon Klyk of Buffalo?"

74

"I once met the mayor at a police department convention in Buffalo. He was the speaker."

"Would that in any way keep you from investigating him?"

Powell was not going to lose this one. "Our meeting was superficial. There would be no conflict."

Loren nodded curtly, then proceeded to explain to Powell that Jon Klyk was the only obstacle in her husband's road to the governor's mansion. She was equally forthright about what she wanted him to do.

"I'll take care of this personally, Mrs. Sturdivant. I agree with you . . . spoilers serve no constructive purpose. I think your word—neutralized—describes the solution. It will be done. I guarantee it."

CHAPTER 11

THERE WERE THOSE who attended Judge Henry Stewart's funeral out of a sense of respect for his position. Henry Stewart had been a pioneer—the Jackie Robinson of the political establishment, the first black assemblyman, the first black state senator, the first black supreme court justice of New York State. There were others who attended because they deeply felt his loss. Judges Sturdivant, Levine and Parker were among these. It had been a rare day when the four did not meet in Sturdivant's chambers for lunch. They were of the same mold, scholars of the law who were held in high esteem by both the bench and the bar. Their legal opinions were intelligently and concisely written, and they took great pleasure in discussing the law and their individual philosophical approaches to it.

As the strains of "Amazing Grace" filtered through the Abyssinian Baptist Church, the three survivors of the daily luncheon meetings sat together, still stunned by the fact of their friend's death. Allen Sturdivant was trying to organize his thoughts. Earlier in the day, before the service began, the pastor had called him into his study. "Judge Sturdivant," he had said, "I was Henry Stewart's minister and friend for almost forty years. Henry used to confide in me. He knew he was dying—"

"I had no idea—"

"He preferred it that way. He accepted it as humbly as he accepted his life. And he was as prepared for his death as he was for life. He asked that you represent his colleagues at his funeral—a short eulogy. I know this is unfair asking you at the last moment but Henry said—I can almost hear him—'Don't give Allen Sturdivant advance notice. He may say no.'"

"Say no?" Sturdivant asked. "Who would say no to such an honor?" And to himself . . . am I worthy of it? What would this wonderful man have thought had he known that his friend Judge Sturdivant was living a terrible lie, that he had actually killed someone? Henry Stewart, whose sense of honor and truth and justice was unparalleled by anyone Sturdivant had ever met, would never have believed his friend capable of committing such an act. Sturdivant felt torn apart.

"Amazing Grace" ended, the minister began to speak. Sturdivant looked around the crowded chapel, saw Henry Stewart's family in the first few pews. He recognized Henry's wife, Emily, who had gone through so much with her husband. Next to her were their children and grandchildren. There were others who bore a family resemblance, from the branch of Henry's family that had never immigrated from Bermuda.

The minister's voice broke into Sturdivant's thoughts, speaking words that must have been spoken over Andrea Blanchard's lifeless body. He'd almost been able to shut out thoughts of Andrea during the past two months, now the nightmare came rushing back. The consolation being offered by the minister to the mourners of Henry Stewart held no consolation, gave no relief to Allen Sturdivant.

He felt himself tremble as the congregation stood to sing a hymn . . . Images of Andrea flashed through his mind, beginning at Lake Como—ending at her apartment on that Christmas Eve . . . He heard the minister call his name and for a moment, in his panic, was tempted to turn and run from the church, then forced himself to go to the front of the church. He had been blessed to have the likes of Henry Stewart touch his life. For God's sake, don't fail him too.

And normally cool, collected Allen Sturdivant startled himself and those who knew him in the congregation by the passion in his eulogy. At the end some thought they detected an altogether uncharacteristic moisture in his eyes—a touching sign of his great sense of loss, they assumed. Except they did not, of course, know the half of it.

Judge Victor Pierce had arrived too late to get into the packed church. Not that he was all that concerned about the passing of a colleague . . . Victor Pierce had other things on his mind, and silently railed at the delay that had forced him to stand outside the church while the people he had to see were inside it.

Judge Pierce was not known for his wisdom, but that bothered him little. He didn't presume to be a Solomon . . . for him it was enough that he was a survivor. As a city councilman he had been close to indictment for failure to file New York State income tax returns for four consecutive years and had pleaded "mistake" to the grand jury, which although it cost him a bundle in legal fees, penalties and interest on his tax bill, as well as the loss of his few law clients, also made it possible for him to walk away comparatively unscarred. A year later came an inquiry into his involvement in a certain valuable variance of zoning regulations that had been granted by the Board of Standards and Appeals. Pierce denied any wrongdoing, was outraged that such an accusation should be made against him. His outrage did not impress, but the arranged lack of evidence did.

Pierce decided against running for reelection to the city council the following year, announcing that he had decided to give up public service because of the pressing financial needs of his family and so forth. Apparently, though, he had not done too badly during his eight years as councilman. He lived in a large apartment in the East Seventies and owned a spacious colonial-style home in Connecticut.

Over the years Pierce had accumulated a number of due bills from his political acquaintances, and when a state supreme court seat became vacant, he made some phone calls. The judicial screening committee, which had to pass on his qualifications, decided that he was unqualified, and the New York *Times* published this finding in a lead story that suggested Pierce's presence on the supreme court bench would be an insult to the legal establishment. No question, these were powerful forces aligned against him, but the power of political expediency was stronger, and the deals he made with political leaders throughout the county insured that he would have enough delegates at the judicial convention to put him over the top. He became a nominee of the party, which assured his election in the one-party Borough of Manhattan, then was elected to sit on the Supreme Court of the State of New York.

Victor Pierce did have a problem that was not so easily fixed: he was a judge who knew no law. Indeed he had not opened a law book since he'd crammed for his bar exam over twenty years ago. His practice had not required that particular waste of his valuable time. And so the court administrators, obliged to find a suitable place for him in the system where his abundant lack of knowledge would not be widely damaging, assigned him to a calendar part where he would not try cases, only supervise plea negotiations. It was an assignment few judges relished, but it was something he could do and in fact he did it quite well. As one lawyer said of him, "Pierce gives you offers you can't refuse."

If not the brightest of judges, Victor Pierce was among the most ambitious. Elevation to the supreme court bench was not enough to satisfy him. Why, he asked himself, if I'm so adept at clearing up the backlog can't I be put in charge of the statewide post of administrator? Under a constitutional amendment passed in 1977 the chief judge had the power to make such an appointment, and, as it had so often in Pierce's life, opportunity struck. The current state administrator had just resigned. Pierce's desire was made known to the chief through subtle and the less than subtle means that Pierce was so experienced in bringing to bear. The chief, while he was quite happy with Pierce's rate of disposition of cases, was understandably reluctant to appoint a man with Pierce's checkered past to a prestigious position in the court administration. Though the chief's reluctance frustrated Pierce, it could not deter him from trying to fulfill his new ambition.

Judge Henry Stewart's death opened the door to opportunity. Pierce was aware of the deep affection and respect that Sturdivant and the chief judge had for each other. He also was aware that Sturdivant didn't play the political game and that any approach made to Sturdivant, even by Charlie Sweeney himself, would be counter-productive. This one had to be handled in the only way Pierce knew: *hondling*. Of course one didn't hondle with a Sturdivant. But if one did something valuable for him, it stood to reason, didn't it, that he would remember it . . .

Part of Pierce's duties as the calendar judge, or up-front judge as he was referred to, was to assign to trial judges those cases that could not be disposed of by pleas of guilty, and therefore had to be tried. Normally he would send the next ready case to the first trial part that was open; to a judge who was waiting for a case to be sent to him. The Jorgensen case, which had to be reassigned after Stewart's death, was due to go to Judge Levine, the one next in line. But Victor Pierce saw his opportunity and he took it. He promptly assigned the case to Allen Sturdivant. What a favor to Sturdivant, he thought . . . it would be Sturdivant's last case before he entered the gubernatorial race. All that free media coverage, all that exposure as a dedicated public servant. And all engineered by his loyal friend Victor Pierce, who expected no quid pro quo, except, perhaps, just a word to the chief judge about friend Victor's qualifications to serve as the chief administrator. Surely in recognition of the significant contribution made to Allen Sturdivant's election that wouldn't be too much to ask . . .

To make the cheese more binding, Pierce had called Tom McPartland of All World Media, the most listened-to radio and television news reporter in the city. By giving the news to McPartland, the widest possible audience would hear that the eminent Allen Sturdivant, as his last official act before resigning to run for governor, was to preside at the most shocking trial in decades. Great stuff for the campaign to come.

It wasn't until early that afternoon that Pierce had been able to contact McPartland to give him the story, then had rushed uptown to Henry Stewart's funeral, where a public address system was needed to carry the proceedings to those who, like Pierce, arrived late. Making the best of a frustrating situation, Pierce picked his spot to work the crowd as they left the church.

His first target was Allen Sturdivant, but he cursed softly as he saw him walk quickly to his limousine with Judge Levine. There were too many people in the crowd between

Pierce and the car as he watched Levine precede Sturdivant into the vehicle, which then pulled slowly away.

Abruptly Pierce saw his alternate target Charles Sweeney walking toward his car. "Charlie, wait up . . ."

Sweeney turned and saw Pierce. Sweeney, a friendly man, usually smiled at people he knew. When he saw Victor Pierce, Sweeney did not smile. He did not like Victor Pierce. Sweeney believed lowlifes like Pierce damned every public servant, elected and appointed.

What especially offended Sweeney was that Pierce was a judge. Charlie Sweeney had respect for the law and the judiciary. Most of the judges he knew were hard-working and honest. The fact that the system, which produced such outstanding men, could also produce a Victor Pierce was depressing to Sweeney.

Now Pierce was running up and grabbing his hand. Sweeney noted that, as usual, Pierce's hand was clammy. A thin line of perspiration hung over Pierce's lip like a watery mustache. You had to think, when you looked at Pierce, that he was two steps ahead of the sheriff and was afraid to turn around.

"How are you, Judge?" Sweeney said, affecting a civil tone regardless of his feelings.

"Great, Charlie, great . . . I just want you to know that I made a significant contribution to Allen's victory today—"

Sweeney smelled trouble. "And what would that be, Judge?"

"I'm putting Allen in a spotlight where he can get all pluses and no minuses. I pushed the Jorgensen case into his part. He's going to try it." Pierce anticipated a smile of gratitude and pleasure on Sweeney's face. He didn't get it.

"Did you consult Judge Sturdivant before you assigned the Jorgensen case to him?" Sweeney asked.

Pierce felt the beginning of an attack of cold sweats. Oh

God, did I piss on the parade again? "No . . . I thought he would welcome—"

"If you had asked him, I think he would have told you that he can only lose by sitting on any case that's lurid and controversial. He was hoping to take only the quiet cases available so he could concentrate on the primary."

"Oh, shit . . ."

"It will be impossible for him to preside at the Jorgensen trial. You'll have to assign the case to some other judge."

Pierce turned gray.

"What's the matter?"

"I . . . you see . . . I thought it was so great for Allen that I gave the story to Tom McPartland. He'll have it on the six o'clock news."

Sweeney turned from Pierce and pulled open his car door. He was not finding it easy to control his anger. He got in his car and slammed the door as Benny Rabe started the engine, then rolled down his window and gazed at Victor Pierce. "Judge Pierce, I won't tell you what's running through my mind now. I'll just say good-by, and that it was my misfortune to meet you today, and that you'd better stay way the hell away from me from here on out."

Pierce was left on the sidewalk opening and closing his mouth like a landed fish.

Inside his car, Sweeney punched the thickly padded seat next to him. "That *idiot*, that *horse's ass*. To push his god-damned pitiful career he's put us all in an impossible position."

Benny handed his boss a cigarette, pushed in the car's cigarette lighter. He knew better than to say anything when the man was this angry.

"If the case lasts more than two weeks we'll be behind schedule," Sweeney lectured Benny. "And the worst of it is that if Allen resigns from the case it will look like he's ducking his sworn responsibility. After all the build-up in the campaign about public service—it would ruin his credibility. Oh that miserable greasy son-of-a-bitch . . ."

Sweeney finally leaned back, grabbed the telephone and placed a call to Allen Sturdivant's Riverdale residence. Getting the housekeeper, he left a message for Mr. Sturdivant to be sure to tune in the six o'clock news.

Allen Sturdivant, with a sense of foreboding after getting Charlie Sweeney's message, tuned into the six o'clock news just in time to hear Tom McPartland say: "This reporter has learned that Judge Allen Sturdivant, a favorite in the gubernatorial sweepstakes, has been assigned to preside at the trial of Peter Jorgensen, accused slayer of society playgirl Andrea Blanchard. Observers see political overtones in this selection. Judge Sturdivant is known as a capable judge, but one can't help wonder why a trial such as this is assigned to a man who plans to resign shortly to run for office. The paths of politics may take strange turns, but no one can really believe that this is a coincidence . . ."

It was worse, far worse, than he'd feared, and he quickly was on the phone with Sweeney. "Charlie, how did McPartland get that story?"

"Pierce."

"I thought so. You know, this is the first I've heard about the assignment . . . you know it can be a long drawn-out trial . . . any way I can pull out?"

"It's a no win situation either way, but it's worse if you pull out. It will look like your motive is political. Worse, it will seem that you caved in under pressure. I'm afraid you'll have to try the case. We'll answer McPartland's insinuations, get Pierce to issue a statement that politics had nothing to do with the assignment. That will be true as far as we're concerned. We have no choice, Allen, but to make the best of that idiot Pierce's mess."

But of course, Sturdivant thought in a panic, he *couldn't*

preside at the Jorgensen trial . . . "I'm not sure I agree with you, Charlie. The truth of the matter is that Judge Levine was next in line to be assigned this case. Let's go with the truth—"

"The truth is whatever the press says it is—or at least what they insinuate it is. Remember, the public is suspicious of every politician and figures any action during a political campaign is self-serving. This is a lousy break, but we'll deal with it."

Of course Sweeney was right . . . any further protest would begin to raise questions, look suspicious. "All right, Charlie, you're right, I'll take the case."

Except how could he preside at the trial of a man accused of his crime . . . all right, an act committed when he was out of control, not even aware of what he was doing . . . but since when was that an excuse, except in the strictly legal sense of diminished capacity. Stop it, he was not a masochist or suicidal. He would, somehow, conduct a proper trial, stay uninvolved, let the evidence clear the man on trial . . . Andrea was gone, nothing could be done to bring her back. Did it help her, anybody, to beat his breast in an orgy of self-indulgence that would serve no one, and end forever the opportunity to serve that he'd prepared a whole lifetime for. The answer to that was clear. Face it, he ordered himself. Face it, and try to make a life that would help atone. Don't let it all have been for nothing . . .

"Can I get you anything, Your Honor," the housekeeper was asking, thinking the judge was looking a bit under the weather.

"No, no thank you, I'm fine. Really. Just fine."

CHAPTER 12

MARC HAMMOND WAS no closer to planning his defense of Peter Jorgensen than he had been the day Charlie Sweeney first called him. Further, it looked as though the prosecution was going to walk into court with an airtight case. Hammond knew the circumstantial evidence had been piling high enough to convince any jury of Peter's guilt. The only break so far was that Allen Sturdivant had been assigned to the case. If nothing else, they at least were guaranteed a fair trial.

Hammond had spent a good deal of time with Peter Jorgensen over the past weeks and had become convinced that Peter was innocent. He felt sorry for Peter, a nice kid if not terribly bright. The real problem was that it seemed the only way to prove Peter's innocence was to prove someone else guilty. But who? The police weren't even looking. As far as they were concerned they'd found their man. Case closed.

If Peter were going to have any chance, Marc decided he'd better start from the beginning, which meant finding out all he could about the late Andrea Blanchard. She'd been, it seemed, the prototypical international good time girl. All right, who had she had a good time with? Marc called a friend at the New York *Post* and arranged to have the morgue file on Andrea made available to him. He figured the *Post* would have much more thorough coverage of a flamboyant personality like Andrea Blanchard than the staid New York *Times*.

The folder was chock full with photographs and gossip columns about parties, openings, trips. Marc noted that her escorts had all been wealthy men well known to the society columnists. Her name was even linked to members of several European royal families. One photograph in particular caught his eye, Andrea in a bikini shoving the crown prince of Saudi Arabia into a swimming pool. In another he read a story about an Italian count who threatened suicide when she refused to leave New York to live with him in his villa on the isle of Capri. Andrea Blanchard had been good copy.

He made a list of the people mentioned with her in the news stories. He made a note next to each name of the dates of the incidents. Who knew what he hoped to find . . . at least it was a beginning.

He returned the file to the morgue, walked outside onto South Street and stood in front of the old granite building. Everything led to the question of motive. Who on the list had a motive to kill Andrea? Who *didn't*? One theme ran through all those stories: an unhappy ending. Any number of her "friends" could have resented her, even hated her. But enough to kill her? Marc scanned the list again. He doubted the motive was something as simple as jealousy, revenge. Possibly, but not likely with someone like Andrea. Otherwise it would have happened long ago. More likely it was someone who had a real *need* to kill her. She might well have come on information that could have ruined someone. Someone important . . . blackmail? Maybe.

He pocketed the list and as he headed north drew a mental profile for himself of Andrea Blanchard . . . beautiful body and face, an exhibitionist. And a survivor until she pressed her luck one time too many. On the basis of the morgue file, he found he didn't much like her, which would make it easier when it came time to present her to the jury as a woman who had earned the violent end that someone—*not* his unfortunate client—had brought down on her.

Marc looked at his watch, hailed a taxi and gave the cabbie Helen Jorgensen's address. So far she had refused to see him, and had gone to Riker's Island only once to see her son. Helen Jorgensen, it seemed, was a deeply religious woman. Believing her son guilty, she had told him that she would pray for his soul and for God's forgiveness but she would not come to see him again. His sin, even as her son, was apparently too great for her forgiveness.

The woman who opened the door to Marc looked deeply tired. She didn't turn him away but she wouldn't let him into the apartment either, holding the door and talking through a twelve-inch opening.

Marc told her he believed in Peter's innocence. No reaction. She appeared stunned, as if she still had not gotten over the shock of finding Andrea Blanchard's body, although two months had passed. Actually, she'd been dealt a double blow; the loss of Andrea Blanchard, who had treated her well and whom she had truly cared about, and the horror of her son being held for Andrea's death.

When Marc tried to question her about anyone Andrea had known who might have had a motive to kill her, Helen became agitated. Marc tried to calm her, to sound casual, but it was no use.

"Mr. Hammond," she said, her voice hollow, "I can't help you. I won't tell you things that Miss Blanchard told me. They've nothing to do with . . . with what happened to her. They will not help my son." She began to close the door. "God will see to it that justice is done. Andrea Blanchard was a good woman, good to me . . . you won't save Peter by destroying her memory. You'll only end up destroying them both."

Marc looked into Helen Jorgensen's eyes. They belonged to a true believer . . . the hardest kind to crack. He would get no help here. He turned and walked away as the door closed. The bottom line, it seemed, was that he and Peter Jorgensen were on their own, far out on a limb, with no help or safety net in sight.

Marc had to catch his breath as he did every time he saw Randy Spencer. He doubted he would ever get used to her beauty, and as she now held the door of her apartment open for him, he decided he never wanted to.

The day after Christmas he'd made up his mind to see her again and had called everyone he knew with any connection to the fashion world. Finally a former and forgiving girlfriend who worked at Vogue told him that Randy was represented by the Dodge Agency. The Dodge Agency, however, would tell him nothing. Then, through a friend of a friend who was dating another Dodge model, Marc struck paydirt.

Randy was not surprised to hear from him. What did surprise—and please—her was the speed with which he had tracked her down. "No one's ever done it in less than two weeks," she said, laughing into the phone.

Somehow she didn't sound conceited, just open and good-humored—traits Marc had given up much hope of finding in a modern single woman that attracted him. "I can be at your place in twenty minutes."

He made it in fifteen.

From that night on Marc and Randy had spent their limited

free time together. There was no game-playing. They enjoyed each other's company, begrudged the crowded schedules that kept them apart.

Now as Marc entered her apartment Randy took one look at him and saw trouble. She took his coat, led him into the living room, without a word poured a very dry martini and sat him down next to her on the couch.

"That bad?" she said.

He took a long sip of the martini. "I'm afraid I'm not going to be very good company tonight. I mean the ballet, all those tutus and—"

She leaned over and slowly kissed him on the lips. "Then we won't go. We'll just have to find something to do right here in the old homestead."

And then she was in his arms, and soon there was no room for anything in his life except the hungry, generous loving of Randy Spencer.

The next morning, stationed in the lobby of the Monte Carlo Apartments, Marc, at a nod from the doorman he had tipped generously, followed a middle-aged woman into the elevator and then to the door of her apartment, directly across the hall from the late Andrea Blanchard's.

Leaving the elevator, Marc had said, "I'm a lawyer involved in the Blanchard case. May I ask you a few questions?"

At first she hesitated, then shrugged. He seemed so nice and clean-cut looking. "All right, but I don't want my name mentioned in court."

"No names, I promise . . . Did you ever talk with Andrea Blanchard?"

"Just in passing. Good morning. Have a nice day. Terrible weather. That sort of thing."

"How did she impress you?"

"She seemed okay, minded her own business. But"—

the woman lowered her voice—"she had visitors, sometimes late at night. I used to hear her door opening and closing."

"Did you ever see any of the people who visited her late at night?"

"Look, I mind my own business. Live and let live is my motto. Don't laugh, I mean it. In this city the less you know, the better off you are. But once, it was real late and there'd been some robberies in the building, I did look through the peephole and saw a man in front of her door. You know, as I remember it now, it looked as if he was letting himself in."

"Do you remember what he looked like?"

"No, I only saw his back. But I can tell you one thing . . ."

"Yes?"

"I'm pretty sure it wasn't that kid that they say killed her. I saw him once, I think it was last spring sometime—maybe May or early June. Andrea was having a party in her apartment. She rang our bell and asked if she could borrow some ice, so my husband and I took a bucket to her apartment. When we saw that Jorgensen kid's picture in the paper we both remembered that he'd been the bartender at that party . . . but like I say, I'm almost sure he wasn't the one I saw letting himself into Andrea's apartment."

"Why do you say that?"

"Different builds. The kid was much thinner, taller." She smiled. "Sort of cute buns, if you follow me. What the hell, I'm still alive, I got a right to look . . ."

Marc had to like her, for what she said and the way she said it. But of course it didn't clear Jorgensen—just meant that the night she saw a man it wasn't Jorgensen. There were, as the prosecution would point out, other nights . . . like the murder night.

* * *

Marc's first question to Peter at their next session was about the party. Andrea had called him to "help out" as bartender at a party she was throwing for some friends. Andrea never asked Helen to work at such social gatherings that were catered. This one would be too, but Andrea said she was afraid she'd underestimated the number of guests and the caterers couldn't provide an extra bartender in time. That's what she said . . .

For Peter the prospect of mingling with celebrities—and being paid for it—was too good to miss. He didn't know much about mixing drinks, so he took a quickie mini-course from a bartender friend.

The caterer and his staff were already setting up, Peter said, when he arrived, and he proceeded to look busy at the bar. Andrea made an entrance after most of the guests had arrived, and she was a knockout in black silk evening pants and cut-to-the-navel blouse. Her necklace was the prize trophy of her marriage to the Saudi Arabian prince—a nineteen carat square-cut emerald encrusted in diamonds and supported by a diamond chain. Her black hair hung loose and full.

Peter recognized many of the guests from movies, or television, the magazines. Soon someone at the piano was playing up a storm, the room was filled with laughter, gorgeous women. He was on a high just being there, and after three vodkas he felt even better.

His high, though, soon dissipated when he spotted a grungy looking character in too much jewelry, including a gold coke spoon held by a solid gold chain. Worse, guests began to approach him for little white packages of pills of all colors. The Candy Man. Later cocaine made its appearance and the beautiful people began to seem considerably less beautiful.

Peter had been around drugs before but he'd never seen anything quite as blatant as this. The worst part was the way 'these hotshots were ass-kissing the sleaze. He felt he had to get away, he couldn't take this place or these people any longer. He preferred his own friends to these characters anytime . . . at least they cared about each other.

As he was about to take off he felt pressure on his arm— Andrea's hand. "You don't look very happy," she said.

"Well, I guess this isn't my thing."

She bent forward and whispered in his ear. "Let's try to find something that is."

She took his hand and led him upstairs. She opened the door of each of the bedrooms and closed them quickly. "We seem to be a little late," she said, and steered him into a large bathroom, locked the door and turned on the light.

She moved quickly then, undressing herself from the waist down and doing the same for him. He had never known another woman who was so sexually aggressive. Andrea Blanchard simply had no inhibitions. She maneuvered him to the carpeted floor, and did things with her mouth and fingers that were new to him in their expertise.

When it was over they went back to the party, she to the guests who were still relatively sober, he to the bar. He was still not entranced by the beautiful people with their guard down, but he was feeling better about himself. After all, that was *Andrea Blanchard* who had just seduced *him* . . . Andrea Blanchard the famous international beauty. She had chosen him. From all the big deals at that party she had chosen Peter Jorgensen. Not too shabby for a three-hundred-dollar-a-week mechanic . . .

Yes, not too shabby, Marc agreed, but he was less interested in the erotic happenings at the party than the possibility of identifying at least one suspect for Andrea Blanchard's murder. Did anybody, he pressed Peter, show resentment at Andrea's behavior, especially her disappearing from the party with him? Did someone seem especially possessive of her—

man or woman? Peter tried hard to remember, but had to tell Marc that he just couldn't remember anybody that seemed to care much what anybody else did, including Andrea. It was that kind of a bash. Sorry . . .

Marc nodded, patted him on the shoulder. "Never mind, we'll come up with something . . ." He hoped he sounded more sanguine than he felt.

CHAPTER 13

SINCE FORMING HIS agency, J. Franklin Powell had restricted himself to handling administrative duties. However, the importance of the investigation of Jon Klyk at the request of Loren Sturdivant had persuaded Powell to handle this case himself, as he had promised to do.

Powell's man in Buffalo met him at the airport, and while they drove to the hotel Powell was filled in on the mayor. Most of what the operative told him was already known by half of Buffalo. Jon Klyk was not a corrupt man, there was no evidence that he had even profited financially from his office. Maybe he was too kind to some political connections who were undeserving of the public trust, but that could normally be expected from the man who wore two hats, mayor and county leader. Klyk understood the fine line between political *quid pro quo* and corruption, and his instincts were sharp enough never to cross that line.

Powell soon realized that if Klyk was vulnerable at all, it must be in his personal, not his political, life. Klyk did, he was told, have something of a reputation as a womanizer, but so far it had not hurt him in an election. If anything, the voters of Buffalo grinned and winked, rather enjoying their mayor's philandering in the otherwise drab unhappy events of the day.

Powell had studied all the reports. Klyk, it seemed, was an extrovert not inclined to be cautious in his connections. Somewhere along the line this could have led him to make a serious mistake in judgment, not just a bit of womanizing—a mistake that if unearthed, could be exactly what Loren Sturdivant was looking for.

If you told Jimmy Powell that he was digging up dirt to blackmail the mayor of Buffalo he would have considered that a bloody slander. The carrying out of this assignment was, in his mind, a legitimate pursuit of his profession . . . he was merely gathering information and delivering it to his client. What his client did with the material was none of his business.

Powell's years as a street cop had taught him to start at the bottom, beneath the public persona. That's where you found the heart of the matter, the unpretty nitty-gritty. His operative had told him about a bar called Louie's, apparently a Buffalo institution. Right around the corner from City Hall, it was an old-fashioned tavern that politicos and civil service employees frequented, a place where they could all get a bag on in a congenial atmosphere. Louie welcomed them all; titles and honors were left at the door. Louie himself was nonpolitical, having realized long before that partisanship in the bar business could be deadly. He solicited the ins and the outs, which meant that the opponents of Mayor Jon Klyk, mostly only a few outcasts from favor, were free to voice their criticism of His Honor so long as it was done, as Louie put it, in a "civilized style." After all, Jon Klyk, a four-time mayor, was by now something of an institution in the city of Buffalo.

Powell's first visit to Louie's was on a chilly afternoon,

making the warm atmosphere at the bar especially welcome. He sat at the bar for four hours. He spoke to no one, and no one spoke to him, except for Louie, of course, who was cautiously friendly. Powell sipped beer the whole time—actually he was a teetotaler, drinking only when the job called for it. He nursed his beer carefully, he would not allow his senses to be dulled.

That first day, and the next two, Powell struck out. He'd buy drinks for occasional prospects and learn nothing. He knew it was time to move on . . . he was even beginning to like the beer. He had given his name as Jim Mortonson and said his occupation was selling steel products, which was enough . . . Louie was not nosy, nor were his customers. Powell was looked on as a pleasant enough guy passing through, and after the first day he more or less melted into the background. Actually he hadn't sat around a bar like this for ages and would have enjoyed himself if he hadn't been working.

The break came on the fourth day, just as he was about to give up on Louie's, and it came from a most unlikely source. It was nearly midnight and the crowd was thinning out when a well-dressed man entered. He was obviously a regular, well known to the remaining patrons who all greeted him. Louie informed Powell that the man was Billy McNiff, Buffalo's water commissioner. More important, he was *the* political aide to the mayor, the number two man. Around City Hall they called him "Avis" McNiff, and like Klyk he was outgoing, ebullient, friendly.

Powell watched McNiff carefully. The man's tongue became looser with every round; he talked a lot, and about a lot of people. As the evening wore on he became more explicit and, so it seemed to Powell, more careless. He was not a good drunk.

At 2 A.M. McNiff was by himself at the bar, sitting leeward. Powell slid down the bar to the stool next to McNiff's and ordered another beer for himself and a double Scotch for McNiff.

The water commissioner of Buffalo turned to his benefactor and smiled. "Why, thank you, friend. I'm afraid I didn't get your name."

"Mortonson. Jim Mortonson. My pleasure."

"Billy McNiff." They shook hands and Powell had to apply pressure to his grip to prevent McNiff from falling on him.

"Wonderful town you have here, Billy."

"The garden spot of the state."

"And your mayor . . . I've heard good things about him."

"All true," McNiff said. "Salt of the earth. Best damn mayor money can buy."

Powell nearly did a double take. "What makes him so popular? I mean four terms—and the way I hear it the last one was a laugher."

"No one's ever going to beat Jonny Klyk in this town. Let me tell you, you got to have it in this game—that special quality. Jon Klyk was born with it."

Powell sensed envy in McNiff's voice . . . that crack about the best mayor money could buy . . . sour grapes? Squeeze 'em and see. He hoped a few more drinks would do it. He ordered another round.

"Make it neat, Louie," McNiff said. He downed the double Scotch in two quick motions. "The ladies love Jonny and he loves the ladies. When he performs at a women's club meeting they damn near come. He's good with them, all kinds, all ages and races. An equal opportunity screwer, our mayor. But that's all right, that's part of what makes him the champ. The blue collar loves him, the white collar loves him, the ladies love him. He can do no wrong. No matter what, in this town, Jonny Klyk can do no wrong."

Powell was reeling in his fish but he had to be careful not to pull out the hook. The little green man was no longer disguised. McNiff was a loser—and a bitter one. He obviously didn't like being known as "Avis."

Another double Scotch was ordered, and was just as quickly consumed.

"Hope I'm not holding you up," Powell said.

"No, no, you're not keeping me from anything. My wife isn't waiting for me. The kids aren't waiting for me. Stopped waiting two years ago. Traveling with Jonny, I went first class. But after the parties and good times and laughs I had to go home. I guess I expected them to wait for me forever. Kind of dumb, right? Look what I traded my family, my future for—lousy water commissioner of the City of Buffalo. Big deal."

McNiff pulled a handkerchief from his pocket and blew his nose. From Powell's experience, once a drunk reached that stage, he wouldn't stop until it all hung out.

"Billy," Powell said, "if you had it to do all over again, would you have done it differently?"

"With what I know now? You bet your sweet ass. I would have been another Jon Klyk, in spades. I was afraid to take chances, he wasn't. You ever meet a guy who always lands on his feet? Oh, his wife finally divorced him—she couldn't take all the broads. It was all nice and quiet. She got her settlement, not a fortune, moved away and nobody got hurt."

"He's had a charmed life," said Powell.

McNiff lifted his glass, saw that it was empty and banged it on the bar. "That's *just* what it is, my friend. A charmed life. No matter how deep a hole he digs he gets out of it . . . take that thing with Norma Policheck—"

"Norma Policheck?"

"Christ . . . don't you know what happened with Norma Policheck?"

"No," said Powell carefully, "can't say that I heard about it."

"Well, we told him not to go near her but he laughed us

off. We worry, he does it, and he laughs. It's one tightrope after another. But he never falls off. Like tonight . . ."

"Tonight?" Norma Policheck could wait.

"Yeah . . . if we told him once we told him a million times. Stay the hell away from Pell." He smiled, perhaps savoring the unintended rhyme.

"Who's Pell?"

"A hundred percent fourteen-carat scumbag. Fat slob's into every dirty action in town. Porno bookstores, massage parlors, numbers—no question he's got racket connections or he couldn't operate. Even worse than that . . ."

Powell waited.

"Kiddie porn. He likes little girls in his movies. The younger, the better."

"Why does Jon Klyk have anything to do with him?"

"Money. Pell's a big contributor to the organization. Oh, Jonny's honest—wouldn't take a dime—never has. But for the organization, his only real family, he draws no lines on who he accepts money from. I think it's a mistake. You got to stop at a snake like Pell."

Powell signaled to the bartender to fill McNiff's glass again, then asked as casually as he could, "What's happening tonight?"

"What? Oh, tonight . . . tonight Pell's holding a meeting of the heavy contributors at his house. Jonny says he can't offend Pell, has to show. Well, maybe he's right and I'm wrong. All the fat cats are going to be there. They don't seem to mind. I guess no one wants to offend that scumbag . . ."

Powell made his move. "Billy, I admire Klyk—have for years. One of the reasons I'm in town is to make a contribution to his campaign. I can understand your feelings about this Pell person, but I can also understand, like you say, why Klyk wouldn't want to offend him. Since I'm leaving late tonight, maybe I should stop by Pell's and just go give Jonny my check personally."

"You're going to give him money for the campaign?"

"Yes. A substantial amount."

"What do you call a substantial amount?"

"Over ten thousand."

McNiff eyed Powell blearily. "You know what I think?"

"What?"

"I think you're full of shit."

Powell stood up and signaled for the check.

"Where ya goin'?"

"It seems you're not interested in my offer."

"Aw, forget it . . . gimme a pen." He couldn't have Jonny hear he'd blown a ten thousand dollar contribution.

The bartender supplied the pen and McNiff wrote Pell's address on a paper napkin. "That's the creep's address. You can get there any time after nine. I'll tell Jonny you're coming. Give your name at the door."

J. Franklin Powell prided himself on using the most advanced surveillance aids available, including the camera he was using for this job, which operated through a shortwave signal from his watch. The camera itself was a black box, one inch in length, width and depth. He wore it strapped to his shirt. The lens opening fell flush behind an opening in an American flag lapel pin that he wore. By depressing the crown of his watch, the shutter reacted and the film was exposed. Through a complicated infrared process photographs could be taken without supplementary lighting and were crystal clear after enlargement.

He double checked his IDs in the name of James Mortonson: social security card, driver's license, credit cards and, most important, a check bearing the name of a nonexistent bank in Ohio with "James Mortonson" printed prominently on its face. He would, for the moment at least, be able to put his money where his mouth was.

101

Powell exchanged his Chevy at the agency for a souped-up Camaro. He wanted a car with a high compression engine, just in case.

Pell's house, on the top of a hill on the northern outskirts of Buffalo, looked like a castle with its watchtowers at the four corners. It would have been an ideal set for a Frankenstein movie, Powell thought. What added to its eeriness was the absence of moonlight and the dense fog shrouding the grounds. Powell noted several cars in the driveway. A faint light over the main doorway pierced the fog.

The woman who responded to the doorbell checked a list when Powell gave his name. "Okay," she said. "You're here. Go on up the stairs."

Powell found a group of paunched and demi-paunched men sitting around a large round table. McNiff, who had, remarkably, apparently slept it off, greeted Powell effusively.

Now Jon Klyk himself was coming up to him, smiling. He put his arm around Powell's shoulder. "Welcome. Billy McNiff tells me you're a friend. We can always use friends."

"It's an honor, Mr. Mayor."

"The honor is mine, Jim. Let me introduce you to our host." He guided Powell to a heavyset man with a round fleshy face. "Stanley," Klyk said, "I took the liberty of inviting a new friend."

Pell nodded curtly, obviously not happy to see somebody new that hadn't been checked out.

Powell was shown a chair and listened as anticipated campaign expenses were discussed, both for the primary and the general election. Then the talk stopped and the checks appeared. When his turn came Powell handed Klyk a check drawn on the Ohio bank for twenty-five thousand dollars.

Klyk smiled his thanks.

Pell did not. He now spoke directly to Powell for the first time. "Mortonson, we're a group of Buffalo businessmen that have a stake in Jon's election. None of us has ever seen you before. What do you want? What's your game?"

"Well, sir, I'm a longtime admirer of Mayor Klyk. I think he should be governor. I'm willing to contribute toward that end. I also represent certain interests who are *not* admirers of Allen Sturdivant, people who would rather Sturdivant not become governor. *That's* my game. And that's all I'm going to say. If that's not good enough, Mr. Pell, I'll leave now and take my check with me—"

"Hey, that's good enough for me," Klyk broke in, laughing. The tension was broken, the subject was dropped.

Finally, with his diamond-ringed finger flashing and the large gold Rolex watch prominently displayed on his wrist, Pell made an announcement. "Gentlemen," he said, "I have a little surprise for you. Enjoy."

He signaled, and one of two bodyguards who had been close to him all evening opened a door at the far side of the room. Three naked girls, none of whom could have been more than fourteen, came bouncing into the room. They jumped from lap to lap, planting kisses on overstuffed faces, rubbing against the men, holding their hands against their breasts. Those not interested in the entertainment left. A handful remained.

One of the girls abruptly moved onto Jon Klyk's lap. As casually as he could, Powell faced Klyk and pressed the crown of his watch as the girl kissed a surprised and uncomfortable Jon Klyk. He especially didn't know what to do with his hands. The young girl promptly steered them to her breasts, all of it captured on film not once but three times, at various angles, so that Klyk's identity could not be disputed.

Powell now began to edge away from Klyk and would have been home free if Billy McNiff's time off the wagon had not been too brief. McNiff, who had been helping himself to Pell's Scotch at the bar, took a step back, stumbled and lost his balance—the only thing available to break his fall being Powell's jacket, which opened as McNiff grabbed it, exposing the small camera and the tape holding it in place. Powell, acting instinctively, tried to cover up the damaging evidence but it was too late. One of Pell's bodyguards saw it and called out, "The son-of-a-bitch is wired . . ."

There followed a rush for the front door by Klyk, McNiff and the remaining contributors, the girls exiting the back door. In a matter of seconds Powell, Pell and Pell's two muscle men were alone. One of Pell's bodyguards went to his waist, produced a blackjack and with his henchman moved slowly toward Powell.

Back to the wall, Powell thought of his words to the Marine recruits at Parris Island years ago when he was in top physical shape, good enough for the Marines to use him as an instructor in hand-to-hand combat. *What I'm teaching you is never to be used unless you want to kill a man or seriously cripple him. Learn this well—it's the art of dirty fighting, it's the art of surviving.*

They were less than three feet from him. No more time for instructive memories. His left leg lashed out in a perfectly placed karate kick. Pell caught the full force of the blow in his groin and dropped to the floor. At nearly the same time the flat of Powell's left hand came into contact with the nose of one of the bodyguards. Powell could feel the bones crunch, saw blood begin to flow. The second man was now swinging his blackjack in a short arc. Powell moved his head to the left, just missing the full force of the blow, which landed on his right arm. And hurt. He extended the second and third fingers of his right hand and drove each into the man's eyes. The man's screams followed Powell as he ran down the stairs and out the door to his car in the still fog-covered driveway.

The Camaro accelerated like a rocket, followed by three cracking noises, presumably shots. Powell did not slow down to find out for certain. He sped down the hill, careened around a corner on two wheels. He would have felt safer if a patrol car had picked him up on radar and stopped him, then thought the thought of a million other civilians before him: *You can never find a cop when you need one.*

CHAPTER 14

CHARLIE SWEENEY AND Mickey Goldman were the classic odd couple. Charlie had grown up conservative Irish, Mickey Goldman had been born into an immigrant family of Jewish liberals. The relationship between the two went back forty years, during which time Charlie had become a liberal politician and Goldman a conservative labor leader. One thing had not changed over the years—respect for each other.

Mickey Goldman was president of the powerful Association of Public Employees but controlled the votes of more than just his members. Any public employee not his came under the umbrella of the New York State Civil Service Confederation, of which Goldman was chairman. Translating his political power into numbers, Mickey Goldman pretty well could deliver the votes of over 100,000 statewide workers. Goldman, though, knew the limits of his power. In a citywide or statewide election other groups rivaled labor in pulling power. A labor endorsement, he knew, while beneficial by no means meant a lock on the election; but, in a close race, it definitely was better to have Mickey Goldman with you than not.

Once agreements were made between Charlie Sweeney and Mickey Goldman they were never broken. Those times when they could not get together on a candidate or issue, they simply agreed to disagree and shook hands on it. Still, each hated turning down the other, which was why Goldman was not happy when Sweeney had asked him to support Allen Sturdivant. Goldman did not want to get involved in the primary. He knew Sturdivant had had a good labor record when he had been in Congress, voting "right" over eighty-five percent of the time. But Goldman also had no fault to find with Jon Klyk, whose labor record as mayor of Buffalo was exemplary. Mickey preferred not to commit himself, even though Sturdivant would be the obvious winner in the primary. If he did, when the smoke cleared he would have to deal with an angry Klyk in Buffalo. He probably would anyway. It was a no-win situation, and he had spelled it out for Charlie Sweeney when they had met in Sweeney's office.

"I know all that stuff," Charlie had said, "but do you want Beale for four more years?"

"God forbid," Goldman replied. "So why don't you just tell Klyk to pull out?"

"I wish to hell I could. You know Jonny. When he thinks he's doing the right thing, Jesus H. Christ couldn't make him change his mind. I understand why he's doing this . . . I don't agree with it but I understand it. And he understands that I have to do my best to knock him out of the box as soon as I can. If he doesn't get twenty-five percent of the delegates at the state convention he won't get on the ballot unless he gets signatures on petitions. With your support for Sturdivant he may not get them, but even if he does it will weaken him for the third-party run."

"You can stop that," Goldman said.

"I don't think so. Some of my leaders in the state are

very fond of Jonny Klyk. And keep this in mind, Mickey . . . if Jonny gets that third independent line he divides our vote and Beale wins."

Goldman shook his head. "I'm sorry, Charlie. I can't do it. It's not in my people's interest."

"At least give me this much—see Sturdivant with me, size him up and then make up your mind. Give me at least that shot at your support."

Goldman had reluctantly agreed, and Sweeney had set up the meeting in Sturdivant's chambers. Goldman had felt strongly about privacy . . . the fewer who knew about the meeting the better. Those were also Sturdivant's sentiments when he had arranged to meet them the next evening. Now he waited for them at the receptionist's desk, where a court officer normally sat during court hours to announce visitors and escort them to chambers.

Sturdivant's chambers were the largest and most opulent in the court building. Victor Pierce, ever the expert in currying favor for what he believed to be his own benefit, and ever the expert in screwing his colleagues, had assigned Sturdivant to those chambers, ignoring the seniority of some judges who had been on the bench for fifteen years or longer and ordinarily would have had the first option, except they happened to have been of no value to Pierce. To Sturdivant's credit, he was unaware of the preferential treatment, and by the time he heard of the rumblings of his colleagues, he was settled in and for all practical purposes could not move.

The size of the room had also given Loren the opportunity to display her taste in furnishings, which reflected, she felt, the dignity and prestige of her husband's position. One wall of the room was covered by a mahogany bookcase, a minilibrary that contained every set of law reference books available. Sturdivant was a student of the law and made personal use of these books, preferring to do his own research. He worked at the job . . . The beige carpeting was thick piled

108

wool, the drapes a soft black-and-beige linen. Two black leather couches faced each other, framed at the ends by metal art-deco tables and lamps. Glass coffee tables were in front of each couch. Sturdivant's black mahogany desk was hand carved. It was probably the only judge's chambers ever to be photographed for *Architectural Digest* magazine.

Mickey Goldman was not impressed by the august trappings. His headquarters in a lower Manhattan union-owned building was furnished in true-blue proletarian. His office was only slightly larger than the quarters he had when he started as leader of a small local. He didn't affect plainness; it was his style.

Charlie Sweeney, on the other hand, appreciated the luxury that the judge's chambers represented. Sweeney, like Goldman a simple man, understood and appreciated wealth, and the power it represented; after all, one learned something from a close association with the Kennedy clan. It occurred now to Sweeney that Allen Sturdivant seemed at least distracted, perhaps nervous, but after the introductions Sturdivant seemed to relax. As if, Sweeney thought, whatever had been on his mind was diminished by the importance of this meeting.

"Allen," Sweeney said, "I'm trying to persuade Mickey to endorse you. I'm afraid he hasn't given me any encouragement."

Sturdivant smiled. "I regret that, Mr. Goldman. I would have thought my labor record deserved your consideration, but I understand—"

"I don't want to be the heavy, Judge," Mickey said. "There's nothing wrong with your record. I think you'd make a good candidate. So would Jon Klyk—at least from our point of view. He's proved he's a friend, and we don't discard friends unless we have no choice. We have, you might say, no visible incentives."

Obviously, Sturdivant thought, Charlie had brought Goldman to him so that "incentives" could be offered: patronage, promises of future consultations on appointments, promises of preference for labor. The ball, as they liked to say, was in his court.

Mickey Goldman broke the silence. "Judge," he asked slowly, "what's your position on pension supplements?" Mickey was referring to labor's sore point . . . for years inflation had been causing hardships to his retirees who had pensioned out five or more years before. In many cases where pensioners weren't able to work the hardships were extreme. Mickey had succeeded in getting a bill passed that provided for an increase in pension payments to equal the rate of inflation—retroactive to the date of retirement. Governor Beale had vetoed it. What made it especially difficult for Goldman to abandon Klyk now was that the Buffalo mayor had instantly reacted to Beale's veto and joined Goldman in his condemnation of Beale, publicly promising that if he was elected governor he would make pension-supplements the law.

Sturdivant, knowing how important this was to Goldman, said, "If I'm elected I would have to make an assessment as to whether an increase in pension costs would diminish essential services in the cities, not to mention what impact a pension supplement would have on the statewide economy. If we can absorb it, we should do it. But the numbers have to be there."

Mickey Goldman had to feel a grudging respect for this man, but he still wasn't getting the right answer. "Frankly, Judge," he said, "I've heard *numbers* all my life. My experience has been that if you try hard enough you can always find the money."

Sturdivant nodded. "If that turns out to be the case, then we're in agreement. If I find that public services won't be curtailed, the pension-supplement bill will be passed. And no veto."

110

"That's not exactly a commitment—"

"But it's the truth." And it felt good saying it.

Sweeney knew that Goldman was not happy, not at all. But Charlie had also anticipated this Mexican standoff, and so had not gone into this meeting without ammunition. The boss had friends all over, including an agent in Beale's camp who kept him advised about doings in Republican headquarters. The latest intelligence, gleaned from an out-of-state labor leader in Beale's camp, could prove helpful to the Sturdivant image.

"Allen," Sweeney said, "did you ever hear of a small town in Appalachia called Owl's Beak?"

Sturdivant's lips thinned. "I've heard of it." His voice was expressionless.

Goldman laughed. "Where the hell is Owl's Beak, and what the hell does it have to do with why we're here?"

"Humor me, Mickey," Sweeney said. "Owl's Beak is a miserable coal mining town in West Virginia where the poverty level is just about as low as you can get in the good old U.S. of A. Last year the only chance those people had to survive without welfare died with the collapse of the mine. It was bad enough that ten men were killed and dozens injured, but the company decided not to reopen. More than one hundred mortgages were in default. The bank had no choice—it had to foreclose."

Sturdivant stared straight ahead.

"Last week," Sweeney went on, "at the eleventh hour, you might say, the bank received a call from a foundation in New York that inquired about covering the mortgages. But before they could get their hopes up the foundation called again and told them that the trustees had ruled against such a grant. Then they received a third call: good news from a donor who said he personally would cover the mortgages as long as he was not identified. Naturally, the bank agreed."

111

Still no reaction from Sturdivant. "You should have known that you can't keep a secret in a small town, Allen. Beale's office had the name of the donor within an hour. The Sturdivant Foundation was going to pull them out of it, then its investment managers changed their minds. So you reached deep—I hear for more than a quarter of a million."

Mickey Goldman whistled. "This I never heard, Charlie. This is dynamite. You can use this—"

Sturdivant cut him off. "This will not be used in the campaign. What I do privately is my business. Period. I'm not trying to be noble. What I did was easy for me. Besides, I've been down there, I've seen those people. They've nothing except their homes. By an accident of birth I've been fortunate enough to be a receiver all my life. If I used this one chance to give back as a political tool . . . well, you get my point. I'm sorry I was identified as the contributor. I doubt the opposition will spread it around. I would appreciate it if you gentlemen didn't let it go any further than this room."

The meeting ended.

Sweeney and Goldman waited in front of the court building for Benny Rabe to bring Sweeney's car around.

"Well," Sweeney said, "what do you think of my candidate?"

Goldman seated himself in the car before he answered. "Charlie, I think he's a *mensch*. And you're a son-of-a-bitch for setting me up."

The following day Mickey Goldman called a meeting of the executive board of the New York State Service Confederation and suggested that the confederation endorse Allen Sturdivant immediately. His "suggestion" was unanimously adopted.

What Goldman and Sweeney couldn't know was that Allen Sturdivant considered his involvement in Owl's Beak as a kind of penance, never mind the illogic of that: after

112

all, he'd made the gesture before he killed Andrea. Never mind, even if it was expiation *ex post facto*, he'd take it.

What Goldman and Sweeney also couldn't know was how the meeting had made Allen Sturdivant realize for the first time that the opposing party was going to be looking closely at everything in his life—past and present—in an attempt to discredit him. So far they'd come up with nothing. But how soon before they came on the truth, or came too close to it . . . ?

___ Chapter 15 ___

WHEN MARC HAMMOND told Peter Jorgensen that his application for bail had been denied, he became despondent. He ate little, slept briefly and fitfully and walked about as if in a trance.

Quad C-74 on Riker's housed juveniles and adults on different floors. Detention facilities consisted of two-man cells and dormitories. Officially there was no preference about assignment, but security cases were always placed in the cells. Peter, because of his first-offender status, was put in one of the two dorms on the floor, each of which housed sixty men and ran parallel to each other, separated by the shower room. It was a noisy, humid hellhole.

The two correction officers who sat on duty in a glassed enclosure at the front of the dorms minded their own business, which made thievery the rule in the dorms. Only the very strong could keep their property, otherwise you got ripped off and you shut your mouth . . .

Correction Officer Ralph Kearney was fighting off sleep as he neared the end of his tour. Two more months—he loved the sound of it, the thought of it. Two more months to pension time and living time. He'd had all he could take—twenty years watching this scum. Let them kill each other off, but be quiet about it. He glanced at the two dorms from his glass cubicle. In two months he'd be away forever from the noise, and the smell and the wretchedness of C-74.

He turned away. Kearney's partner was in the bathroom and he was alone. He reached for his copy of *Field and Stream*, became so absorbed in the magazine that he hardly noticed the scraggly thin blond kid who entered the shower area. The inmates in the dorm were work crew and were allowed to use the showers any time until lock-up at 11 P.M. Now two inmates followed the kid into the showers.

Peter used the showers every chance he got, his only escape from C-74 where he had been roughed up and his shoes, a jacket, a shirt, even his hairbrush and comb had been stolen. As he let the hot water soothe his body, he wondered for a moment if his punishment was somehow deserved even if he was innocent of Andrea's murder. Oh, he had committed a sin, his mother was very big on sin. She'd taught him too well . . . but what had he done to deserve this? He'd fornicated with married women, skipped church, had impure thoughts. But did all that add to *this* . . . ?

Peter's ankle ached, even though it had pretty well healed. After six weeks the cast had been removed and the swelling had all but disappeared. His scarecrow appearance resulted not from his injury but from his near-complete appetite loss. He had dropped fifteen pounds since his arrest—his eyes were hollow sockets, his skin was dry and pulled taut over the bones of his face. Once self-assured, even cocky, he just didn't give a damn, his depression such that he even thought about the relief of a peaceful death—

It started with a whisper.

"There you are—you sweet thing."

Peter turned in the direction of the voice and was struck hard on his forehead with a solid object. He fell to the floor, instinctively reaching to cover the wound in his face that was gushing blood. He almost passed out, but was aware of being turned around. When he felt the hot water on his back he tried to scream but couldn't, not even when he felt pain from his rear, a tearing humiliating pain. Still he could not scream. He heard another voice. "Get off him, man—leave some of that sweet stuff for me."

Peter felt weight lift off his legs, replaced seconds later by another, and then the pain again. He tried to call out for help, for death, for anything that would stop this invasion of his body but no sound came out. The second weight had left him . . . he lay there, blood coming from his head and from his buttocks, turning the water crimson.

The voices were gone, Peter's mind slowly cleared, full consciousness returned. He felt the pain in his body, but the pain in his mind overwhelmed him as he realized what had been done to him. And then the scream he had been denied found his voice, over and over again.

Three inmates ran into the shower room, followed by Correction Officer Kearney and another officer. They found Peter lying in the bloody water, still screaming.

Kearney bent over to take a good look at Peter. "Holy Christ, kid. What a mess." Peter lost consciousness then.

When he awakened he was in Riker's Hospital lying on a hard table. He heard someone say "X-rays." He heard someone else say, "The Doc says they really tore him up." He passed out again.

When he woke up the second time a man in white was standing over him. "Jorgensen, I'm Dr. Sloane. You've got to take it easy. You're going to be all right, but you've got a lot of healing to do. We'll change the bandages after you sleep. Take this now."

116

Peter shook his head. "I want to see Marc Hammond, my lawyer. I have to see him now."

"I'll do what I can, Jorgensen. Take the pill."

Peter took the sedative and closed his eyes. In a few minutes his heart stopped pounding and, for the first time since he had been arrested, he felt a strange calm . . . And he thought of one friend he had made at Riker's, a kid named Hank. Hank was nineteen but could have passed for fourteen. He was slight, small. Since his sentence for grand larceny auto, Hank had been robbed, beaten and sodomized. He had done four months and with one-third off for good behavior he had only four months to go. Hank never complained, always wore a scary little smile, scary because under that smile Peter could see something really terrifying. One day after discovering that the little money he had had been stolen from its hiding place, Hank told Peter that he wasn't going to make it.

"Don't be a fool," Peter said. "You've got only four months to go—"

"I've had it. I can't wait four months. I can't wait four days."

"We're talking about your life."

"So?"

Hank had the right to ask. He had told Peter that when he was twelve his mother had left him with a neighbor while she went back to Puerto Rico for a visit. It must have been some visit, because she never came back. The neighbor handed him over to the Bureau of Child Welfare, which placed him in several homes, where Hank learned about sexual abuse. When he was fifteen he ran off to the streets.

"Look," he told Peter, "it's easy. You cut the bedsheets into strips—like this. Then you wet the parts you're gonna tie together and let the pieces dry so they stick good and don't fall apart. Be sure the slip-knot for the noose is smooth. You gotta test it first. Put all your weight on it. If it don't

117

break when you do that it'll hold you. Then you slip the noose over your neck, make sure the knot is pressing against your Adam's apple"—he demonstrated to Peter—"kick away the chair, twist around and it's over. You're home free." He even laughed at the black joke.

"Just four months—"

"It ain't the four months. I can't make it out there, I know I'll be back."

Peter had reported Hank's intention to the correction officer in the quad, a suicide watch was ordered but there weren't enough correction personnel to maintain a twenty-four hour watch on every potential suicide.

Two days later they cut Hank down. He had that scary smile on his face. A few days later a correction officer handed Peter an envelope. He opened it and saw written in a semiliterate scrawl: "Dear Peter. Dying ain't no big deal. Good luck. Your friend, Hank."

As the sedative worked its way through him, Peter began to understand Hank's feeling about death. He found comfort that he, like Hank, at least had a choice. He had asked Marc Hammond what sentence a conviction of murder in the second degree would bring. Reluctantly Marc had told him that the minimum was fifteen to life. There was no way, not after what had happened, that he would face that time in prison. Before he slipped off into unconsciousness Peter thanked Hank for the message that "dying ain't no big deal."

Marc Hammond's relationship with Randy Spencer had built into something more than he had quite bargained for, especially at this time when he needed to concentrate on the upcoming Jorgensen trial. He found, though, that whenever he was not with Randy he was thinking about her, a serious distraction. When he mentioned his dilemma to Randy, she provided a solution. She moved in with him.

Not that he was so opposed to the idea . . . the chauvinistic stereotype of a blond blue-eyed model having the mental capacity of a tsetse fly had been thoroughly shattered by Randy—a warm, intelligent woman involved in her own career yet genuinely interested in his. She had an inquisitive mind, as well as the ability to assimilate what she gathered. For one of the few times in Marc's life, the pleasures did not end with bed.

On this particular night, however, bed and its pleasures were all that they had in mind. They had eaten dinner at home and retired early. What was on the agenda was no less and no more than serious sex—

The phone rang.

Son-of-a-bitch. He tried to ignore it.

"Marc," Randy whispered, "the phone."

"Let it ring, maybe they'll go away."

But the phone rang and rang. "I don't think they're going away," she said.

Marc sighed, lifted the receiver.

"Mr. Hammond?"

"Yes."

"This is Captain Cleary at Riker's Island Hospital. Is Peter Jorgensen your client?"

"Yes."

"Well, he asked us to notify you that he was attacked by two inmates tonight. Wants to see you—"

"Attacked? How?"

"Well, the report states that he was raped."

Marc was stunned into silence for a moment, then said, "I want to see him now."

"You mean tonight?"

"Yes."

"I'm sorry, Counselor, we don't make provision for evening visitors at the hospital—"

"Well, you better make provision, Captain. I'm going out there now and I'm going to get a statement from my client.

119

And if you stop me from seeing him I personally guarantee that the shit will hit the fan on the front page of every newspaper in this state."

Silence, followed by: "Wait a minute. I've got to check this out."

While he waited Marc filled Randy in.

"I'll go with you," she said, feeling his distress.

"It won't be pleasant—"

"Nevertheless, I'm going." Her tone was one he'd learned not to argue with.

Cleary was back on the line. "All right, you can come out."

"Good, and by the way, Captain, I want to transcribe my client's statement. I'm bringing my secretary along."

"She'll have to stay in the waiting room, she can't go into the ward."

"Okay," Marc said, and heard Cleary muttering to himself as he replaced the receiver.

Marc tromped the accelerator of his Honda as they sped out toward Riker's. A sudden temperature rise had created a dense fog that made driving hazardous. When he crossed the bridge connecting the island to Queens, Marc's headlights could not penetrate the maze of heavy moisture that covered the road and he almost drove into a man standing in front of a small guardhouse. Marc slammed on the brakes as the man, a correction officer, approached the driver's window and flashed his searchlight into the car. Marc identified himself and was directed to the main entrance, where an officer escorted them to an outer waiting area of the hospital. The correction officer then told Marc to follow him through the main gate, leaving Randy to wait on a wooden bench.

The hospital ward was dark except for a lighted alcove just large enough to contain a bed and a chair. Peter Jorgensen lay on the bed dressed in hospital pajamas. A ban-

120

dage covered his head wounds. He became agitated as soon as he saw Marc, wanting to verbalize the horror he had just experienced but not being able to. He would start to talk, then stop, then start again.

Marc stood by the bed, his hand on Peter's shoulder, trying to calm him down. After some time Peter did relax a bit and began to tell his story. Once started, the words flowed in torturous detail. After he'd said it all, he turned his head toward the wall, exhausted, and closed his eyes. Marc gave him a few minutes, then promised to visit again in the morning. Peter did not look at him.

Back in the waiting area a shaken Marc told Randy what had happened to Peter only hours before.

"My God," she said, "this is straight out of Dickens. Violence and brutality put people in Riker's, and violence and brutality follow them there."

As he drove in the fog over the connecting bridge toward the Midtown Tunnel, Marc said, "Randy . . . I'm sorry you came with me tonight. You don't need—"

"I don't need what? What do you think I am? A piece of delicate china? A china doll? Will I break if not handled with care? Come on, Marc, this is now, modern times, although the people who run Riker's apparently haven't yet gotten the message."

He looked at her and smiled, properly chastened. "Forgive me, my love. From this day on, I promise I will spare you nothing."

She lifted his hand to her mouth and kissed it. "I'll hold you to that, my love, beginning with when we get back to what we'd started."

CHAPTER 16

THE DESIGNATION OF Allen Sturdivant as the guest speaker at the party's annual dinner was Charles Sweeney's public statement that Sturdivant was his candidate. Loren was delighted, knowing the message would not be lost on Jon Klyk and his supporters. As she saw it, the only problem now was Allen himself, still displaying a peculiar and worrisome lack of enthusiasm and drive that would be needed in this campaign.

On the morning of the dinner the Sturdivants drove into Manhattan, Loren dropped Allen at the Carlyle where he would review his speech and rest, and she would go on to Sweeney's office to meet with him and the rest of the county leaders . . .

Allen Sturdivant let himself into the suite, the housekeeper took his bags, unpacked them and left him. Allen preferred to be alone when he was preparing a speech . . . otherwise he felt foolish speaking aloud, gesturing into a mirror.

He looked at his watch. Eleven-thirty. Half an hour until

the sun would be over the yardarm. His nerves were stretched thin. He had slept little since that terrible Christmas Eve and was beginning to show it. In a fashion he had almost learned to live—well, at least exist—with the fact of Andrea's death, but now he was having even more trouble with the notion that an innocent person was being accused, detained, and about to be tried for *his* crime . . .

Sturdivant turned on the television set, switched it off, went into the bedroom. His dinner jacket was hanging on the closet door. Beside it was Loren's black strapless Yves St. Laurent gown. Her elegante would reinforce her husband's—

But not tonight. Sturdivant had at last made up his mind not to pursue the nomination. If he accepted the party's nomination he would have to preside at Peter Jorgensen's trial. If he walked away from the nomination, he could then walk away from the trial. And he *couldn't* go through with the trial.

Now, somehow, he had to tell Loren and Charlie Sweeney before the dinner.

When Loren returned to the Carlyle at five her husband met her at the door and handed her a martini, then led her into the living room. She did not like the look on his face. She liked much less what he proceeded to say.

"Loren"—voice clear, controlled—"I'm going to call Charlie and tell him I'm out. He'll have to back Klyk."

Loren said nothing, just stood and stared at him.

"I know this is a disappointment, it must seem to you as though I'm throwing away everything we've worked for all these years. Believe me, if there were any other way . . ." He took a long sip of his drink, over the rim of the glass looked for an understanding from her that he knew was impossible.

Loren crossed the room and stood in front of him. Her

cheeks were only faintly flushed. She was still in control. "If I don't disclose it, Allen, is there anyone else who knows about your relationship with Andrea Blanchard?"

Sturdivant took an involuntary step backward. "My God, you know? How . . . ?"

"Oh, come on, Allen. How long is it that we've had our little ladies and gentlemen's agreement? Of course, it's been rather one-sided, but I haven't really minded, not as long as we stayed on course, not as long as you did what was expected of you. That was, after all, darling, our bargain, was it not? As for Andrea Blanchard, I salute you for your discreetness there . . . I'm pretty sure you've managed to keep that one quiet, except, of course, from me. I've made it my business to know your ladies, for future reference, so to speak. As for the divine Miss Blanchard, or should I say the late Miss Blanchard, I followed you one night, saw you enter the Monte Carlo, well-known as the residence of Miss Blanchard, and didn't have to be Miss Marple to deduce who you were paying a visit to. So now, it seems, you're afraid that the truth of Allen and Andrea will somehow leak out in the wake of her murder, that it will embarrass you and your distinguished family and you're doing the noble thing and not running so as to spare us all. Forget it, Allen, my lips are sealed, or will be so long as you do the correct thing by me, or, if you like, the state and nation."

It was a long speech for Loren, but he was grateful just now for the opportunity to regroup, to collect himself and realize that at least she apparently knew nothing about Andrea's . . . death. He tried to think of it in the abstract, not always very successfully, but somehow it seemed to help to think the word "death" rather than "murder." He was, after all, a lawyer. Words counted . . .

"It seems I've underestimated the extent of your ambition to—"

"Oh, can it, Allen. We're not talking ambition here, not

124

ordinary garden-variety stuff. You know what's at stake. The party is building on your record and background to carry you beyond the governorship to the White House. As for Andrea Blanchard . . . maybe you had more than, as they say, carnal knowledge of her. You might even have had something to do with her death. I could not care less. What was she, after all, but a prettified tart? What counts, Allen, is that *we* not lose sight of our objective. I trust you follow me."

Sturdivant looked at her wonderingly. Yes, he had under-estimated her. He doubted if he'd ever really known her. Her father, Morton Phillips, had been a tough calculating son-of-a-bitch who never let anything stand in the way of what he wanted, but . . . well, clearly the fruit did not fall far from the tree.

"Look, Allen, I've never pretended to you what I want or why I want it. You needn't look shocked at this late date. As for you, I concede you have nobler motives. This is me, Allen. Remember how many times you've said you'd like to be president to have the chance to do something about poverty, hunger and pain in America. 'I'd like to try to turn things around,' you said. Well, you have the ability, the intelligence and now the opportunity to do it. It seems, though, that you may be a little short in the guts depart-ment."

"It could also be that I'm coming to my senses, that I even have a conscience—"

"Stop that nonsense. You can't afford the luxury of in-dulging in such things. You are *not* quitting. If you really believe in what you've been saying, then face up to your . . . indiscretion . . . and live with it."

"I need time to think—"

"There's nothing to think about. No time to think. Make your speech tonight. We'll campaign *and* we'll win."

"I said I need *time*—"

"You still don't seem to understand. I'm removing the options. We will proceed as planned, because if not . . . well, then I'm afraid your little secret will somehow become front page news. And what the papers don't spell out to your daughters, I will."

He raised his eyes and looked at her, shook his head. She knew how to reach him . . . she was aware of his love and concern for the girls, just as she was aware that what he did was at least in part motivated by his desire to win their approval. It seemed impossible, though, that she could use their children this way. He shook his head again. "I can't believe you said that. I can't believe you would—"

"Believe it. That's right. Blackmail."

He sat on the couch, put his head in his hands.

"Come, come, Allen. It's not so bad. I'll be with you every step of the way. And I've got enough balls for both of us."

At seven that evening the Waldorf's lobby began its parade of men in dinner jackets and women in formal dress heading for the elevators to the grand ballroom. Most who had paid three hundred dollars for their tickets saw no advantage in making such a large contribution without getting the maximum benefit. Get to the cocktail party on time to maximize the chances for politicking.

Charlie Sweeney, true to a custom that he had instituted when he first became democratic state chairman, stood in a receiving line greeting anyone who wanted to make his or her presence known. In many instances that was all they got for their three hundred bucks, but to many it was enough. They certainly did not come for the overdone filet mignon or the soggy carrots.

If there had been any doubt who the organization was going to support for the governorship it had been dispelled when Judge Sturdivant's name was listed as guest speaker on the dinner invitations. The significance of such a designation was lost on no one, including Victor Pierce. Despondent over his recent faux pas, Pierce had made up his mind to corner Sturdivant and explain how well-meaning he had been and how sorry he now was. His opportunity came sooner than he had hoped. He saw Sturdivant's limousine pull up to the Park Avenue entrance of the Waldorf. Loren stepped out first, then her husband. Pierce smiled at Sturdivant, advanced quickly and extended his hand. Sturdivant moved past him, leaving Pierce's outstretched hand grasping the night air. Pierce stayed for the cocktail party, shook Charlie Sweeney's hand and left early to lick his self-inflicted wounds.

Meanwhile, Loren and Allen moved into the VIP room where the county leaders, large contributors and other important guests were congregating. The three-hundred-dollar ticket did not alone assure entry to this sanctum. Two burly members of a union friendly to the organization were at the door, turning away all who did not have the special invitation issued for this elite gathering.

Half an hour later, at the request of the chairman of the dinner committee, the guests began to filter into the dining room, slowly at first, then in larger groups, the band striking up the inevitable "Happy Days Are Here Again" at maximum decibel count.

Charlie Sweeney called out to Benny Rabe. "Benny," he growled, "tell the bandleader that if he doesn't cut the noise, I'm personally gonna stick that trumpet up his ass." Benny delivered the message, the music diminished only slightly.

At a cue from the dinner chairman the dais guests began their march into the banquet room, the band switched to "For He's a Jolly Good Fellow," and Allen Sturdivant as guest speaker was directed to a seat to the immediate right of Charlie Sweeney. Jon Klyk sat to Sweeney's left. Sweeney, despite Klyk's stand, would not permit him to be eased off into seating in Siberia. Sturdivant was the party's choice, but the significance of Klyk's position on the dais would not be lost on his supporters. Quite aside from their friendship, Sweeney was well aware that Klyk spoke for a good percentage of the party faithful and so was still a valuable political asset. Sweeney never burned bridges.

A quick look at the seating list surprised Marc Hammond. Sweeney had put him at table one. Seating, he knew, at these functions tended to spell out the pecking order. If the place was filled to the rafters and you were seated so far from the dais that you needed binoculars, or so high in the third tier of tables that your nose bled . . . well, the message was clear. Up front or at table one, where the family and guests closest to the chairman were seated, provided a quick readout that you were at least somebody. The others at Marc's table were Sylvia and Mickey Goldman, Loren Sturdivant, Peg Sweeney, her daughter and son-in-law, and the majority leader of the city council and his wife. Randy's was the tenth seat at the table, and Randy was a knockout in her formfitting strapless Halston white silk jersey. Her face, framed by her natural blond hair, was familiar to most everyone, and the paparazzi primarily there to get shots of the dais guests turned their lenses to table one when they spotted Randy Spencer there.

Peg Sweeney, a gentle lady who could, if the occasion called for it, be as tough as her husband, saw Randy's discomfort, left the table and had a few words with the photographers, who promptly dispersed. Randy was sitting next to Loren Sturdivant and Marc noted that before long the two women seemed deep in some conversation. Not bad, he thought, his girl and the future First Lady of the state apparently getting on so well.

The music, down only a few decibels, and the conversational rumble of over two thousand people talking and milling about in the Waldorf-Astoria ballroom made it impossible to converse with anyone unless you were nose to nose, where Marc found himself with Mickey Goldman, who urged him to come closer.

"Son-of-a-bitch," Goldman said. "If I wasn't deaf before, I'll be deaf after tonight. Listen, Charlie tells me you're a damn good lawyer."

"I hope he's half right."

"Me too, because I may be throwing some business your way." He eyed Marc, then in his direct style said what was on his mind. "Is Marc Hammond your real name?"

"No, I changed it. Why?"

"Why. Yeah, that's my question. Why?"

"Moshe Himmelfarb, Counselor at Law . . . I guess I copped out on that one. I'm not too proud of that . . ."

"Yeah, well, I had an uncle by the name of Moshe. He was a horse thief in the Ukraine. He was terrific, though. So if you don't mind, to me from now on you're Moshe. Still, I admit a campaign poster reading Moshe Himmelfarb for District Attorney—or for Judge, or Senator might not play so well. It depends on what you're after. What makes Moshe run?"

Marc appreciated the frankness.

"I don't know yet."

"A honest answer. I like that. You could have given me bullshit. Maybe that's why Charlie likes you. He says he has plans for you. You must have something, kid. In all the years I've known him, I never saw Charlie so high on a kid before. He talks about you like you're his son. But you know what really impresses me about you? I'll tell you . . . your taste in women." They both glanced at Randy, who was still talking to Loren Sturdivant. "How'd you land such a beautiful lady? I mean, I've seen and met plenty of women in my time, but I can't remember anyone stacks up to this *shiksa* you brought tonight. What does she see in you?"

"I'm not asking," Marc laughed. "I just hope I don't lose it."

Goldman shifted gears. "You're trying the Jorgensen case?"

"Yes."

"How do you see Sturdivant as a judge?"

Marc's response was immediate. "He's a good man. He has the full respect of the bar."

"He'll be a good governor?"

"He'll do the right thing," Marc said, using a colloquialism that was often used in the jargon of labor leaders.

Mickey thought, the kid's cute, I like him. He said, "I hope you're right."

Ten minutes later the dinner committee asked everyone to rise for the singing of "The Star Spangled Banner" and the invocation.

As soon as the guests were reseated the waiters began serving dinner, being as they were under strict orders to move quickly. Judge Sturdivant's speech had to be completed no later than 9:30 P.M. to make the ten o'clock and eleven o'clock television newscasts. They were already behind schedule, so Charlie ordered the maître d' to serve dessert and coffee after the speech. Charlie had been there before.

At nine o'clock the dinner chairman introduced Charlie Sweeney, who quickly got down to the nitty-gritty.

"Tonight, Allen Sturdivant will talk to us about the coming election. We're all looking forward to what he has to say because he represents everything we'd like our party to stand for—service, integrity and courage. Ladies and gentlemen, I give you Judge Allen Sturdivant."

The band went to "Happy Days Are Here Again," and Loren stood and turned to face the applauding crowd now on its feet. They smell a winner, she thought. The outs want in. And *I do too . . .*

The applause increased as Sturdivant made his way to the podium, stood up to his full height, put his shoulders back and smiled his smile as he waited for the crowd to quiet.

"Mr. Chairman, distinguished guests and friends, we live in the greatest nation in the world and the greatest state in the nation. Yet we're losing that status because we have problems that have to be solved, and the present administration is not solving them. Unemployment is too high. We have seen a decline in low-income housing. Our hospitals are inadequate, public health services are deteriorating. Services in our major cities are a scandal. One could go on with this litany, but the essential message is that this administration has permitted New York to decline for eight years. Our citizens have been taxed to the limit and have gotten precious little return for it."

Then he came to the heart of his speech. "Ours is a great party. I believe that. History proves it. I'm proud to be part of it. I'm grateful to be standing here now—addressing you now—and announcing now, that after my current assignment is completed I plan to resign from the bench and seek your support in obtaining the nomination for governor, and, if successful, to go on to victory in November." Loud applause. "I want you to know that as much as I would like your support, if I don't receive it I will back the party's candidate in every way possible for me. This party, I truly believe, is more important than any one man—this party that speaks for the people, that has always spoken for the people, must win . . ."

Allen Sturdivant, who meant what he said, was in. He was, they decided, a party man.

Charlie Sweeney, smiling broadly, signaled the band leader to go for it and "Happy Days Are Here Again" rocked the ballroom as Allen Sturdivant, standing tall at the podium, symbolized for the gathering the Moses who would bring the party out of the wilderness.

Nobody noticed that Loren Sturdivant, sitting quietly, had no smile on her face. For her Allen Sturdivant was no Moses. He was her vehicle for getting what she was entitled to. And God help him if he forgot it.

Tom McPartland, holding his tape recorder, made his way with his cameraman to the exit. He was looking to pounce not on Sturdivant, toward whom all his competition was moving, but on Jon Klyk. McPartland realized that the big story of the night would likely come from Klyk. Finally he cornered Klyk, and the good mayor, never shy with the press, eagerly took directions from McPartland when asked to stand in front of a dark drape.

McPartland began: "Ladies and gentlemen, we have with us Jon Klyk, the mayor of the city of Buffalo. Mayor Klyk has also announced for the party's nomination, and will face Judge Sturdivant in the primary." McPartland turned to Klyk. "Mr. Mayor, we'd like to hear your reaction to Judge Sturdivant's speech."

"It seems that Allen Sturdivant has gotten party religion."

"Can we infer that you mean his conversion is for political expediency?"

"I never question people's motives."

"You saw and heard the reception that Judge Sturdivant received. Will this deter you from entering the race?"

"No. I applauded the judge, as did many of the people here tonight who are supporting me. He made a good speech. But, of course, speeches don't decide primaries. We've got four months to go and the members of this party will have an opportunity to hear both of us, as well as from any other candidates, before they make up their minds."

"Mr. Mayor, how about the possibility of a Sturdivant—

Klyk ticket? That's being talked about as an unbeatable combination."

Klyk's booming laugh was followed by a playful punch on McPartland's arm. "Tom, I suspect that the only talk about that comes from you. Running for lieutenant governor never crossed my mind—it won't happen."

"Mayor Klyk," McPartland persisted, "now for the sixty-four thousand dollar question. Will you support the winner of the primary, no matter who wins?"

"Of course I will. I'll be the nominee." Then, with a broad smile and a pat on McPartland's back, Klyk walked out of camera range.

Before Klyk reached the bank of elevators Loren Sturdivant had made her way up to him. Klyk embraced her, as people do who meet each other repeatedly at such functions, yet he understood that they were natural enemies. His game plan was to knock Sturdivant out of the box, even if he had to hand the election back to the incumbent Beale.

The reality of the situation, however, did not erase his sexual fantasies when he looked at this beautiful woman. He was attracted to her, had wanted to get her into the hay from the first time he had laid eyes on her. Without question, the mayor of Buffalo had a bad case of the hots for his opponent's wife.

Klyk was both pleased and surprised when Loren took his hand and guided him away from the flow of traffic. "Jon," she said, her voice low, surprisingly intimate, "there's something you should know before the campaign goes any further. I'd like to talk to you privately—soon."

Klyk continued to smile, but was puzzled and even a bit alarmed. They had never exchanged more than a few words. What was the lady up to? For a moment he considered avoiding the meeting, but he was too curious. And, face it, too attracted by the possibility of getting to know Loren Sturdivant in a way he had long fantasized.

"Where and when?"

"Are you going back to Buffalo tonight?"

"Yes, but I'll be back in New York next week."

"Where can I get in touch with you?"

"Here, at the Waldorf."

Taking his hand, and giving it a brief squeeze, she said, "Expect my call."

CHAPTER 17

It was a Tuesday afternoon when Loren Sturdivant called Jon Klyk at the Waldorf. The clerk told her that the mayor had checked in but was not answering his phone. She called again that evening with the same result. The third time she called, at eleven, Klyk did answer his phone.

"Mr. Mayor," she said, "this is Loren Sturdivant. I'm sorry to call so late but you weren't in when I tried earlier."

"That's okay, okay. I was looking forward to your call, but I'm afraid we're not going to be able to get together. I'll only be here for the day tomorrow and I'm booked solid. I'm disappointed as hell but there won't be enough minutes in the day for us to meet."

"It's important that I speak to you." She paused a moment, then said, "I can come over now if you'll see me."

"Well, uh, sure . . . I'm in suite twelve-seventeen." Christ, he thought, what the hell is on her mind?

"And, Mr. Mayor . . . it's personal. You will be alone, won't you?"

"I'll be alone."

Jon Klyk had friends at Democratic headquarters who were loyal to him; he had put them where they were. And they had reported to him Loren's meetings with Charlie Sweeney. They also had told Klyk to "watch her."

Which intelligence only confirmed Klyk's instinctive impression of Loren. Through years of political wars and infighting, he had developed his own radar. Loren Sturdivant was danger. Yet, Jon Klyk was looking forward to this battle, if that's what it was to be. Besides, he had never been able to resist a beautiful woman, or more to the point, to overlook the possibility of a piece of ass.

Blackmail was a business that Loren well understood. She had, after all, already practiced a form of it against her husband. Of course, she realized, one should be careful not to overuse it, but if necessary, if her gentle persuasion didn't work, she had every intention of using the photographs to bring Jon Klyk around . . .

When Loren knocked at the door to Suite 1217 she was wearing a light-blue silk dress that managed a tasteful seductiveness. Jon Klyk registered his appreciation as he opened the door. "Welcome," he said, following her into the room, "I'm sorry we couldn't have time for dinner."

Loren nodded and sat in the chair he indicated. "I want to talk to you about the election. There's no reason why you and my husband need to be adversaries. Running against Allen and giving the election to Beale is stupid."

Klyk poured two martinis and handed one to Loren. "You came here tonight to tell me that?"

"I came here to try to settle the differences between you two."

"What would you suggest?"

"I suggest a joining of our forces in a ticket that can't lose—Sturdivant for governor, Klyk for lieutenant governor."

136

"How about Klyk–Sturdivant?"

"We both know that's not realistic. Your people take polls as well as ours do. My husband is going to win the primary."

"Polls have been wrong."

"Come on, Jon. Not by the twenty-eight percent margin that our polls show. I don't know why you're being so stubborn. We're rational people, we can work together and we can win together."

"But only on your terms."

"On the only terms that make sense. The numbers don't lie. You won't destroy my husband . . . but you could end up destroying yourself."

The not so subtle threat was not lost on him. "Loren," he said slowly, "the only thing I appreciate about this conversation is your frankness. I'll be equally frank. We come from different backgrounds. You and Allen are Newport and Southampton. The combined assets of the Phillips and Sturdivant fortunes could probably wipe out the state debt."

"Pretty close," she said.

"I was born in a poor section of Buffalo. My father was a car mechanic who had to support a wife and six kids, and he barely made it. But I had a lot of respect for my father. He was a politician—a ward leader—and he taught me about people. And you may not know it, but that's what politics is all about. You really have to like people. I carried designating petitions from door to door with my father when I was six. I've been going from door to door ever since. I wonder how many doors your husband has knocked on? My point is—with all due respect—when Allen Sturdivant calls for social change and justice and a square deal for the little man it's well meant but what does he really know about the little man? When I say it I know what I'm talking about. Allen's not an F.D.R. or a Harriman. He's offended by the nitty-gritty of politics. He thinks he can be above it. F.D.R.

didn't. He was rich and well born but one helluva politician."

"You obviously believe that you're the type of politician the party needs."

"Modesty aside, yes, I do."

"So it would naturally follow that if anything happened to affect your credibility, it would affect the party as well as yourself."

"You could say that . . ."

Loren reached for her bag, opened it, and put her hand inside. The gesture had its intended effect.

"Drop the other shoe, Loren."

"I will, Mr. Mayor, because you've given me no alternative."

"So what have you got?"

"The party at Pell's," and she handed him a photograph of himself fondling the breasts of a naked fourteen-year-old.

Klyk's initial reaction was confusion. How in hell could she have gotten hold of . . . and then it fell into place . . . the big spender . . . Jim Mortonson, or whoever he really was. They'd quickly learned that Mortonson's check was drawn on a nonexistent bank, but he'd never had reason to think the guy was a plant, setting him up for something like this. He'd figured Mortonson was just a guy trying to be a big shot—a phony but not a pro . . . Jesus, he should have smelled something . . . obviously he was worried about the wrong Sturdivant.

He knew exactly what the photograph would mean to his career. It would destroy him . . . "Would it make any difference if I told you that was the only time, a few minutes?"

"I'm afraid not, Jon. The black-and-white of it says sex with a minor. Not too popular a notion these days."

He looked at her, said nothing.

Loren's voice now became almost soothing. "Jon, you're

138

a realist. You understand your situation. If you want to stroke your ego by running against my husband in the primary, go right ahead. But running against him in November, on a third-party line, splitting the vote and thereby assuring the victory for the opposition, well, that I can't permit. Be sensible. You've done good things, you've had a fine career—"

He snapped his fingers. "And you'd end it like this."

"You force me to."

"Look, Mrs. Sturdivant—"

"What happened to Loren?"

"I'd say we're past that now."

"I'm sorry. You're quite a fascinating man, I like you."

"And you're amazing. Talk about ice. You're blackmailing me and coming on to me at the same time. I'll bet your husband doesn't even know about this visit—or about the photographs."

"You'd win the bet. I've told no one about these photos since they've come into my hands. I sincerely hope I won't have to."

Too much.

He stood up and angrily threw his glass against the wall. He moved toward her and raised his hand as if to strike her. She did not flinch, but calmly looked into his eyes. He lowered his hand. She had won.

She took his hand in hers. "Jon," she said softly, "you're going to be the next lieutenant governor of the great State of New York. That's not so bad, is it?" She opened the fragile buttons of her dress, guided his hand onto her bare breast and kissed him.

"Would you call this compensation pay, Mrs. Sturdivant?"

She smiled faintly. "Let's call it an added incentive, Mr. Mayor."

* * *

139

The blinding flashes of the cameras did not bother John Klyk, nor did the barrage of reporters' questions. Klyk thrived on them.

"Okay, fellas, I have a statement for you if you settle down and give me a break. If you've got questions after the statement I'll answer them . . . Okay, here we go. In the interests of party unity, in the interests of good government, but *most* of all in the interests of the people of the State of New York I am withdrawing as candidate for governor. I've consulted with Allen Sturdivant, the next governor of this state, and have agreed to run with him for the office of lieutenant governor. The most important objective of the upcoming election is to return government to the people. Judge Sturdivant and I, as a team, will restore New York State to its prominence under previous Democratic administrations."

The cameras continued to roll and the reporters threw their questions. One asked the obvious: "Why isn't the judge here to make this announcement with you?"

"Because he's still on the bench," Klyk answered. "You guys know he's presiding at an important trial. Judicial ethics prevent his appearance. But this trial will be over shortly and the judge has informed me that his resignation from the bench will be tendered the day that trial is over. I assure you that you'll be seeing a lot of him—of both of us—immediately after."

When Klyk called Charlie Sweeney to inform him of his decision, Sweeney was ecstatic—his conflict of loyalties was out the window. He had the best candidate and could keep an old party stalwart and friend. Both on the same ticket. Beautiful. He had refused even to think about the inevitable confrontation with his old political comrade-in-arms. No need to now. He had been in the game too long to believe that dislodging an incumbent would be easy, but this ticket with its broad base would be the closest thing to the best of all possible political worlds.

Wanting to celebrate, Sweeney set up a dinner meeting at Cambiere's, an intimate overpriced French restaurant. Normally such a place was not Sweeney's cup of tea, but the owner was an old henchman of the boss. Also, Sweeney wanted this particular meeting to be away from the public, and the private dining room at Cambiere's was perfect for that.

Sweeney and his Peg arrived early, Loren and Allen Sturdivant a few minutes later, then Klyk. The door was shut, and with the exception of a waiter who entered and exited invisibly, the five of them were alone in the room. Silk gold brocade covered the walls, edged off by double welting and matched by thick pile carpeting. The dishes were blue-and-white Limoges. Red, white, and yellow roses made up the centerpiece, giving sharp color contrast to the snow white linen tablecloths. The sterling silver and the Waterford glass glistened in the light of the chandelier.

When Klyk came in he and Sturdivant shook hands formally, a bit stiffly, and then Klyk and Sweeney embraced, clearly two men who liked each other, felt close to one another.

But Klyk's laugh was less uninhibited as he said, "I'll bet you're wondering how come I changed my mind, right, Charlie?"

Sweeney waited.

"Well, to be truthful, it was Loren here . . . I mean she made a lot of sense, Charlie, and she said what I'd been thinking myself but not wanting to face up to. I'm a party man. This ticket will win. And bucking you . . . well, it was bothering me. I don't want to run against my friends, be a spoiler. Not my style . . . " He smiled too broadly, said, "I'm not the most patient man in the world, so if we all live long enough I hope my day will come."

141

"You can go to sleep on it," Sweeney told him, and meant it, feeling warm and damn near euphoric about the way things had turned out.

But after Benny had driven them home, Sweeney's good feeling began to give way to an uneasiness. It was two A.M. and he was staring at the ceiling. Peg, also awake, watched him.

"What's the problem, Charles?"

"Problem?"

"Forty-one years of marriage, Charlie."

"I could never fool you."

"Not from day one, my sweetheart. Give."

"Well," he said, "I should be a most happy fella. No more spoiler . . . nothing's a sure thing, but I see us winners. So why do I feel I missed something tonight?"

"Meaning?"

"Meaning that I've known Jonny Klyk too long and too well. This sudden sea change isn't like him. He was stonewall when I first asked him to pull out. A wimp caves, Jon Klyk's no wimp. He's a strong, determined and very stubborn man. Normally if he makes up his mind he's right you can't move him with a bulldozer."

"He seemed happy to me," Peg said. "And what he said made pretty good sense . . ."

"Oh, he was laughing and scratching all right. But his eyes weren't laughing. They looked positively grim to this old friend."

"Let it pass, Charles," Peg said.

He detected something in her voice, raised his head from the pillow and faced her.

"You know something, don't you? I think you caught what I sense I missed. Come clean."

"Well, darling, your problem here is you're not a woman. You're not built to catch on to certain things . . ."

He looked at her closely, and then the light bulb went

142

on. "Sweet Jesus, that's it, sure . . . Jon's problem always was the ladies . . . Something's going on between the fair Loren and Jonny Klyk."

"Bingo. They avoided looking at each other all night, except for a few times that I caught and that said it all. At least to this longtime sideline observer."

He hugged her. "But when? And how? For a while there I had the idea they didn't like each other."

"That was then, this is now."

Charlie still was trying to put it together. Sex couldn't be the whole story. Not even with Jonny and his famous roving pecker. "There's got to be more to this. But what?"

"There probably is, sweetheart, but your smart wife suspects you should mind your own business, lie back and enjoy your good fortune. Some things you're maybe better off not knowing. Now get some sleep."

Sweeney turned over, but he didn't sleep.

CHAPTER 18

MARC HAMMOND HAD hoped to surface someone besides Peter Jorgensen that had seen the man with the wide-brimmed hat leaving Andrea's apartment, but the snowstorm, the late hour, the way the man had left Andrea's floor all pointed to the dismal probability that he'd been seen by no one but Peter.

A twenty dollar bill to the superintendent and Marc was able to trace Peter's steps that Christmas Eve. He also traced the route of the person with the hat, who he was convinced was Andrea's murderer. He timed the man's movements down the stairs, through the basement, out the gate in the service entrance, and into the street. Less than three minutes. And no one in sight.

The superintendent lived on the first floor and said he had seen and heard nothing. Hammond tended to believe him even though he'd been faintly evasive, almost frightened. Obviously he'd also been instructed by the D.A. not to discuss the case with anyone.

This man with the hat was one lucky son-of-a-bitch. The

only person who *had* seen him was the one person the jury was not going to believe. Marc had a sick feeling in his stomach. He was going into this trial with nothing—zilch. And this was the one he had to win. For his client, of course, who he was convinced was innocent. And also, to be truthful, for the career opportunity. This trial had all the ingredients . . . drugs, sex, a beautiful and rich celebrity murdered in her own apartment late at night. What was so bad if one could serve justice and one's career at the same time? Too often for a lawyer the two were natural enemies. When the media pressed him about his plans, he gave them a smiling "Wait and see." But he was whistling in the dark.

The trial was scheduled for the first week in June, and so far the only issue he had shot at was a request for the suppression of the original statement that Peter had given to the police. Marc told himself that in the following days he had better get lucky, or Peter Jorgensen's future was all in the past . . .

Fortunately Randy was around to help divert him at times from the case. She planned, for example, an escape for Memorial Day weekend, arranging for an invitation to a friend's wedding that was being held on Fire Island. Charlotte Hall's father had just sold his company for over thirty million dollars and seemed intent on spending as much of it as he could as quickly as he could. The wedding guests were invited to stay for the weekend, some being put up at the bride's house, some at cottages rented for the occasion, some at neighboring homes owned by friends of the Hall.

Randy and Marc left early Friday in time to catch the 12:30 ferry from Sayville, Long Island. The weather was perfect: a blue cloudless sky with a bright warm sun cutting a golden swath through the waters of the Great South Bay. They were met at the ferry dock by the bride's cousin, who escorted them by foot—no vehicles permitted on Fire Island—to the enormous house. Built on two low levels that maintained the integrity of the terrain, the sprawling building contained two living rooms, a cavernous den, a gym, minimoviehouse, a dining room as large as Marc's entire apartment, a restaurant-equipped kitchen and twelve bedrooms—not counting the servant's quarters; the tennis court, swimming pool and guest house were at beach level.

Charlotte Hall, the bride-to-be, was attractive but knew she would never make it as a professional model so settled for living vicariously through the lives of her friends like Randy Spencer, who were at or on their way to the top. Charlotte's feeling toward Randy was not envy; on the contrary, she adored and admired Randy and was obviously delighted when Randy and Marc arrived. They were given the royal treatment and led to one of the largest of the many guest rooms facing the ocean.

Marc was uncomfortable with the fawning. "Do these people owe you money?" he asked.

"Oh, that's just Charlotte's way of making you feel at home."

"Then let's camp here for the summer."

"Very funny."

They were into their bathing suits in record time. It was unusually warm for a Memorial Day weekend, more like mid-July weather, the thermometer edging ninety and the beach and the pool areas populated by sun-worshippers getting an early start on their tans.

Strolling with Randy on the warm sand, breathing in the salt air, for the first time in weeks Marc felt the tension begin to ebb. Indeed, how sweet it was, walking with this bikini-clad vision who was his lady, on a Fire Island beach, with nothing to do for the next forty-eight hours but delight in themselves.

The next day was also unusually bright and beautiful. The wedding took place in a miniature open-air chapel con-

146

structed on the large deck adjacent to the pool area, the ceremony conducted by the local judge who managed to stay sober until after the ceremony.

The father of the bride had imported French champagne that flowed from fountains on each of the tables. Gin, Scotch, bourbon and wines were transported in movable bars by formally attired waiters. The buffet was a glutton's dream, running the gamut from lobster and steak to quail and caviar.

When the party moved indoors Randy introduced Marc to her boss, Madeline Dodge. Marc had heard of Madeline; she had been a top model in her younger years and now was the owner of the preeminent modeling agency in New York. She surprised Marc by bringing up the Jorgensen case.

"When does it start?" she asked.

"Tuesday . . . when this beautiful weekend is over and we're back to reality."

"You know, Andrea and I worked together some. I knew her fairly well."

Marc tried to sound casual. "She must have been an unusual woman."

"Well, certainly one of a kind." Her tone suggested that no love had been lost between Andrea Blanchard and Madeline Dodge. "She was tough," Madeline was saying. "As tough as they come. When we came up together in this business, we used to talk about what we wanted out of life. Andrea said what she wanted was to travel first class. And she did that. Whatever Andrea wanted, Andrea got. She was a collector, collected all sorts of things, including people."

"May I ask a personal question?" Marc asked.

"Go ahead."

"Did Andrea ever collect something that belonged to you?"

She laughed. "Right on, Counselor. There was a man . . . it doesn't matter who he was, it was eons ago, but the day I casually introduced him to Andrea, well, that

147

was the day I lost him. No, sir, her death didn't exactly reduce me to sackcloth and ashes. Give her credit, though. She was great at what she did. I'd have given a lot to read that diary she kept."

"Diary?" The wheels rolled. "Did you ever see it?"

"No, but she once told me about it. She recorded the times and places of her dates. She used code names, she told me, just in case it fell into the wrong hands. Sometimes she'd write a couple of pages about a particularly interesting person or event. She said she was planning to write her autobiography, an annuity for her old age. And she was right. It would have been a sure bestseller. Andrea said that when the time came she was going to name everybody— and when Andrea said everybody, she meant presidents, kings, the *works*. Look, Marc, I know what you're after, and believe me, I wish I could help you. But if you're hunting for someone who had a motive to kill her, well, you couldn't count the number of men *and* women who breathed a deep sigh of relief when they heard the news of her death. But like I said, I never saw the diary. Frankly, I doubt if anyone else saw it, at least while she was alive."

Just then the bride and groom joined them and conversation turned from the Jorgensen case to honeymoon retreats.

After a while Randy motioned to Marc, who was pleased to get the message, and they slipped quietly away and headed for what he had hoped was their room. But Randy detoured them onto the beach. It was late afternoon and the sun was low over the horizon, reflecting off the snow-white clouds drifting in the brisk easterly wind. The waves were building, the birds were beginning their chatter.

As they walked along in silence Randy suddenly turned to Marc and grasped his arm. "Marc, where *are* you?"

"In paradise," he said, and kissed her.

148

"This is me, okay? Your head is miles away. It has been ever since Madeline talked to you."

He tried to laugh it off. "A mentalist, yet. I'm in big trouble."

She didn't smile.

"Look, darling, I confess. I've been scared to death a whopping miscarriage of justice is about to happen, and if it does it will be my fault. My client didn't kill Andrea Blanchard—he told me that from day one, but I'm convinced of it now. The kid's telling the truth, but I'm the only one who believes him, including his mother. Up to now, I didn't have any lead, but now the diary—that diary maybe opens the door, maybe a lot of doors. The possibilities keep rattling around inside my head. I've got to start running them down and it can't wait until Tuesday."

"I agree," she said. "We're leaving tonight."

He kissed her long and hard. Then: "At least now I know where to start. Peter's mother . . . she cleaned the place . . . she was loyal . . . chances are she has the diary or knows where it is . . ."

When Helen Jorgensen answered the knock on her door at nine o'clock on Memorial Day morning she quickly showed her displeasure. "I told you I'm not going to talk to you anymore—"

Marc pushed past her into the apartment, not able to control the anger in his voice. "For God's sake, Mrs. Jorgensen, we're not dealing with a stranger here, this is about your *son*. I've found out something that may be important, important for him. I need your cooperation. Where is Andrea Blanchard's diary?"

She turned away. "I don't have it."

"Do you know who does?"

"I gave it to one of the men from the district attorney's office."

149

"Did you get his name?"

"No. He asked me if Andrea kept a diary and I told him that she did, but that Andrea told me not to turn it over to anyone if anything ever happened to her. But this man insisted, told me I was withholding evidence, so I gave it to him—"

"Why didn't you tell me about this before?"

"Well, he told me no one else would ever know about it. And I guess I was scared. He's the law, you're just a lawyer—"

"Did you read any of it?"

"No."

"Did Andrea ever talk to you about what was in it?"

"No, *never.*" Helen sat down heavily on a worn chintz-covered couch. She took a deep breath. "I have nothing more to say to you. Please leave, Mr. Hammond."

Marc did not move. "I really don't think you understand, Mrs. Jorgensen. This can help clear your son."

She avoided his eyes. "I *told* you, if he killed Andrea, then I no longer have a son."

"Mrs. Jorgensen, have you been reading the papers about the murder?"

"Yes."

"Everything you've read or heard or seen has helped convince you that Peter is guilty. But you haven't talked to Peter the way I have. That boy wouldn't kill anyone, you as his mother should know that."

"I don't know anything. Not anymore. Today's kids . . . wild . . . I don't know . . ." And she began to cry.

"Please listen to me. The more I look into this case, the more I talk to your son, the more I'm convinced that he's being put through this hell for something he didn't do—"

"Why did he lie to the police?"

My God, he thought, she's like a prosecutor. Fire and

brimstone . . . "He lied because he was frightened, like you were of the D.A. Andrea was dead before he got there. Yes, there was something going on between them, but certainly you can forgive him for that . . . Andrea had many lovers. Andrea used drugs. Andrea associated with strange people. I know it upsets you to hear me say it—but Andrea was *not* a saint."

Helen's eyes filled with tears again. "She treated me like I was family. She was good to me. All that other talk, I don't care, I don't want to hear it."

"Is all that any reason to turn your back on your son?"

He let the question sink in. She was the jury now. It was as important to convince her now as it would be to convince the jury during the next few weeks. He lowered his voice. "At least *consider* the possibility that your Peter is innocent. Consider all the men that Andrea knew, not boys like your son but immoral men, any one of whom could have had a motive to kill her. Peter is your son, dammit. Your son. He loves and trusts you and he needs you now. I guarantee you, he's finished if you don't help him. It's *you* who will be committing the sin if you forsake him now."

She began to sob uncontrollably, and after a few minutes turned to him. "All right, what do you want me to do?"

"Testify at the trial. Tell about the people you saw at Andrea's apartment and the things they did. Tell the jury about the diary, *and* the circumstances under which it was taken from you. I know it won't be pleasant for you. I realize how you felt about Andrea. All I ask is that you tell the truth, because if the jury hears the truth, then we've got a chance to save your son."

She wiped her eyes. "I want to see him."

Marc nodded. "I'll drive you to Riker's tomorrow."

* * *

After Marc left he tried to recall a case he had recently read about concerning a diary . . . the court had held that the diary could be considered discoverable material if helpful to the defense. He had even made a note of it at the time, for future reference. Little did he know . . . He would find the write-up . . . Now he finally had something to latch onto. And, even if the entries were in code, as Madeline had said, at least the jury could be made to see how *many* people might have had reason to want Andrea Blanchard dead. Get the diary, or some of its references, into evidence. It was the stuff that reasonable doubt was made of. For the first time, Marc believed that they had a shot.

___ CHAPTER 19 ___

JUDGE VICTOR PIERCE assigned the largest courtroom in the Supreme Court Building on Centre Street for the trial of the Jorgensen case. Ostensibly performing his administrative duties, he inspected the courtroom with two aides before giving the okay for the press to enter, hoping, of course, that the press might want to interview him. They didn't; indeed, the only one who even acknowledged his presence was a reporter for the New York *Daily News,* and that was only because he stepped on her foot. This was not his year.

Three front rows on each side of the courtroom were reserved for the press; they were also provided with a table behind each of the counsel tables. Every wire service and local news program wanted its people there. The Jorgensen trial was going to be a major media event.

After the press people entered, the spectators were permitted to file in slowly, duly warned by the court officers that anyone creating a disturbance would be asked to leave— the admonitions were in stern language, all of the officers suddenly becoming *basso profundos*. It seemed the full presence of the press had its effect on the court personnel—even the court clerk stopped chewing gum.

Among those filing into the courtroom to take up the limited number of seats available to the general public was a young Italian, recently graduated from the University of Bologna law school, who had arrived in the United States only the previous day, on Monday, and had immediately determined to attend this trial. He was attracted by this early opportunity to see America's judicial system in action—a system he had long admired, along with the U.S. Constitution on which it was founded, and this admiration very much in spite of the unpopularity of his pro-American sentiments at the University of Bologna, where the prevailing winds were distinctly pro-Communist and anti-American. But there was another attraction that this particular trial held for Vito Mondo. It concerned the murder of Andrea Blanchard, and not only had he read about the case in the Italian press . . . she was, after all, an international personality . . . but she was the American lady whose beauty and whose smile in particular he had never forgotten during the years since he had first been its bedazzled recipient after doing her a favor in the passport division of the U.S. Consulate in Milan. What a loss, he thought. And what a terrible way for the beautiful lady to die. He supposed as much as to observe the way of American justice he was also here to see her avenged, and in the beginning he, like most others who had read of the case, was inclined to believe that Peter Jorgensen was the guilty party.

Also among those taking seats was a large group of social security recipients who spent much of their retirement in the pursuit of human drama by attending criminal trials. Day in and day out they made the Criminal Court building their second home. They were known to rate the lawyers at the many trials they had watched, and high on their list for best trial lawyers was Marc Hammond. Marc, in turn, found their reactions to witnesses helpful, realizing early on in his career that since they thought like jurors their impressions could be valuable. More than once he had consulted with them in the corridor at recesses to get their insights.

Assistant District Attorney Brian McCarthy was already seated at his table when Marc walked to his table and removed the case file from his briefcase. The difference between the two was marked. McCarthy was impeccably dressed in a dark blue suit, white cotton shirt and solid blue tie. There was not a wrinkle on him—as though his suit had been pressed with him in it. Marc could never quite achieve that Harvard look. He wore his clothing with relaxed ease. He simply was not as formidable looking a man as McCarthy with his West Point carriage. Their styles contrasted, but they were both outstanding lawyers, intelligent and able.

When everyone in the courtroom was seated the court officers brought in Peter Jorgensen from the adjoining room. Peter now had the gray-white pallor of a long-term prisoner. He halfheartedly waved to his mother, who sat in the rear of the courtroom, and she responded by nodding her head. Marc could only hope Peter's mother now shared his belief that her son was innocent.

"How you doing?" Marc asked as Peter took his seat at the defense table.

"I'm scared." Peter's voice was weak.

"Keep the faith. We have a few things going for us."

"Sure."

Allen Sturdivant stood at the window in his robing room, looking out at lower Manhattan, the Brooklyn Bridge and the morning traffic flowing slowly on the East River Drive. He was trying to psyche himself into a state allowing him to go forward with the trial. He was not underestimating his own fear, or guilt, or what the two might do to him. Loren . . . her threats . . . an innocent boy . . . Somehow he had to resolve them all . . . Stop thinking and *start* . . .

He buzzed the clerk, the court officer escorted him into the courtroom, all stood until he took his seat. The clerk intoned: "People of the State of New York against Peter Jorgensen. Appearances, please, counsel."

"Brian McCarthy, Assistant District Attorney for the People."

"Marc Hammond for the defendant."

The ritual completed, Peter was told to be seated by the court officer.

"Are the People ready?" Sturdivant asked. The routine was almost soothing, something to submerge himself in.

"The People are ready," McCarthy said.

"Is the defendant ready?"

Marc said, "No sir, we are not. We are not ready because the district attorney has not furnished the pre-trial discovery material that we're entitled to view under the law."

A low murmur in the audience, the court officers warning the spectators to be quiet or leave . . . Sturdivant concentrated on Marc's announcement, not surprised at the ploy but not liking the prospect of a delay that would prolong the trial . . . prolong his trial . . . he had no idea how either would come, in a way felt as much a defendant as a judge . . . "This was the date mutually agreed on, Mr. Hammond. You and Mr. McCarthy were consulted before it was fixed."

"That's true, Your Honor, but if I may be heard, I believe I will establish to Your Honor's satisfaction that my request is made necessary by the district attorney's neglect, not mine. As Your Honor is aware, I moved for all documents the district attorney had in his possession that would be relevant to the prosecution of my client. I'm entitled to that

156

by statute. May I direct Your Honor's attention to item number thirty-seven of my discovery motion in which I request all *Brady* material." Marc was referring to the United States Supreme Court's decision in *Brady* vs. *Maryland*. The court had held there that any material that could be helpful to the accused's defense had to be turned over to him before trial. "We maintain that such material has been withheld from the defendant."

McCarthy had waited long enough. "Your Honor, I take exception to counsel's unfounded remarks. There is no *Brady* material that has been withheld from the defendant, and I resent the implication that I've acted unethically by keeping something from him."

"I don't question Mr. McCarthy's ethics," Marc said quickly. "But I believe he's wrong on the law as to what constitutes *Brady* material. I'm referring, Your Honor, to a diary kept by the deceased. I'm ready to swear a witness, Mrs. Helen Jorgensen, the mother of the defendant, who will testify that she had the diary in her possession and that she surrendered it to the D.A. I maintain that that diary is essential to the defendant, although I would not even have known it existed if not for my personal investigation. Denial of the defendant's access to that diary is just what *Brady* vs. *Maryland* tried to avoid. We expect to establish from the pages of that personal record that there are people walking about freely today who had a real and substantial motive to kill the deceased, and that *one* of them should be sitting in that chair instead of my client."

McCarthy shook his head. "I don't deny, Your Honor, that we took the diary, but on examination we found it contained a record of events that have no bearing whatsoever on the issues in this case. No names are mentioned, only single initials—there's not the remotest possibility that any person could state with any degree of certainty that the deceased was referring to a particular person in any particular entry. In good faith, we came to the conclusion that it could be of no value to either the prosecution or the defense. What it did contain would only be the basis for speculation, not evidence, and I think Your Honor will agree that such speculation would be potentially damaging and should be avoided. The court of appeals in *People* vs. *Kanefsky* backs up our position . . . since the entries in the diary have no bearing on the criminal transaction with which this defendant is charged, they do not belong in evidence."

Marc spoke up. "Your Honor, the prosecutor is usurping your role. He's taken it on himself to determine that the contents of this diary will not be helpful to the defendant. How can he be so sure? Perhaps if the diary were in my hands instead of his there's the chance that I might be more vigorous than he was in following up leads that could cast meaningful doubt on my client's guilt."

Sturdivant had been caught off guard. This was the first mention of a diary. McCarthy said there were no names, but initials . . . his palms began to sweat. "It seems to me, gentlemen, that I can't rule on the possible relevancy of this diary unless I read it. The court of appeals also said in *Kanefsky* that the court must make that determination. I direct the People to produce the diary. I'll read it and decide whether it should be made available to the defendant. However, Mr. Hammond, under no circumstances will this trial be delayed beyond the time it takes me to examine the diary. Counsel will return at two P.M."

McCarthy delivered the diary to the judge's chambers in a matter of minutes, and Tony Fortuna, Sturdivant's law secretary, promptly brought it in to him.

"Tony, no calls, no interruptions of any kind."

Fortuna nodded and quietly closed the door.

Allen Sturdivant's hands were unsteady as he opened the diary. It went back five years. He read it twice, the first time quickly checking for his name. He was there, of course, referred to only as *A*. Beads of sweat covered his forehead as he turned each page for the possibility of evidence that could link him to her. Nothing. Andrea had made clever use of her code. . . .

On the day of their meeting in Milan she had written: *Met A today. Met him once before in the Hamptons. Think I'll see him again. He's rich, distinguished, good-looking.*

On their idyll at Lake Como, which he had thought at the time was a genuine romantic adventure: *Went to Lake Como with A. Spent the night at a little inn. Great view. A was great in bed.*

On still another date: *Beginning to get used to A—maybe too much. Should I ditch him? Before he ditches me?*

Other similar entries were scattered throughout the diary, the final a month before her death: *A is coming around less and less. I'm sure he wants to end it. Well, he won't get out so easily. He'll learn, if he hasn't already, that he can't have it both ways.*

That, he reflected, could apply to almost anyone. He read through a second time, checking for any references that he might have missed that possibly could identify him. There were still none that he could see. Andrea hadn't even designated any of the occupations of her men—no lawyer, doctor or . . . judge. Only single initials, dates and, in some instances, places. Another time he probably would have been upset to see the number of her paramours— "paramour," what a nice old-fashioned term for a judge who'd compromised his whole life and family, he thought grimly—even though he of course had never thought he was the only one, except while he was seeing her. That was quickly dispelled by the dates he noted, several of which were during the time period when he'd been seeing her. Well, like they said, there was no fool like an old fool, and he had managed to deceive himself that he'd been number one while he was—*stop it,* he ordered himself. You've no right, or the luxury of such absurd self-indulgent ruminations. Are you actually trying to justify what you did . . . ?

He switched his thoughts to Andrea's reasons for being so circumspect, even in her own diary. She herself gave the most compelling one on the last page . . . *"Dear Diary, if anyone is going to get mileage out of what's here, it's only going to be me."* Nobody could steal her diary and make it pay without her input. Andrea had, it seemed, covered all the possibilities, except one . . .

He wiped off his perspiring hands with his handkerchief. McCarthy was probably right . . . Hammond would have great difficulty finding anything useful in this diary. But as Hammond himself had pointed out—and he respected the young attorney's bulldog qualities as well as his well-known enterprise—something in the diary might well open a door to him, indicate a compromising line of investigation. Who could predict what leads would turn up . . . ? He could not risk letting the door be opened, no matter how slim the odds that anything compromising would eventuate. His job, and intent, was to see justice administered to Jorgensen— not to convict himself in the process. But he would need to be reasoned in his ruling not to admit. Yes, reasoned and judicial. He began to write . . .

At two o'clock Sturdivant ordered the court officers to bring in the defendant once again and directed the attorneys to appear before him. He looked down and silently reread what he had written on his legal pad . . . "The Court has examined the diary and its contents. I find that no portion of the contents of the diary is relevant to the issue of the defendant's guilt or innocence. Therefore, no portion of it will be admissible in this trial. The request of counsel for its delivery is denied . . ."

Those were the words he was prepared to read into the

record. But as all waited he found he couldn't. It was all self-serving rationalization . . . not to mention panicky. He crumpled the paper containing those words and spoke as he knew he must.

"I have read the diary. I find that the contents neither exculpate the defendant nor point the finger at anyone else. But I cannot say with certainty that those contents could not possibly lead to something that might be helpful to the defense. In my judgment the spirit of the *Brady* decision requires that the defendant be given the opportunity to pursue any leads which could possibly establish his innocence. I therefore direct the district attorney to deliver the diary to counsel for the defendant at the close of these proceedings."

McCarthy rose. "May I be heard, Your Honor?"

Sturdivant nodded.

"May I first say that no one has more respect for Your Honor's judicial knowledge than I. Nevertheless, I most respectfully disagree. These were the intimate and personal memoranda of the deceased. Out of common respect, they should remain private unless disclosure would serve a definite purpose. I share completely Your Honor's evaluation of the entries. They are not probative or admissible at this trial for any purpose. Conceivably those entries might doom the defendant instead of helping him—"

"Just the point," Sturdivant replied quickly. "You have the material. You can pursue leads from that information, innocuous as it may seem now, to doom the defendant. His counsel must have an equal opportunity to pursue an opposite conclusion. However, respect for the deceased is a point well made. Mr. Hammond, after you receive the diary you are directed not to disclose those contents to any one other than your client. What is contained there is for your eyes and his only. You are not to reveal to anyone what you find there."

Marc nodded, pleased at the ruling. "I appreciate and

161

respect Your Honor's concern. There will be no revelation or discussion of the contents to anyone other than my client."

Sturdivant routinely set the next Monday for pre-trial hearings, then walked slowly into the robing room.

"I'll be fine, Fred," he said to the court officer. "You can go."

The officer was puzzled. It was his duty to escort the judge to his chambers.

"Are you sure, Judge?"

"Yes, thank you."

Alone now, Sturdivant stood once again at the window. At least for one brief moment this afternoon his self-respect had returned. Not that he had by any means wiped the slate clean. Still, for the minute or two it took him to render the decision he at least was a judge again. He had decided an issue on its merits, where the criterion was fairness. Only a brief moment, but it reminded him of what he had been, what he had always wanted to be.

CHAPTER 20

MARC READ AND reread the diary, trying to find some pattern, a lead to follow. The judge was right. Single initials made it impossible to identify anyone, and she gave no physical characteristics. Still, he would have liked to discover who "A" was. A was ditching her, apparently, but why would A kill her if he was breaking off contact with her?

There was an interesting entry in late November, a month before she was murdered. He read it once again.

A is coming around less and less. I'm sure he wants to end it. Well, he won't get out so easily.

A threat? Blackmail? Andrea Blanchard, so far as one could tell from newspaper clips, was not above it. And if so, retaliation by A would not be so farfetched . . .

But it was speculation, it was all he had. He knew from the diary A was rich and distinguished, but the other references were uninformative. He considered giving the information to an investigator to attempt to clue in on the identity of A, as well as P and J and R, but that would require breaking his commitment to Judge Sturdivant that he would reveal nothing to anyone. And once the judge learned he hadn't kept his word . . . well, judges didn't take kindly to that sort of thing. And antagonizing the judge could hardly help the defense of his client.

Still, the thought of an investigator persisted, not to develop the entries but to dig into Andrea's relationships independently.

He called Charlie Sweeney, who understood the problem and told Marc to leave it to him, that he would see to it that Peter Jorgensen got the best. . . .

J. Franklin Powell welcomed the call from Sweeney. It was a banner season . . . Loren Sturdivant and now Charlie Sweeney. When Sweeney asked that he put his resources behind Hammond at a reduced fee, Powell considered it a rare opportunity to have the state chairman of the Democratic party in his debt.

But after meeting with Hammond, Powell knew he had his work cut out for him. All he had were news clippings and a few short days in which to come up with something useful. He reviewed clippings, again and again, until he finally saw something that looked like a possible lead. Possible, but thin.

Two weeks before her death Andrea Blanchard had been involved in a dust-up at the Oasis Club. Apparently miffed at her escort, she had thrown a glass at him, missed her target and the glass ended up breaking an eight-foot mirror. The police were called, and Andrea, her escort, and the owner of the restaurant were escorted to the precinct. The owner, after apologies and assurance of compensation, had dropped the charges. Powell decided the first step was to talk to the police officer who had responded.

Because of his background and connections, there wasn't a precinct commander that Powell didn't know, and consequently there wasn't a cop who was unavailable to him. The C.O. of the precinct that had responded to the Oasis imbroglio was especially cooperative—Powell had been able to be of some help to him in the past regarding his wife. The officer who responded to the "disturbance" call at the Oasis was promptly called into the captain's office.

"Commissioner Powell," the C.O. said, using Powell's title from his police department days, "this is Pat O'Connor. Pat, you know Commissioner Powell?"

"Never had the pleasure. But sure proud to meet you, Commissioner."

"The commissioner wants to ask you a few questions about that little fracas at the Oasis," the captain said, and discreetly left the room.

"Sit down, Pat," Powell said easily. "I understand you responded to the disturbance call involving Andrea Blanchard?"

"Yes, sir."

"I know no arrest was made, but I'd like to know what happened. The newspapers were skimpy on details."

"Well, I'd say the lady was a bit under the weather, sir. The maître d' told me she came in alone about five and sat at the bar for an hour until her date arrived. An hour later it started. Her date kept his cool, but that only made her angrier and she threw her glass at him. After she talked to the restaurant owner and apologized and promised him compensation he cooled down and left. Then her date left, not happy. And then she went into a crying jag. I drove her home."

"You drove her home? How come?"

"Well, she seemed really upset and asked me and—"

"Okay, okay, what did she talk about?"

"Well, she said she was depressed, and that if it wasn't for her shrink she didn't know how she could make it."

"Did she mention the name of the shrink?"

"Like a goddamn broken record . . . you'd think he was the messiah. Gerald Kossulth. Who could forget it?"

Powell had heard of Kossulth. He had even met him on a few occasions at city affairs. He was one rich and well-connected shrink.

Back at his office Powell called a meeting of his people and laid out the problem.

"So that's where we stand. I want you to talk to as many people on the list I'm about to give you as you can. They're all people who have been connected one way or another to Andrea Blanchard in the newspapers. Most of them will probably run from you like the plague, but get what you can. Obviously the most useful information would come from Dr. Kossulth, but he'll never reveal confidential information from a patient."

"But maybe someone else who had access to it would." This came from Maggie Nelson, an ex-cop who had been with Powell since her retirement three years earlier. She was intelligent, attractive and innovative; and, being divorced with no dependents, was able to lose herself in her work. Powell had come to rely heavily on her.

"Kossulth has a secretary," Maggie said. "Been with him for ten years. She's a nice lady but made the mistake of marrying a bum. He's always been a cheap hustler—pimping, selling coke, running numbers, con games."

"Can you locate him?"

"Matter of fact, I can. Don't laugh, but he won a John Travolta look-alike contest at a male strip joint on Forty-sixth Street and they gave him a steady job. He *is* good-looking, that I'll give him. His name is Matty Ruffino, but he goes under the name of—are you ready for this—Peaches Travolta."

Powell smiled. "How do you know him so well, Maggie?"

"I collared him years ago for procuring. He became an

informant—a damned good one. I dealt with him a lot, although to tell you the truth he made my flesh crawl. He used to tell me about his conquests, blow-by-blow, and about the confidential info he made his wife give him about Kossulth's patients. The son-of-a-bitch threatened to leave her if she didn't talk. He has this hold on her—it's all sex, I'm sure. She's scared to death he'll take off. Of course if Kossulth ever knew she talked to this slime he'd fire her fast."

"You think she may have told him something about Andrea Blanchard?"

"It's possible. She has access to the files. She's efficient. Kossulth relies on her. She's in charge of the office."

"Can you get him to talk?"

"He'd sell his mother if the price was right. We wouldn't have to look for him if he knew what we wanted him for, he'd be looking for us."

"What we need," Powell said, feeling a little better, "is evidence that someone, other than Jorgensen of course, wanted Andrea Blanchard dead. How soon can you see him?"

"Tonight."

"How much will it take?"

"I don't know. He's doing pretty well now so he can afford to hold back."

"Do what you have to do," Powell told her.

Maggie Nelson arrived at the Macho Club a few minutes before the first show started. According to the billboard out front, Peaches Travolta was a featured act.

The room was relatively small, but every square inch of it had been utilized. Small tables were placed together in long tiers. The male waiters, in brief briefs and black bow ties, slipped through the narrow rows serving drinks. There was an implied understanding that a pat on the buns from a patron would automatically earn the waiter a tip for the

167

familiarity. The room was painted red. Lining the walls were enormous photographs of steroid-enhanced muscle men in jockstraps. The decibel level was near-deafening even before the three musicians began playing their electronic instruments.

The women sitting at the tables kept time to the music by waving their hands and their bodies while jumping up and down. They pounded the tables with their fists, and the floor vibrated from their stomping feet.

Maggie spotted one of the few vacant seats and managed to squeeze into a space alongside a heavyset woman whose face was bathed in sweat, partly, Maggie guessed, because of the inadequate ventilation but mostly because of her anticipation of the impending action. Maggie had only seen this intensity at a revival meeting she had attended when she was working undercover on a church-scam operation. The woman was calling out, "Bring 'em on, take it off," over and over again.

Now the lights lowered, the noise level heightened as the musicians turned up the mikes. Then, as suddenly as they began, the musicians stopped and a flashing red spot played on the small stage. A woman's voice, coming from behind the curtain, announced: "Ladies, this is it. No long introductions. You want action, not talk. For our first attraction we bring you that hunk from Canarsie, that dreamboat, the one you want to take home to mother when mother isn't home, Mr. Perpetual Motion"—a beat for effect—"PEA–CHES TRA–VOL–TA."

The red spot changed to white, and there was Peaches in skintight jeans. The music launched into fast rock. Peaches's pelvis rotated in all directions, he played with the zipper on his fly, then slipped out of his jeans and stood revealed in a mini-bikini, hands and arms extended as he accepted the adoration of his admirers. Now it was money time. As Peaches moved toward the end of the runway the women next to Maggie lunged forward. "I've got a hundred here—a hundred!" Peaches saw the hundred dollar bill and smiled at the woman as she tried to push herself in front of the women already waiting at the end of the runway. They would not budge. Peaches, not about to lose that hundred, moved to the very end and extended his pelvis to give the hundred-dollar woman the opportunity to insert the bill and, as he would have described it with his characteristic humility, get a feel of the promised land.

His maneuver was a mistake. The women in front still would not move, intent on making their own donations. In her anxiety and frustration, the heavy woman now moved her arm in a downward position, over the heads of the women in front of her, her clenched fist containing the hundred dollar bill landing flush on Peaches's groin. Peaches, a stricken ox, fell to the floor, clutching himself. A colleague and another performer carried him behind the curtain into the small dressing room they all shared.

Maggie left the club and using a facsimile of her old shield gained entrance from the doorman through the rear door. The music had restarted out front, as well as the other action. Peaches was, it seemed, soon forgotten.

When Maggie entered the dimly lit room, Peaches recognized her immediately. The pain had subsided enough so that he could talk.

"You see what happened in there?" he asked.

"Yes. I guess a thing like that could put you out of commission."

"Did that fat broad leave the C-note with anyone?"

"I don't think so."

"Son-of-a-bitch. A total loss. Let me get out there. She cost me three hundred, minimum." He tried to get up from the couch but the pain held him back.

"You'd better take it easy," Maggie said. "There'll be other nights."

"Geez, nothing ever happened like this. Maybe a few scratches from the long nails but never like this. I won't be able to have sex for a week."

"They say abstinence makes us strong, Peaches. Anyway, I'm your good samaritan. How would you like to make plenty more than you lost tonight?"

"Talk to me."

"No, you talk to me."

"What about?"

"What Rhonda told you about Andrea Blanchard."

"You mean the broad who was killed by the kid?"

"I do."

Peaches managed a smile. "You're asking for highly confidential information, Miss Maggie. Information that was given to me in the heat of passion, if you know what I mean. My Rhonda most especially didn't want to talk about this Blanchard dame. I told her if she didn't come across I wouldn't come across. Naturally that did it. But it took a lot out of me, so this won't come cheap."

You disgusting son-of-a-bitch, Maggie thought. Aloud she said, "How much?"

"A grand."

"Five hundred."

"No way."

"Forget it then." Maggie moved toward the door.

"Seven-fifty."

"Six."

"Deal. Let's see the money first." Maggie counted six one-hundred-dollar bills taken from her bag but held onto them in her hand. He reached for the money, she pulled her hand back.

"Talk now, pay later."

"Hey, Miss Maggie, you got a real way with words. Well, Blanchard had been seeing the doctor for a long time, usually once a week, sometimes more. She was a real screwed-

170

up broad, even with all that bread and looks going for her. She boozed too much, did drugs."

"We know all that," Maggie said.

"Yeah, but here's the good stuff. She said she was really gone on some special guy. Claimed she loved him. She told Kossulth she would never reveal his name, not even to the doc, because his deal with her could ruin him if it got out. She also said she was afraid she was losing him, that she figured the only hold she ever had on him was sex. Rhonda felt sorry for her. Sort of two of a kind. Anyway, when this guy started to cut down on his visits, she began to lose it. She told the doc this guy was her last shot at happiness and she was going to do everything she could to hold him. I remember Rhonda telling me that she was really hitting the booze and who knew what else. Rhonda said she looked lousy on the last visit to Kossulth, the one before she was killed."

"When was that?"

"Well, let's see . . . oh, yeah, I remember reading she was killed on Christmas Eve. I guess it was about a week before. Like I say, she was a screwed-up broad. But one thing you got to say for her—she never gave him up, never told his name. I tell ya"—Peaches laughed—"when they fall in love with ya, you can get away with murder."

Maggie Nelson threw the six hundred dollars in his lap and walked out.

Brian McCarthy and Marc Hammond were waiting in the anteroom of Judge Sturdivant's chambers. McCarthy was annoyed. He thought the issue about a further delay in the trial had been put to rest. He hadn't taken kindly to Hammond's call advising him that he was going to make another request.

Marc was equally on edge. Powell had submitted Maggie Nelson's report of her interview with Peaches Travolta. The

171

last line was: "Given time, it's possible that we could get closer to the identity of this mystery man."

Marc was aware the comment was mostly self-serving, but he couldn't overlook any possibility. He needed another postponement, which he realized would not sit well with the judge, never mind the prosecution. Sturdivant was behind schedule already—the trial had to be finished before he could resign and begin his campaign. Yet Marc had to hope that Sturdivant would still be guided by a sense of justice. That was his reputation.

Sturdivant called them now into his chambers, motioned for them to be seated while he finished rereading Maggie Nelson's report, which Marc had been obliged to show him to back up his request for a delay in the trial. He hoped his face masked the fear stirred up by the report. He told himself that at least he had acted properly in ordering the diary to be delivered to Hammond, even at the risk of eventually exposing himself. But now the thought of a further delay, a prolonging of the tension of this trial, was intolerable. He knew that time was running out, that he could endure this situation of being pulled in two directions only so long. He wanted it over with, praying that he wouldn't fall apart before it was ended.

The judge placed the report on his desk. "Mr. Hammond, there's nothing in this report that could serve as a valid reason for further delay. This trial will begin on Monday. That's all, gentlemen."

Brian McCarthy, with a restrained smile, walked toward the door.

Marc Hammond stood and looked at Sturdivant.

"That's all, Mr. Hammond."

"No, dammit," Hammond said, "that is not all."

McCarthy stopped at the door. Hammond was asking for trouble.

Sturdivant's face showed surprise, then anger. "Mr. Hammond, I appreciate your concern for your client, and your emotional involvement is understandable, but I've made my determination and I advise you—"

"But the report states that further investigation may lead to identifying a man who might very well be guilty of the crime my client is on trial for. To deny me the opportunity to—"

McCarthy moved back into the room and pulled Hammond's arm. "Marc, for Christ's sake, cool it."

Hammond pulled his arm free. "I know what I'm saying. I believe my client is being deprived of the right to establish his innocence." And then he went too far, knew it but couldn't stop himself . . . "Judge, are we taking shortcuts here so you can keep a timetable in your campaign?"

Two court officers entered, and on Sturdivant's instructions led Marc out. McCarthy was about to leave, too, but hesitated. "Judge, Marc Hammond went too far, and after he cools off he'll realize it. You'd be more than justified to take steps to discipline him but . . . well, frankly it could happen to any of us, and besides, I want to beat him even up."

"Don't worry, Mr. McCarthy, you'll have your chance. I'll take no such steps. Leave now, please."

Allen Sturdivant sat at his desk, not moving. "To none will we sell, to none deny or delay, right or justice." Words from the Magna Carta, words he had lived by, still believed in. Believed in, but couldn't afford to live by . . . Oh, he could rationalize his ruling, the report hadn't contained any hard evidence, but there was the statement of the investigator that something more might turn up with time . . . time . . . he couldn't face it . . . couldn't, face it, risk it . . .

173

He poured himself a drink from a flask he kept in the bottom drawer of his desk, but Scotch was no solution. He knew it, and knowing it, poured another and bigger drink. Loren had called and arranged for them to have dinner together at the Carlyle that evening. Just a nice little family get-together . . .

CHAPTER 21

OFICER JOSEPH LAWRENCE was to be McCarthy's only witness for the Huntely hearing, so-called because of the court of appeals decision in *People* vs. *Huntely*, which required a pre-trial hearing before the selection of a jury to determine whether a confession the prosecution sought to enter into evidence was made voluntarily by the defendant. Marc Hammond's motion for the hearing had been granted on the basis that Peter had been suffering extreme pain when he made his first statement and, therefore, the statement should not be admissible into evidence because it could not have been made voluntarily.

Joe Lawrence was sworn by the clerk and McCarthy began his examination. "Officer Lawrence, will you state for the court your assignment on December twenty-fourth, last Christmas Eve?"

"I was working R.M.P., Radio Motor Patrol, with my partner, Officer Dave Darby."

"Did you have occasion, sometime after midnight on that day, to make an arrest of the defendant, Peter Jorgensen?"

"Yes."

"Will you tell the Court the circumstances surrounding the arrest?"

"We were proceeding north on Central Park West and turned west onto Sixty-third Street. After completing the turn I saw the defendant holding onto one of the spikes of a fence that guarded the side entrance of the Monte Carlo Apartments. I saw him lose his hold and fall to the ground."

"What did you do after you saw this?"

"I left the vehicle and placed the defendant under arrest."

"Why did you take this action?"

"Based upon my experience as a police officer I believed that the defendant was either attempting to enter those premises unlawfully or already had and was attempting to leave."

"When you say you placed him under arrest, what did you physically do, if anything?"

"I spread-eagled him over the hood of the car and frisked him."

"Is that normal police procedure after an arrest is made?"

"Yes."

"Proceed, please."

"I directed him to enter the car, which he did, and I followed him into the rear seat. Officer Darby had remained in the driver's seat. At that point I gave the defendant his Miranda warnings."

"And then he made a statement to you?"

"Yes, he did."

"What was the substance of that statement?"

"That he was a mechanic and that he had entered the premises because he wanted to steal some tools from the basement."

"Did he use the word 'steal'?"

"I believe he used the word 'cop.'"

"Was that the entire statement?"

"He said that when he realized how foolish he had been,

176

he decided to get out the same way he got in—by climbing over the fence."

"Was the fence locked when you inspected it?"

"Yes. The superintendent had a key. I called him and he opened it."

McCarthy consulted his notes. "Actually, the defendant gave you two statements. One after the arrest for the burglary, and the second the next day when you rearrested him on the homicide charge. Is that correct?"

"That's correct."

"In the second statement did he refer to the manner in which he entered the basement?"

"Yes. He said that the deceased had given him a key to the fence door and that he used it to enter, but that when he went to the apartment and discovered Andrea Blanchard's body he panicked and lost the key and tried to get out by climbing over the fence."

"Objection." Marc was on his feet. "Judge, we're not concerning ourselves here with the second statement in this hearing. It's irrelevant to the central question of whether the first statement was given involuntarily."

"I only wanted to accommodate counsel," McCarthy said evenly. "If he wants to move to strike the second statement as well, in the interest of saving time I would have no objection to making that statement a part of this hearing as well."

McCarthy was pulling a *schtick*. Both attorneys knew that the first statement was a lie and cover-up, and if the jury heard it, it would leave an unfavorable impression. They also both knew that the second statement was, in essence, Jorgensen's defense and that under no circumstances would Marc want to suppress a statement that he wanted the jury to believe. And one that he now believed.

"Don't do me any favors, Mr. McCarthy. You try your case and I'll try mine."

Sturdivant said impatiently, "All right, gentlemen, let's try to remember that this is a courtroom. Mr. Hammond, your objection is sustained. For the purpose of this hearing, I will not hear any evidence concerning the second statement given by the defendant. The only issue in this hearing is whether the defendant's statement given after his arrest for burglary was made voluntarily. Mr. McCarthy, confine your proof to that issue."

"Very well, Your Honor. Officer Lawrence, did you ever reduce the statement to writing and have the defendant sign it?"

"Yes, sir, I did."

"When and where did he sign it?"

"In the station house, about twenty minutes after I placed him under arrest."

McCarthy, anticipating the defense strategy, asked the question that he knew Hammond would ask.

"Did he at any time, before or after you gave him his Miranda warnings, tell you that he did not understand what you were saying to him?"

"No, sir."

"Did he, before or after you gave him the Miranda warnings, say that he was in pain because of an injury to his foot?"

"No, sir."

"When he signed the statement, did you read it to him?"

"Yes, sir. I read it to him, and then I made sure that he read it. Then he signed it."

"Did he at the time he signed the statement indicate that he was in pain?"

"No, sir. He had mentioned that he thought he might have sprained his ankle, but he didn't complain about it being painful. He was just anxious to make the statement—"

"Objection."

"Overruled."

178

Marc couldn't believe it. Lawrence's answer had been speculation about Peter's state of mind—inadmissible testimony. Ordinarily he would have claimed "exception," but he knew he'd better be careful, though, after his recent outburst in the judge's chambers over a delay. He wouldn't push it. Not now.

McCarthy had done well with this witness. He ended his questioning with, "Officer Lawrence, did you at any time threaten the defendant, or in any way induce him to make any statement to you—oral or written?"

"No, sir, I did not."

Marc began his cross-examination.

"You say you saw the defendant for the first time when you turned west onto Sixty-third Street?"

"Yes, sir."

"How were you able to see him?"

"The headlights of the car picked him up. The entrance to the building's basement is only about fifty feet from a street lamp. He was easy to spot because he was hanging from the top of the fence. By that I mean he had one hand on the top of one of the spikes, and he was dangling. Then my partner put the spotlight on him."

"Then you saw him before he fell."

"Yes."

Marc produced a photograph from his file. He said, from the defense table, "Officer Lawrence, will you look at the photograph? Is that an accurate photographic reproduction of the gate as it appeared to you at the time you said you inspected it on Christmas Eve?"

Lawrence inspected the picture. "Yes, it is."

"Your Honor, may I have the photograph now marked as Defendant's Exhibit A for the purpose of this hearing?"

"No objection," said McCarthy.

"Officer, after looking at this photograph, will you estimate for us the height of the fence, from the base to the top?"

"About fifteen feet."

"That's an unusually high fence, isn't it?"

"It's higher than most, yes . . ."

"In your arrest report, you estimate the defendant's height as approximately six feet."

"Yes."

"Now, would you say that his arm was extended about two feet over his body while he was holding onto the tip of the spike?"

"That's about right."

"So, with his natural height of six feet, adding another two feet for the arm extension, when he slipped he would have fallen about seven feet. Is that correct?"

"Yes, I guess so."

"Did you see how he landed?"

"I'm not sure I understand what you mean."

"Did he land on one foot? On both feet? On his face? How?"

"I believe he landed on his left foot."

"Did he remain on the ground when you put the spot on him?"

"Yes."

"You testified that you had him spread-eagled over the hood of the car to search him, correct?"

"Yes."

"Did you order him to get off the ground to do that?"

"Yes, sir."

"Did he need your assistance to stand?"

Lawrence frowned. He appeared to be concentrating on the answer. "No," he said finally, "he stood by himself. I didn't assist him."

"So it's your testimony that in spite of the fact that the

defendant complained about the pain, he didn't need your help to stand?"

"He didn't say a thing about pain. After he was in the patrol car he said he thought he had sprained his ankle."

"Are you sure that's all he said?"

"Yes, to the best of my recollection, that was all he said."

"Are you sure that he didn't tell you that he thought he *broke* his ankle?"

"No, I'm sure he never said that."

"And that the pain was so intense that he needed medical assistance immediately, at a hospital?"

"No, he never said anything about a hospital until after we got to the stationhouse, and then only after I suggested that his ankle should be checked."

Peter pulled at Marc's sleeve. Marc bent down.

"He's lying," Peter whispered. "I can't believe how he could lie like that."

"I can," Hammond whispered back.

Lawrence kept a straight face as he watched them, but he was thinking . . . Fuck you, Counselor. I'm getting a gold shield out of this. Your client is guilty. So what if I stretch the truth to prove it? The son-of-a-bitch is guilty and we all know it . . .

Marc straightened and faced Lawrence again. "How long was it, after you made that compassionate offer to the defendant, that you actually took him to the hospital?"

McCarthy rose to object to Hammond's sarcasm, then decided to let it pass. He was way ahead, why not be generous.

Lawrence answered, "About two hours from the time we first placed him under arrest."

"Are you aware that the diagnosis at the hospital was that the defendant had suffered a compound fracture of the ankle?"

"I took him there. The doctor mentioned it."

"And yet you're telling this court now that he wasn't in

181

extreme pain before and after you took his statement." Marc raised his voice. "Do you really expect this court to believe that?"

"Objection."

"Sustained. Mr. Hammond, you know better than that. Don't do that again."

Hammond paused, collected himself. "Officer Lawrence," he said, "is it your testimony then that in spite of suffering a compound fracture, the defendant never complained about being in severe pain?"

"That's my testimony, yes, sir."

"Officer Lawrence, isn't it a fact that you are testifying to this untruth because the defendant gave both his oral and written statement under painful duress after being told that he would not be permitted to receive medical aid unless he made a statement. And isn't it a fact that the defendant would have admitted to anything from the assassination of Abraham Lincoln to the killing of Cock Robin just to get relief from his pain—?"

McCarthy's "Objection" was near the top of his voice.

Sturdivant pointed his finger at Marc. "I am warning you, Counselor, that you are about to be held in contempt."

Hammond, noting that Sturdivant's hand was shaking slightly, once again restrained himself. He realized he'd better do more . . . "I want to apologize to this Court. It's just that the witness' testimony is so difficult to believe—"

Sturdivant was back in control. "Mr. Hammond, there is no jury here—bear that in mind with your comments. I do not appreciate the dramatics. This is *not* a stage to perform on. Any redirect, Mr. McCarthy?"

"No, sir. For the purpose of this hearing, the People rest."

Lawrence stood up, preparing to leave the witness stand.

"Don't go quite yet, Officer Lawrence," Sturdivant said. "I have a few questions."

At last, thought Marc, it's finally bothering him.

"Officer Lawrence, when a person is placed under arrest and is in apparent need of medical treatment, what is the correct police procedure?"

"He's given medical attention as soon as possible."

"When you say as soon as possible, could that be done even before the booking procedure if his condition called for it?"

"Yes, if his condition called for it."

"So you're saying in your judgment the defendant's condition did not require immediate medical attention after he was placed under arrest."

"That's correct, sir."

"Yet from your testimony it became apparent to you at some point that his ankle needed looking after?"

"Yes, sir."

"Can you recall at what point you concluded that?"

Lawrence frowned. He understood that the question was not entirely friendly. "I can't really recall that, sir."

"Thank you, Officer. You're excused."

Sturdivant appeared to be making notes on his pad; he was only writing his name, doodling to buy time to think. He felt a sweaty combination of relief and anxiety over his questioning that had pointed out the weakness of Lawrence's testimony. It was the right thing to do, but an awful feeling was growing in him that what served the defense somehow threatened him. He had told himself that justice for the defendant and his own skin could somehow both be preserved . . . but now there was the frightening temptation to safeguard his position by compromising the defendant's. No, damn it, he wouldn't do it, and even as he tried to reassure himself of that, he felt an enormous uneasiness, a desire to give in to the easy way . . . As he turned to Marc Hammond to continue the hearing he felt like an observer, a bystander waiting to see what this Judge Sturdivant would do. Perhaps this way he could go on, by not being himself . . .

"Do you have any witnesses to call for the purpose of this hearing?" he asked Marc.

"No, Your Honor. The defense rests for the purpose of this hearing."

Sturdivant pushed himself back in his chair. "I will hear any final arguments."

Marc stood up and took a few steps from the bench.

"I'm aware that it's usually difficult for the Court to grant the motion to suppress the statement based on the lack of credibility of the arresting officer's testimony. But I'm also reasonably sure Your Honor has granted such motions when the lack of credibility is apparent on its face. This is such a case. To believe Officer Lawrence's testimony, in the light of common experience, simply defies common sense. The fact is that the defendant suffered a compound fracture of his ankle as a result of his fall from the fence. He could not possibly have hidden his agony from Officer Lawrence. Yet he was forced to give his statement before he could receive as much as a Band-Aid. He would have said anything to get medical attention. Yes, Miranda warnings were given to him, but that process in this case was a sham—a compliance with the law but a travesty of the spirit of the law. It was an involuntary statement. The Supreme Court in *Miranda* vs. *Arizona* told us that the Fifth Amendment does not permit an individual to be coerced into testifying against himself and that inducement of a confession by threat or promise or any other involuntary means is not admissible in evidence against him because it *is,* in effect, a means of compelling him to testify against himself. Such procedure violates fair play and justice. The defendant's statement was involuntary and therefore inadmissible as a matter of law."

Sturdivant turned to McCarthy, who spoke crisply, without emotion. "Counsel for the defendant would have us believe, from the testimony elicited at this hearing, that the only reason the defendant made his admittedly false statement to the officer was his painful condition and the promise of medical aid. We suggest that the defendant had a far different motive for making the statement to Officer Lawrence. I submit to this Court that the last thing the defendant wanted to do was remain silent. On the contrary, Your Honor, I submit that in his panic he made his statement not because of his painful injury and the need for medical attention but because he believed that with the admission of a relatively innocuous criminal act he could conceal his presence in Andrea Blanchard's apartment and the act of murder that he committed there. I respectfully submit that to keep this statement from the jury would deprive the People of the opportunity to demonstrate that the defendant's *admitted* lie was nothing more than an attempt to deceive, and that, with respect, the jury should make that determination. So it is the People's position that not only did the defendant make the statement voluntarily, he reached out to make it to serve his purpose of covering up the truth. For these reasons I respectfully urge Your Honor to deny defendant's motion to suppress the statement and allow it to be introduced as evidence at the trial."

Sturdivant waited until McCarthy was seated. "I'll reserve decision on the motion and direct the court reporter to provide me with a copy of the record of these proceedings. I will review the testimony before rendering my decision on the motion, which will be done tomorrow morning at nine-thirty A.M. Court is recessed until then."

Marc felt a spark of hope. He had to feel at least somewhat encouraged by the way Sturdivant had put his questions to the officer. He was also cheered by the way McCarthy, in his closing argument, seemed to avoid commenting on Lawrence's credibility. Apparently McCarthy as well as the judge had some doubts about Lawrence's truthfulness. And if Pe-

185

ter's first statement was suppressed he could take the stand and have a shot at persuading the jury to believe him, without being confronted with his first phony admission.

Marc was able to smile at his client before he left the courtroom and say with some conviction, "It's a ballgame now, Peter. I don't want to build up false hopes, but I can tell you that we have something to work with. Hang in, buddy."

Marc decided to risk a little celebration. He knew he might be courting the displeasure of the gods, but he felt positive enough about Sturdivant's ruling to call Randy and arrange to meet her at Elaine's, the Upper East Side restaurant noted for its clientele of achievers.

Elaine herself met him and escorted him to the table where Randy was waiting. He was under no illusion about who was the celebrity, and he loved it. This was Randy's turf, and she deserved the attention she got. Randy kept the conversation light throughout dinner, understanding Marc's need to be diverted from the Jorgensen trial.

It was only much later, at home, after they had made love, that she asked him what had happened during the day to chase his glooms about the trial.

"It's not what happened today," he told her. "It's what will happen tomorrow."

All were in place when Sturdivant entered the courtroom. Marc continued to feel good. Peter sat tight-lipped. McCarthy looked straight ahead, not looking too confident.

The judge proceeded to read from the papers in front of him without looking up. "After hearing on the Huntely issue, the following is the decision of this Court: The credibility of the officer's testimony is a question that must be determined. But let us assume that the officer did in fact suggest to the defendant that giving the statement first would expedite his receiving medical aid. If such were the case,

186

defendant claims that the statement should be suppressed and not admissible at trial because it was acquired involuntarily. The People take the position that the defendant's statement was not only voluntarily made but was designed to divert police attention from further investigation as to what in fact occurred in Andrea Blanchard's apartment on the night of December twenty-fourth." Sturdivant scarcely paused for a breath, racing ahead to get through it . . .

"Counsel for the defendant is correct that reference to the second statement is not germane to the issue before us—the voluntariness of the first. Nevertheless, we can't operate in a vacuum and block the knowledge from our minds that a second statement—inconsistent with the first—was in fact made. To that extent this second statement is relevant, because this Court is called on to determine the defendant's state of mind. Was the defendant's motive in talking to the police officer his desire for relief from his pain or was it an intent to deceive? From the testimony here I am not able to determine as a matter of law that either is the case. This decision will remain, as it should, a function of the jury. They will answer the question along with other questions raised by the testimony in the case. They will decide where the truth lies—that is their province under our law.

"The motion to suppress the defendant's statement at the time of his first arrest is denied. The People may introduce this statement at the trial. We will proceed with jury selection as soon as the panel arrives. Mr. Clerk, please call for the panel now. Until then this Court stands in recess."

Marc was immediately on his feet. "Your Honor, I'm having difficulty understanding your decision. During the course of this hearing you saw fit to exclude reference to a second statement, yet in your decision, sir, you yourself refer to it."

"Mr. Hammond," Sturdivant heard himself responding, "your exception to my ruling is duly noted on the record.

187

To repeat, we will proceed with jury selection when the panel arrives."

Outside the courtroom reporters were surrounding McCarthy, whose first reaction, which he was not advertising, was also surprise—though in his case a pleased surprise. Marc was too hot to talk to anyone. He didn't wait for the elevator, ducked into a stair exit and began hurrying down. He heard the door open behind him, heard his name called and stopped. It was Tom McPartland.

"Tom," Marc said, "give me a break. Talk to McCarthy. This is his moment, not mine. If I talk to a reporter now I'll be disbarred."

"Listen," McPartland said, "you want to talk? Then talk. It'll be off the record."

"No 'reliable source' stuff?"

"You got it."

"All right, I can't understand it," Marc said. "He rationalized in there, it even might seem to make sense to a layman, but it was a wrong decision and he's too good a judge not to know it. What makes it even harder to understand is that this man has a record of being concerned with the civil rights of defendants. I don't get it . . . unless maybe his candidacy—"

McPartland interrupted. "Maybe? Don't be naive, sport. No maybe. You and the distinguished judge are now in the world of politics. What's the number one issue in this state? Crime, law and order. Is *candidate* Sturdivant going to make a ruling that will make him appear soft on crime? Marc, the man is running for governor of the state of New York. He's going to win, you know, and after that—everyone knows what he's really after. So just look at what's on the line here and then consider how a Peter Jorgensen figures in the picture. Stop kidding yourself. For this trial Judge Allen Sturdivant will not be the judge you know. Willy-nilly, maybe without even realizing it, he'll be campaigning

188

from the bench, and I bet you that every ruling he makes will reflect that."

Marc shook his head. "I just can't believe that a man like Sturdivant—"

"Believe it," McPartland said, gave Marc a friendly pat on the arm and left.

Marc continued down the stairs and out to the street. Could McPartland be right? Could Allen Sturdivant compromise for the sake of winning an election? He didn't want to believe it, but it seemed the question answered itself.

Marc stopped in front of the Supreme Court Building at 60 Centre Street. Looking up, as he had so many times before, he read the inscription carved in stone over the massive entrance to the busiest court in the world: *The True Administration of Justice is the Firmest Pillar of Good Government.*

He turned quickly and, head down, walked back to the courthouse.

CHAPTER 22

JURY SELECTION WAS completed in one day. Judge Sturdivant had the reputation of not tolerating delay in the picking of juries, but it was not a concern in this case because neither Marc Hammond nor Brian McCarthy was inclined to waste time.

McCarthy opened to the jury in the soft tones that had proven so effective for him in the past. He stated succinctly and clearly the case of the People of the State of New York against Peter Jorgensen, leading the jury through the events of the night of Andrea Blanchard's murder, presenting them as he wanted them to be seen.

He concluded: "Ladies and gentlemen, this is what lawyers call a circumstantial evidence case. The People will present no eyewitnesses to the actual killing because there were none. But we submit that the fingerprints of the defendant found at the scene of the murder, the untruths told by the defendant to cover up his guilt, and other evidence that you will hear in this case, will convince you that whatever happened between the defendant and the deceased that evening, it ended in the death of Andrea Blanchard at the hand of the defendant. We will not speculate as to what may have caused the defendant to choke the life out of the deceased—we need not establish *why* he killed her, only that he *did* kill her. And, ladies and gentlemen, we *will* prove that Peter Jorgensen is guilty beyond a reasonable doubt of the murder of Andrea Blanchard."

When McCarthy had taken his seat Marc slowly walked to the jury box. He made eye contact with each of the jurors. "Ladies and gentlemen," he said, "all I ask is that you listen carefully to the evidence presented in this case, with an open mind, just as you promised you would during the jury selection.

"You will hear testimony about the deceased, Andrea Blanchard, and her relationship with the defendant. You will hear the defendant, himself, who will testify at this trial. I am going to ask you to assess this witness to determine if he is lying or telling the truth. And I will also ask you to take into account how the deceased conducted her life—"

McCarthy was up quickly. "Objection, Your Honor. The reputation of the deceased is not on trial here, nor is it an issue in this case."

"Your Honor," Marc replied patiently, "would the district attorney prevent this jury from hearing about the numerous men intimately involved with the deceased? Men who, *unlike* the defendant, might well have had a real motive to kill her? Especially one who acted out his feelings?"

Sturdivant was genuinely annoyed. "I tell you, Mr. Hammond, this will be the first and last time during this trial that I will tolerate this type of theatrics and innuendo. You know better." Then facing the jury: "What you have just heard, ladies and gentlemen, is not evidence in this trial and you are not to consider it as such. You may draw reasonable inferences and conclusions from the testimony and the evidence, but only the evidence that is ruled admissible. Statements by lawyers cannot be considered as evidence and are to be disregarded." Sturdivant turned back toward Marc: "Continue your opening statement, Mr. Hammond."

Marc decided some appeasement was in order. "I want to apologize to Your Honor and to this jury. Sometimes zeal in the defense of one's client causes one to lose perspective."

"All right, fine, now proceed."

Marc continued his opening statement without further interruption. Really, the best he could do was to impress on the jury their obligation to keep an open mind. When he was finished Sturdivant directed McCarthy to call his first witness.

"The People call Mrs. Helen Jorgensen."

Murmuring from the spectators, Sturdivant called for order. The first witness called by the *prosecutor* was the mother of the defendant. It made for good drama, and it was also the most natural thing for McCarthy to do. To present his case in logical sequence he would have to begin with the person who had discovered the body—the defendant's mother.

But McCarthy was vaguely bothered by something about Helen Jorgensen. He remembered clearly their conversation in his office when she was first brought to him for an interview . . .

"Mrs. Jorgensen," he had said, "I understand how difficult this must be for you. But you do have a duty to testify truthfully."

She had looked at him grimly but had assured him she would tell the truth on the witness stand. She had cooperated with him, and her testimony to the grand jury was succinct and effective.

192

But then in preparing her the day before for her testimony at the trial, he had detected a reserve—possibly even hostility. Her changed attitude puzzled and bothered him. He realized that Hammond had probably worked on her, and of course it *was* her son he was trying to convict. But she had also impressed him as an intensely religious woman. She had, many times, referred to her supreme obligation to God and her loyalty to Andrea Blanchard. She also had nothing to lie about . . . she was being called merely to set the case in motion. Nothing in her testimony need incriminate her son . . .

McCarthy now led Helen Jorgensen into testimony concerning her employment and her relationship to Andrea. Marc did not object to the leading questions—they had no relevance to the issue of Peter's guilt or innocence.

Finally McCarthy got to that Christmas morning.

"Now, when you arrived at the apartment, did you observe anything unusual?"

"Yes, the door was open. A few times before Miss Andrea had forgotten to lock her door so I didn't pay it much mind. I walked in and put my hat, coat and boots in the hall closet. And then I saw . . ." She could not finish the sentence.

McCarthy waited a beat, then proceeded. "Mrs. Jorgensen, please tell us what you saw after you put your clothes in the hall closet."

"I saw . . . a hand showing past the couch in the living room. I walked toward the couch and I saw Miss Andrea on the floor . . ."

"I know this is painful for you, but please tell us how Miss Blanchard looked."

"Her eyes were open . . . I saw red marks around her neck . . . she bruised easily, she had fair skin." Helen Jorgensen took another minute to gain control of herself, then went on. "Her neck looked twisted, sort of out of shape. I lifted her up and I held her. I closed her eyes. I knew she was dead. I called nine-one-one, like you're supposed to."

"Did you see anything else on the floor?"

"I saw an ashtray. I guess it had fallen from the cocktail table near the couch. It was upside down."

"Did you touch any object, on the floor, or the cocktail table, or the couch?"

"No. When I called nine-one-one I was told not to touch anything and I didn't."

"After you called nine-one-one what did you do?"

"I just sat there with her . . . on the floor . . . holding her head in my lap."

"How long would you say you waited until the police arrived?"

"Ten minutes, maybe less."

"Were you questioned by a police officer at the scene?"

"Yes, by Detective Higgins."

"And did you respond to his questions exactly as you have testified this morning?"

"Yes."

"I have no further questions, Your Honor."

Marc felt sorry for Helen Jorgensen. The woman had not looked at her son once during the entire questioning, probably afraid she would reveal what she was feeling for him. Nevertheless, he had to cross-examine her.

"Mrs. Jorgensen, Peter Jorgensen is your son, is he not?"

"Yes."

"And you understand that it's my obligation and duty to ask you certain questions about the testimony you just gave?"

"Yes . . ."

"You understand that these questions are not intended to upset or distress you in any way?"

194

"Yes, I guess so."

"Now, I believe you testified that you found the body of the deceased on Christmas morning."

"Yes."

"Isn't it unusual for a housekeeper to work on Christmas Day?"

"Not for me . . . I can't remember one day of the year that I didn't drop into her apartment, holiday or any other."

"That was because of your relationship to the deceased?"

"I don't understand."

"You were more than an employee to Andrea Blanchard. Your relationship was much closer than that, wasn't it?"

"Yes, yes, it was."

"So when you went to the apartment on a daily basis, sometimes you talked with her about your personal lives, isn't that true?"

"Yes, we talked about some personal things."

McCarthy objected. "Judge, this is entirely irrelevant."

Which was the opening Marc had waited for. He spoke to the judge but looked at the jury. "Your Honor, how can conversations concerning others who may have had a reason to kill the deceased be irrelevant?"

McCarthy's face was redder than usual. "May we approach the bench?"

Sturdivant nodded.

"That was a cheap shot," McCarthy said at the bench. "Counsel knows that any conversation the witness had with the deceased would not be admissible under these circumstances."

Sturdivant agreed, then added, "From now on, gentlemen, you will state your objections and that's all you will do. If I need an explanation I'll ask for it and you will give it at the bench, but no further debates in front of the jury. Understood?"

Marc nodded. Yes, he thought he did understand. It was

like McPartland said. Ambition was turning a good judge sour . . . All right, to get an even break in this trial he was going to have to get his message across to the jury any damn way he could, and if that meant getting held for contempt, well, so be it . . . He walked back to the witness. "Mrs. Jorgensen, let's get back to Christmas morning. You say you came to the door and were alarmed when you found it open. I presume you had a key to the apartment . . ."

"Yes."

"Did you know anyone else who had a key to the apartment?"

"Nobody I knew of."

"Did you have a key to the rear gate leading into the basement?"

"Yes, I did."

"Why was that necessary?"

"Well, if there was a delivery I would open the gate and show the men where to bring things. Miss Andrea was always having things delivered to the apartment."

"And in order to enter you would open the gate and walk through the basement to the service elevator. Is it an automatic elevator?"

"Yes."

"Did you ever use the service elevator when you were alone?"

"Yes, a few times."

"All right now, tell me this, Mrs. Jorgensen—if someone entered the building by opening the rear gate, could he or she go on to the apartment without being seen by anyone else?"

"Yes, I guess so."

Marc walked two steps toward Helen Jorgensen and looked her straight in the eye. "Were you aware that Andrea Blanchard gave keys to—friends?"

196

"Except for the superintendent, I don't think so."

"You have testified that you saw a turned-over ashtray on the floor beside the body of the deceased. That ashtray would normally have been on the cocktail table near the couch, is that correct?"

"Yes . . ."

"Was there anything else that belonged on the cocktail table that you saw on the floor?"

"No, not that I remember."

"Where was the telephone, the one you used to call nine-one-one?"

"It was on the end table—"

"Are you sure it wasn't on the floor beside the body?"

"Objection," said McCarthy. "This has been asked and answered."

"Sustained," said Sturdivant. "The witness has testified that the only object she saw on the floor was the whisky glass."

Marc looked at the judge. "Maybe I heard her incorrectly, Your Honor. I thought she said ashtray."

Sturdivant felt the sweat through his shirt. Was he *trying* to incriminate himself? What the hell was happening to him? Obviously he couldn't take much more of this. "I stand corrected, Mr. Hammond. I was the one who misheard. Please continue."

Helen Jorgensen had raised her hand, as if she were in a classroom trying to get the teacher's attention. "Wait a minute," she said. "I think there *was* a whisky glass on the floor. I didn't remember until now. I'm sorry."

"Are you saying," Marc said, "that His Honor's mistaken reference to a whisky glass caused you to remember it?" He wondered if Helen Jorgensen didn't have a powerful capacity for responding to suggestions. What the hell, he'd follow this and see where, if anywhere, it lead.

"Yes," she said in answer to his question.

"Well, please describe this whisky glass."

"It was an ordinary whisky glass."

"But you recognized it. I mean, you'd seen it before?"

"Yes, Miss Andrea had lots of them."

"Please try to remember now . . . did you leave the whisky glass on the floor, the way you did the ashtray?"

She hesitated. "I can't be sure. I might have put it back on the cocktail table."

"Even after you were told not to touch anything?"

"I think I might have done that before I called the police."

"Do you remember if there was any whisky in the glass before you moved it?"

"No, I can't remember that."

So much for the whisky glass and the possibility of fingerprints other than Andrea's and Peter's and Helen Jorgensen's. Maybe more later. Marc changed his line of questioning. "Do you remember if Andrea Blanchard had a party planned for Christmas Eve, either in her apartment or elsewhere?"

"I know she didn't."

"How can you be so positive?"

"Because she had reservations for a flight to Palm Beach leaving in the afternoon of December twenty-fourth. The flight was canceled on account of the snowstorm."

"How did you learn that?"

"I called her about four P.M. She told me she'd rescheduled her flight for Christmas day."

"So, as far as you know, she had made no plans for Christmas Eve because she had a flight scheduled. Is that your testimony?"

"Yes."

"Well, you now know that your son, Peter, visited her sometime after midnight. She didn't happen to mention in your telephone conversation on the afternoon of the twenty-fourth that she was expecting him?"

"No, no she didn't . . ."

"Did she happen to mention that she was expecting anyone else—or perhaps more than one person?"

"She *was* expecting someone." Neither Hammond nor McCarthy expected that. The courtroom rustled.

"How do you know that, Mrs. Jorgensen?"

"Because I received a call from Miss Andrea."

A *second* call. She had never said that Andrea had called *her*. "What time did you get that call?"

"About eleven-thirty."

"You already knew that her flight was rescheduled for the next day?"

"Yes."

Marc glanced at McCarthy, whose telltale flush showed his anger. Obviously the D.A. thought this was a conspiracy cooked up between Helen Jorgensen and himself. I wish it were, thought Marc. I also wish I knew where the hell I was going with this . . . for sure, though, McCarthy will never believe that Helen's testimony is as much a surprise to me as it was to him . . .

He pressed on. "Mrs. Jorgensen, please tell the Court and jury the substance of that conversation."

"Miss Andrea was very upset, she was crying. She said that she was depressed and that she was trying to drown her sorrows."

"What did that mean to you?"

"That she had been drinking. I'd heard her use that expression before. I'm sorry to say it, but when she felt bad she drank."

"Did she tell you why she was depressed?"

"She said that a man she loved—for a long time—was coming to see her that night and she was afraid he was going to end their affair."

A reporter for the *Daily News* scribbled his hoped-for headline: SECOND MAN IN BLANCHARD CASE.

199

And that man, known only to himself in that courtroom, felt suddenly naked, not only to every spectator, to the attorneys and to the defendant, but worst of all to himself, and in that awful moment he was immobile, unable even to call for quiet among the spectators in the courtroom who had begun to murmur and talk.

In the few minutes it took for court officers to restore order Marc had an opportunity to analyze the situation . . . He knew Helen Jorgensen was telling the truth. Earlier, for her own misguided reasons, she had been protecting Andrea Blanchard's name even at the expense of her son, no doubt because, as she'd indicated, she had believed her son was guilty, and according to her religious convictions, guilt deserved punishment, even if it were her own son. Now, it seemed she at least was beginning to doubt. Her own testimony had to affect her . . .

When quiet was restored Marc said, "How long did that phone conversation last, Mrs. Jorgensen?"

"I think about fifteen or maybe twenty minutes. Then she said, 'That's him at the door now, I have to go.'"

So the second man, surely the murderer, had arrived before midnight. From day one Peter had said he arrived at 12:15 A.M. If the jury believed Helen there was now doubt— reasonable doubt, he hoped they would agree. "Your witness, Mr. McCarthy."

Brian McCarthy, for all his Irish temper, was better at controlling his anger than Marc. He was now positive that Hammond and Helen Jorgensen had concocted this story, a story that seriously threatened his case. Okay, folks, the gloves are off . . . he had no alternative but to do his best to destroy her—he had to be careful not to arouse jury sympathy for her in the process.

"Mrs. Jorgensen," he began, "do you recall the first time we spoke about this case in my office, on or about the fourth of January last?"

"Yes, sir . . ."

"And did there come a time when I asked you if you spoke to the deceased, Andrea Blanchard, on the evening of December twenty-fourth?"

"Yes, sir."

"And do you recall what you told me?"

"Yes, sir . . . I said that I called Miss Andrea at four o'clock and she told me that on account of the snowstorm her flight was canceled and it was rescheduled for Christmas day."

"Now, do you recall me asking you, in my office, whether that was the *only* conversation you had with her that day?"

"Yes . . . you asked me that."

"And do you recall what you answered?"

"I said that was the only time I talked to her on December twenty-fourth."

"In light of your testimony here—that there was a second phone conversation shortly before midnight that evening— you were not telling me the truth, were you?"

"No, I was not."

"Well, Mrs. Jorgensen, were you lying then, in my office, or are you lying now in this courtroom, and I remind you that you are still under oath?"

"I was lying then."

"Why then, and not now?"

Helen Jorgensen tried and failed to fight back her tears. "Because . . ." She shook her head. "You would have to know the feelings I had for Miss Andrea and she had for me. We were together a long time . . ."

"Mrs. Jorgensen, that's all very well and good, but you haven't answered my question. Why did you lie to me in my office?"

"Because when she called me that night she made me promise never to reveal what she told me about that man."

"Did she mention his name?"

Sturdivant was frozen in his seat.

"No, she *never* told me his name. She didn't say anything about him except that he was an important person and she really cared for him but she was afraid he was going to stop seeing her . . ."

"Had you known about this relationship before she told you about it in that phone conversation?"

"No."

"And you're telling us that up to this minute you have not disclosed that confidence of your former employer?"

"She was more than an employer, Mr. McCarthy. She was my friend, I loved her. I don't care what people say about her, I knew her. She was good to me—"

"Well, then why *now,* Mrs. Jorgensen, do you choose to betray that confidence of your friend that you loved so much?"

"Because"—her voice receded to a whisper—"I love my son more."

McCarthy was ready and waiting. "Exactly, Mrs. Jorgensen. Exactly. You love your son more. So much so that you're concocting a telephone call that was never made to introduce a mystery man who never existed—*to protect your guilty son.*"

Marc was on his feet. "Objection, Your Honor, I move for a mistrial. The statements by the prosecution are inflammatory and prejudicial."

"Denied. You may answer, Mrs. Jorgensen."

"Answer what? Your Honor. The prosecutor didn't ask a question, he made a statement with the sole purpose of prejudicing the jury."

Sturdivant took hold of himself. Hammond was right and he was wrong. It was inflammatory, but not the basis for a mistrial. "Motion denied. Mrs. Jorgensen, would

202

you like the court reporter to read back Mr. McCarthy's words?"

"No, sir. It's all right. I did not make up that call. Miss Andrea called me, she told me about the man that was coming to see her."

Judge Sturdivant chose that moment to declare the luncheon recess. He faced the jury.

"Ladies and gentlemen, we will resume at two P.M. Do not discuss this case among yourselves or with anyone else. If anyone attempts to communicate with you or speak to you about this case you are to report it immediately to me." As the jurors filed out of the box and into the jury room he turned to Helen Jorgensen. "Mrs. Jorgensen, you are still a sworn witness. You have not finished your testimony. You may not converse with either the district attorney or defense counsel until your testimony is completed. Do you understand?"

Helen Jorgensen nodded solemnly and left the witness stand. And now, for the first time that day, she looked directly at her son, and that look told Peter that she had not forsaken him. No matter what happened to him now, no matter how it ended, at least he was not as deserted as he'd thought.

Back in his office Brian McCarthy chewed on a dry turkey sandwich, reflecting on what had happened in the courtroom. No question, even though he had brought out that Helen Jorgensen was not telling the truth to protect her son, she had hurt him with this second man stuff. What had been a lock case was now a ballgame, although he still felt that the evidence against Jorgensen was overwhelming.

Still, he had a nagging feeling—he'd had it more than once in other cases—that something in the woman's testimony needed further probing. He reached for it now . . . She had testified at one point—he'd made a mental note about it, but damn it what was it? He closed his eyes, concentrated on the testimony about what she said about things found at the apartment, on the floor . . .

"Mrs. Jorgensen," McCarthy said when the trial continued, "let's get back to the apartment at the time you found the body of the deceased. I believe you said you saw an ashtray on the floor?"

"Yes."

"And a whisky glass?"

"Yes."

"But you testified to the whisky glass only after His Honor erroneously referred to it."

"Yes, but that reminded me."

He moved closer to her, made direct eye contact. She looked away.

"Please think again, Mrs. Jorgensen"—McCarthy's voice was even but intense, and he clearly was following a line of questioning whose destination he was confident of—"was there anything else on that floor that you saw and didn't mention in your testimony?"

She looked away again.

"Mrs. Jorgensen, I remind you you're still under oath. Was there something else on that floor—something you took—and didn't tell the police about?"

Still no answer.

"Something like a *key*, Mrs. Jorgensen? Or, to be more exact, a set of keys that you recognized? Keys whose owner you knew?"

The keys, of course, were what the district attorney had been reaching for earlier in his office. McCarthy had requested, after hearing Peter Jorgensen's second statement, that the police search the route Jorgensen took—from the basement into the elevator into the Blanchard apartment

204

down the stairs and back out again—to look for the keys he had said he'd lost sometime that night after he let himself in at the gate. Obviously he was telling the truth about losing the keys because he certainly would have let himself out with the same key he had used to get in. McCarthy also believed that Andrea Blanchard had given him a key to her apartment. Yet Jorgensen had no keys on his person when he was arrested, there were no keys in the area, no keys anywhere. The keys had to have been left in the Blanchard apartment . . .

Helen Jorgensen still did not answer his question. She could only sit there, tears in her eyes.

McCarthy softened his tone. The last thing he wanted to do was snatch defeat from the jaws of victory by stirring up sympathy for Helen Jorgensen and needless animosity toward himself. Juries were, after all, human.

"Let me put the question another way, Mrs. Jorgensen. When you found Andrea Blanchard's body, you saw something that belonged to your son, isn't that true?"

Helen sighed, straightened in her chair. She found it difficult enough to lie in response to a direct question at any time, and now she was worn out, drained. She could keep this up no longer. "Yes, I found something."

"They were your son's keys, weren't they, Mrs. Jorgensen?"

"Yes."

"How did you know they were his keys?"

"From the key chain, I gave it to him."

"And when you saw those keys, you knew your son had been in that apartment that night, and you did what any mother would do, you took the keys and hid them from the police because you knew they were evidence that would incriminate your son."

Helen half rose from her seat, tears starting again. "Yes, I hid the keys because I was frightened for him. At the time
205

I thought maybe he did it . . . but Peter *didn't* kill Andrea Blanchard. That man, that man who came to her that night— *he* killed her. I'm sure of that now."

"Are you, Mrs. Jorgensen? This man killed her . . . this mystery man you never saw, never met, and that Andrea Blanchard never spoke about until the night of her murder? You're so sure—?"

"Yes, *yes*." She collapsed back into her chair, altogether spent.

McCarthy's next statement was to the witness but he faced the jury. "I understand your concern, Mrs. Jorgensen. And I'm sure this jury does too. I have no further questions of this witness, Your Honor."

McCarthy was good, Marc was thinking. Whatever benefit he had gained from the mention of a second man had been diluted by Helen's admission that she had withheld evidence pointing to her son's guilt. He couldn't let her go without some attempt to redress the damage. To let this testimony be the last the jury remembered would be disastrous.

Marc approached Helen. "Isn't it a fact, Mrs. Jorgensen, that Andrea Blanchard had a diary and that the diary was seized by the police—?"

McCarthy was instantly on his feet. "Objection. Your Honor, I request that the jury be excused so that I can make this application."

"We'll let the jury stay where they are," Sturdivant told him. "We'll go to the robing room." He then motioned to the court reporter, who followed the judge and the two attorneys into the small robing room next to the courtroom.

McCarthy waited for the reporter to set his machine, then said, "Your Honor has ruled on the issue of the diary, and Mr. Hammond is well aware of that ruling. I'm going to ask that Your Honor instruct the jury as to that ruling, although a certain amount of damage has already been done. I'm also going to ask that Mr. Hammond be instructed as to what the consequences will be if he fails to follow your rulings in the future. I play by the rule, Judge, and I expect Mr. Hammond to do the same."

Mark took it up quickly. "Judge, before Mr. McCarthy has apoplexy, let me remind him that Your Honor's ruling only made the *contents* of the diary inadmissible and inaccessible to me. You never ruled that the diary did not exist, or that I couldn't ask a witness whether it did. I'm just asking for some even-handed justice here. During the course of this trial the People have brought out that objects were found in the Blanchard apartment—an ashtray, a whisky glass and now a set of keys, all of which is damaging to the defendant. Isn't the defendant entitled to have the jury hear testimony about *all* the objects that were recovered from the apartment, especially if the jury could draw a possible favorable inference on the issue of reasonable doubt?"

All right, Sturdivant thought . . . so Marc Hammond was, technically, right. Referring to the mere existence of the diary did not violate the letter of his order. But it did the spirit of it. And the point of it. He had to be consistent . . . that was it. He wasn't going to be pushed either way by these attorneys. He was, by damn, still the judge. And thinking it, at least for the moment, actually believed it . . .

"Mr. Hammond, there will be no further reference to the diary," and before Marc could object he had turned and walked out of the robing room into the courtroom, resumed his seat and turned to the jury:

"Ladies and gentlemen, you will disregard any references

to a diary contained in counsel's last question. I have already ruled that it is irrelevant. You are not to consider it in determining the issues of this trial."

It was at that point that Marc Hammond decided he was facing two prosecutors. Go figure the odds on beating *that*.

_____ CHAPTER 23 _____

ALMOST UNEASILY, OR at least with an optimism compromised by guilt? . . . fear of exposure? . . . Allen Sturdivant came to understand that there was, apparently, little doubt that as the political situation shaped up, he would win the primary and likely go on to prevail in the general election. He did not know why Jon Klyk had dropped out and thrown his support to the ticket—though he suspected persuasion by Charlie Sweeney or Mickey Goldman—but whatever the reason, Klyk's joining instead of bucking the ticket seemed almost surely to translate into a November victory. And who knew what more from there . . .

But the rose color was tainted by Allen's persistent fear that the D.A.'s office might still somehow connect him to Andrea's death, that someone would, for example, pick up on his slip in mentioning the whisky glass during the Helen Jorgensen testimony. There were times when he came across McCarthy in the halls of the courthouse that he felt himself actually searching the man's face for some telltale sign that he was about to spring a damning revelation on him, or that the defense counsel Marc Hammond was. The anxiety was getting near-intolerable, and he found himself increasingly escaping, hiding out in his chambers on the twelfth floor of the courthouse, the place that he had done the work he was most proud of, the place where he was the judge, pure and sure and uncompromised, and where he was now playing out the most bizarre double trial of his life, his own as well as the defendant's.

On one such evening, long after court hours, he began to fantasize himself getting into the district attorney's office, examining the file on the case to assure himself that there was nothing there waiting to jump up and destroy him. The illogic of it occurred immediately . . . why in the world would the D.A. be hiding something incriminating of the judge if he had it, or why wouldn't he, if he had it, have let the judge know, but logic was not all that persuasive at ten P.M. of a Friday evening alone in his chambers, wondering when, when . . . ? Or at least what if . . . ? He began to see himself in a scenario . . . walking down the private stairway from his chambers to the seventh-floor offices of McCarthy, slipping by Paul Conover, the officer on duty, notorious for sleeping away his hours, a retainer with protective political connections, slipping inside the D.A.'s office, finding the file, including the grand jury testimony, searching it for any mention of that damn whisky glass—

"Good evening, Judge, didn't expect to find you here so late on a Friday. Tough case, huh?" It was the security officer, who, fortunately, this night was not sleeping, at least not yet, and so broke into the reverie that had it been acted out could have surely had him running a terrifying and irrational risk . . .

"Good evening to you, Paul. Yes, it's been quite a day. And it is a difficult case. Well, I was just finishing up here. Thanks for looking in on me. Yes, thank you very much."

Chapter 24

It was Benny Rabe who had suggested to Charlie Sweeney that Loren Sturdivant fill in for her husband while he was still on the bench and ineligible to campaign. Sweeney owed Benny for that one. Loren did the job so well that the thought occurred to Sweeney, only partly in jest, that she might have been a better candidate than her husband.

The opportunity to project her own personality seemed to have opened new horizons for Loren. She was becoming an expert at campaigning. She was electric, vibrant, and her speeches were as earthy as they had to be, always, of course, in the cultivated tones of her private school, multi-generationed WASP family background. The content of her speeches was always keyed to the attributes of her husband, but Charlie could see that she was becoming an attraction in her own right. A typical reaction was Mickey Goldman's phone call to the boss after he had heard Loren deliver a speech at the annual luncheon of the Association of Public Employees.

"You know what you got here, Charlie?" Mickey had

said. "This broad is gonna be a superstar. I can't remember the last time my people even *listened* to a speaker. I think you lucked out."

"I know I did, Mickey. Maybe something to keep in mind for the future."

"Yeah . . . but handle her with care, Charlie. All the while she was holding my people in the palm of her hand, she reminded me of someone—"

"Who?"

"How about Eva Peron?"

Charlie laughed.

"Don't laugh. I was in Buenos Aires at a labor conference in the forties and I saw that one in action. The combo of style, charm, the beauty—they're very damn similar."

"What do you suggest?"

"Just know what you got, in all respects. Start building her up after the election. Her husband's position as governor should make that easy. There's no telling where the lady could go, I kid you not. But keep an eye on her at all times."

Sweeney was impressed, and grateful for Mickey's call, but he was also soon brought back to face his current problems with Allen Sturdivant. He just didn't appear to be with it during their last few meetings. He was beginning to have doubts about Sturdivant's ability to put it together once his personal campaigning began. For sure, this wasn't the Allen Sturdivant who had campaigned for congress and beat Sweeney's organization . . . Still, Sweeney reminded himself, Sturdivant had been damn good at the Waldorf dinner only a few weeks before. And he was, after all, a professional. When the moment of truth came, he'd respond and be his old self. Besides, while Loren couldn't carry the ball indefinitely, for the time being she was doing one hell of a job.

* * *

Loren Sturdivant leaned back into the soft leather of her limousine and closed her eyes, trying to grab a short-short nap for the brief time it took to get from the Hotel Pierre on Fifth Avenue, where she had just lunched with an old prep school chum thrilled to be seen with Judge Sturdivant's wife, to the Carlyle on Madison and 76th Street. Before she'd become involved in the campaign she had been blessed with the ability to take catnaps, but now her mind was too stimulated. She opened her eyes and gazed idly at the people on the streets, but her mind was elsewhere. Until now she thought she could be content with the reflected glory of her husband. That was, after all, the way it was supposed to be. But sitting back in the limo as it silently moved up Madison Avenue, she wondered if she had, perhaps, been selling herself short . . .

Her thoughts were abruptly dislodged by the sight of two men on the street, not just part of a passing crowd but two men she recognized. She did a double take, turning her head as the car passed them going into the grill entrance of the Sherry-Netherlands Hotel, which contained a discreetly lit bar. Yes, no question . . . Marc Hammond and J. Franklin Powell.

Loren realized it was possible that the defense counsel's meeting with the private investigator might be a routine matter . . . attorneys often consulted outside investigators, perhaps the two men were old friends . . . except that she knew better. The timing ruled out a plausible coincidence. Marc Hammond and J. Franklin Powell had to be talking about the Jorgensen case . . . And, very likely, that meant exploring the possibility that someone other than the defendant Peter Jorgensen had killed Andrea Blanchard. That would surely be Hammond's interest. What if they managed to link Allen's name to Andrea? She was not amused at the irony that the shoe was apparently now on the other foot. The same means she used against Klyk could, potentially

213

at least, be used to knock Allen out of the political picture. And she was acutely aware of Powell's capabilities as a bloodhound. The superb job he'd done for her left no doubt about that. But how much did Powell, or Hammond, know? She had to see Powell immediately, and her thoughts raced as she considered what she would say to him. She was dealing with a clever man, and any inquiries she might make about his investigation into the Blanchard murder would in itself set his own wheels in motion about the reason for her curiosity.

Knowing the danger, she nevertheless decided that she had no alternative. An investigation by someone with Powell's resources and techniques could expose her husband's relationship with the late Andrea Blanchard. And for him, her and the campaign, that would be a disaster.

Late the same afternoon J. Franklin Powell greeted Loren Sturdivant with warmth and deference, then led her from the large reception room into his plush office.

"It's very good to see you, Mrs. Sturdivant. Can I be of any further service—"

"Yes, Mr. Powell, you can, by answering honestly a direct question. Are you involved in any way with an investigation into Andrea Blanchard's murder?"

Powell was not ready for this one. "Well, Mrs. Sturdivant, your direct question places me in a difficult position. You can well understand that I'm obliged to—"

"Please," Loren interrupted, "I'm aware of obligations to maintain client confidentiality and so forth. But *I'm* a client of yours too, Mr. Powell. And perhaps the most important client you will ever have, if you follow my meaning and I believe you do. Now, as your client, I am here to tell you that I have a special interest in any investigation connected to the case being tried before my husband. His legal and political careers are not unrelated. I have learned to trust

214

you, Mr. Powell, based on your fine work for me . . . You accepted that commission without question or explanation. Now I wish you to accept in the same way my request that you discontinue any investigation related to the case you may have begun, and if you indeed have begun, I want to know what you have learned up to now. Please don't give me reason to alter my high opinion of you, Mr. Powell."

Her voice was soft, there was a smile on her face, but Powell knew a threat when he heard one. He'd heard plenty when he was still on the force. "With all due respect, Mrs. Sturdivant, disclosure of such information under these circumstances would be as wrong as, for example, if I disclosed to anyone the results of the investigation I recently made on your behalf."

He too had a smile fixed on his face when he spoke.

A threat for a threat. She was ready for it. "Mr. Powell, you're a worldly man. As such, I'm sure you're aware that any action taken to injure me, or my husband, will be met with the fullest use of our combined resources. And those are considerable resources, Mr. Powell, as I believe you know. The Phillips and Sturdivant families have effectively joined together in the past to protect themselves against those who would do them harm. We can do it again if necessary."

Powell flushed, fighting to restrain himself. There was little question that Loren Sturdivant meant what she said. And could back it up. He was no coward, he had faced up to his share of danger in his time, but the look on this one's face was a look he had seen only once before . . . on Benny Gatton, a mob hit-man who had admitted to twenty murders. To Benny the life or death of a human was of as much significance as the life or death of a housefly. Loren Sturdivant had the same look. And, to be honest with himself, it scared the shit out of him.

Powell lived a life of measured values, and had long ago learned that to survive there were times when one had to

215

pull in one's horns or they would be lopped off. He withdrew as gracefully as he could. "It appears that we may be right on the brink of a misunderstanding, Mrs. Sturdivant. You're a highly regarded client, and I would certainly not want to compromise our relationship with any action."

"Thank you. But perhaps one of your colleagues has been less astute than yourself. Perhaps he or she has learned something that might be of interest to me."

The lady was good. And he'd run out of options. There was no smile on his face as he said, "Andrea Blanchard had numerous lovers . . . rich and sometimes important men. It seems there was one in particular. I don't know who that person is. Neither I nor my staff will be interested in any efforts to discover this person's identity. We are, after all, not on the case."

"I'm pleased to hear that, Mr. Powell. I assure you your cooperation will be remembered."

Powell buzzed Maggie Nelson on the intercom and asked her to bring in the Jorgensen file. Maggie came in all excited about continuing the investigation. "I think I can lean on Peaches," she said without waiting for her boss to speak. "If he doesn't know who Mr. Big Shot is, or if his wife doesn't know, he'll work on her for leads. I know we're short on time but I've got that good feeling in my bones that we're closing in. I want to hit the Monte Carlo again. I don't think the police dug deep enough. We may be able to save that poor bastard Jorgensen in the nick of time, just like in the movies—"

"I'm afraid not, Maggie."

"What?"

"We're ending the investigation."

216

"You're not serious?"

"It's over. We have other more important cases to work on—"

"When you called us together you said the case had the highest priority."

He took the file from her hand. "Priorities can change."

____ Chapter 25 ____

IN THE FOLLOWING days of the trial McCarthy efficiently proceeded to tighten the noose of circumstantial evidence around Peter Jorgensen's neck.

Officer Joe Lawrence repeated the testimony he had given at the grand jury and pre-trial hearing about Peter Jorgensen's two statements, which he recited in detail, making the point that Peter would lie if he found it to his advantage.

Marc kept his cross-examination of Lawrence brief. Lawrence gave off good-guy sincerity, a not uncommon attribute, Marc had discovered, of practiced liars. There seemed little purpose in making an indelible imprint of Lawrence's testimony on the jury's collective mind.

Next McCarthy called the forensic people. Since the defense was not disputing that Peter had touched the telephone, and since Peter's presence in the apartment was also conceded, Marc's questioning was minimal.

By the end of the third day's testimony Marc had decided

that Powell had better come up with something or his client's goose would be cooked by the piling on of damning circumstantial evidence. He called Powell from the courthouse and got him just as he was about to leave his office and quickly told him Peter Jorgensen was dead if he couldn't come up with the identity of Andrea Blanchard's lover. "Have you got anything new?"

"I'm doing everything I can," Powell said, his voice flat, "but you have to understand that I have obligations to other clients, too, clients who also have time problems . . . Look, Mr. Hammond, I'm sorry to have to cut you short but you caught me on the way out to a meeting I'm already late for. I'll be in touch."

The line went dead.

Powell, Marc thought, had sounded colder than the I.R.S., and he recognized the brush-off for what it was. What the hell was going on? Had everyone gotten together to bury Peter Jorgensen? Had the mystery second man gotten to Powell?

Marc's next call was to Charlie Sweeney. The boss detected the urgency in Marc's voice and agreed to meet him for an early dinner at the Downtown Athletic Club. Marc decided to bring Randy. He was curious about her reaction to Sweeney's reaction to what he had to say.

Marc waited until coffee to tell Sweeney about his dealings with Powell, concluding with the abrupt telephone conversation of a few hours earlier.

Sweeney listened intently, then lit a cigarette, inhaled and exploded into a fit of coughing. "Got to stop," he said. "These things are going to kill me."

"Charlie," Marc said, "when you stall around it's usually bad news. Am I right this time?"

"Marc, you're a smart man and a good lawyer. But maybe you'd better brush up on the law of political contracts."

Randy looked puzzled. Sweeney smiled at her, thinking

what a lucky son-of-a-bitch young Hammond was, and went on to develop his thesis. He was rather enjoying the opportunity to lecture the counselor and his lady. "A political contract isn't quite like a legal contract. A political contract is *never* in writing. It's an agreement that never can be enforced in a court of law. The *quid pro quo* is a person's word, and the power and desire to deliver on it. It's sealed by a handshake. If one party reneges, he can't be sued. He can't be subject to legally fixed monetary damages. But the word is passed, and his value in the political market depreciates to zero. On the other hand, like a legal contract, there's an exchange of consideration, and once a person performs the contract for you, you owe him." Sweeney looked directly at Marc. "And you can't ask him to do two for the price of one."

"But Powell didn't perform the contract—at least not completely—"

"Didn't he? According to your own version he supplied you with the information that Andrea Blanchard had a special lover. You thought that was good enough to request the judge to delay the trial. To get that information for you Powell must have used man hours and the facilities of his office. *And* the price was right . . . he did it on the arm— no fees, no expenses, no nothing. This from the biggest guy in the business."

Marc was silent.

"In this business, you need to learn to appreciate what gets delivered. You need to keep things in perspective. Powell fulfilled the contract, Marc. He extended himself for me, for you. The way I see it, I owe him. Under my rules, I pay him back before I go back to him again. I'm sure you understand."

Marc understood, and there was nothing he could do about it.

"Now, folks," Sweeney said, breaking in a sunnyside

smile, "you stay and enjoy the view. I've got two heavy meetings tonight and Benny Rabe is probably figuring his overtime in the car downstairs."

After Charlie left, Randy and Marc sat quietly for a while, looking at the lengthening shadows on the water as the sun began its descent. Randy knew Marc was hurting. His options were turning into dead ends. The house was falling in on Peter Jorgensen, and there didn't seem to be anything Marc or anyone else could do about it.

On the fourth day of the trial McCarthy called the two doormen who had been on duty Christmas Eve at the Monte Carlo Apartments. Both testified that they had not seen Peter enter through the main entrance the night of the murder, and that they were certain that they had never seen him before that night. It was "salad dressing" testimony, because Peter's statement admitted that he entered through the rear gate. Nevertheless, the testimony served McCarthy's purpose by emphasizing to be jury that Peter tried to avoid recognition by sneaking around to the back. Marc did not bother to cross-examine either of them.

Dr. Myron Lee, chief Medical Examiner of the City of New York, was the next witness to be called by McCarthy. Lee was a leading authority on forensic medicine and made an excellent witness. He was at once colorful and authoritative as he answered questions, conveying to the jury what McCarthy wanted—acceptance of him as the last word on the subject.

It was unusual for the chief to perform an autopsy personally, but because of the public attention given to the Andrea Blanchard case he had not trusted the assignment to anyone else. Lee, often more than necessarily graphic, was beloved of the prosecutor because, in a homicide case, the rule was the gorier the better. Before Dr. Lee's testimony began Marc made the gesture of conceding his qualifications. There would have been no percentage in having the jury hear about the doctor's numerous degrees and honors in the field of forensic pathology.

"Dr. Lee," McCarthy began, "did you perform an autopsy on the deceased some time on December twenty-fifth last?"

"Yes, I did."

"Will you relate to us what your findings were?"

Dr. Lee gave his testimony with a fixed smile. "The body was that of a well-developed, well-nourished white female, with a scale weight of approximately one hundred-sixteen pounds. She had a measured height of five feet four inches. Her general appearance was consistent with her stated age of thirty-seven years. The head hair was black, the eyes were hazel with equal pupils. Examination of the anterior lateral and posterior aspect of the neck revealed sharply demarcated discoloration of the skin, specifically, purple in color. Also evident was hemorrhage in the bubar conjunctiva—the area of the eyes. We also found evidence of hemorrhage in the epiglottal, glottal, and trachea area—used in the swallowing process. As a matter of fact, there was blood congestion in the entire facial area. Further examination revealed a fracture of the hyoid."

"Now, doctor," McCarthy followed up, "based on your experience and on this autopsy which you performed and just described, did you come to an opinion as to the cause of death of the deceased?"

"I did."

"Will you state that opinion to this Court and jury?"

"The cause of death was asphyxiation by strangulation."

"Since most of us here are laymen, please tell us exactly what caused the deceased to choke to death?"

Dr. Lee faced the jury, and proceeded to use his own neck to illustrate. "The hyoid bone is located right here—a little above the Adam's apple. When the bone is fractured the larynx, commonly known as the voice-box, becomes compressed. A compression of the larynx causes a blockage of air coming through the trachea—the windpipe. When the windpipe loses its rigidity it doesn't function and oxygen is cut off from the brain. When I examined the deceased the congestion of the blood in the facial area was evidenced by the purple discoloration to her face, especially in the area of the eyes. The hemorrhages were caused by the stoppage of normal blood flow, and the ensuing discoloration was the expected and usual manifestation of asphyxia, or death by choking. It clearly indicates that that was the cause of death."

"Thank you, Doctor. Your witness, Mr. Hammond."

"Good morning, Dr. Lee," Marc said.

Dr. Lee said with a wide smile, "Good morning." It was evident, Marc thought, that the good doctor was having a ball.

"Doctor, how many cases of death by asphyxia due to strangulation have you come in contact with during your career?"

"Over a thousand."

"Is there a difference between ligature strangulation and manual strangulation?"

"Oh, yes, indeed."

"Would you define them and tell us the difference?"

"Ligature strangulation is effectuated by the use of some foreign object such as a scarf or a leather belt or even a towel that is twisted around the neck in a tourniquet fashion. Manual strangulation is just what it implies—caused by the use of hands."

"The strangulation of the deceased, Andrea Blanchard, was manual, was it not?"

"Yes, that was my diagnosis."

"Why did you come to that conclusion?"

"Because the shape and form of the contusions and abrasions on the neck leave a definable imprint, and an experienced pathologist can easily tell the difference as to the means by which the strangulation was effectuated. Also, there are other more subtle ways that I can detail for you if necessary."

"No, you've convinced me, Doctor." Marc turned to McCarthy. "Will the district attorney stipulate that the death in this case was caused by manual strangulation?"

"I will. And will Mr. Hammond stipulate the entire testimony of Dr. Lee so that we can proceed to the next witness?"

Sturdivant asked the two lawyers to approach the bench. McCarthy noticed the redness of Sturdivant's face, his forehead bathed in sweat. Could such testimony be upsetting him? He wondered why . . . the judge certainly had heard worse in his courtroom.

Sturdivant addressed Marc. "Mr. Hammond, *is* there any point in continuing to question this witness? I find this cross-examination repetitive and time consuming."

Marc was irritated at the effort to cut him off in the middle of his examination. "Your Honor, I really feel I should be allowed to complete my cross."

Sturdivant fought inwardly to control his feelings. The doctor's graphic testimony had thrown him, and he suspected his reaction was confusing the attorneys. Finally he managed to right himself. "All right, Mr. Hammond, if you believe there is any good purpose served in continuing to question this witness, proceed with your cross-examination."

McCarthy returned to the prosecution's table. Marc faced Dr. Myron Lee, but decided he did not want to question him then. He needed time to think out an idea that was beginning to form.

"Your Honor, may I have a recess?"

McCarthy got to his feet. "Judge, I have no objection to

a recess, but Dr. Lee has many duties, and if he can be excused now, the City of New York would be appreciative."

Marc scored that one for McCarthy. The son-of-a-bitch was cute. He played a little dirty, but he was good. But this was no game. Give McCarthy an opening, which he had done, and he could turn it against you. He decided to let Dr. Lee go. Continued cross-examination of Lee along the lines that were forming in his head would probably not be as productive as using his own witness. He had determined who that witness would be, but didn't know whether he could produce her. He needed to get on it.

"Your Honor, I don't want to detain Dr. Lee from his important city duties. I'll end my cross-examination at this time but I would like to reserve the right to recall him tomorrow if necessary."

"Could you be more definitive, Mr. Hammond?"

"I would like to be, Your Honor, but I need a little time."

Sturdivant looked closely at him. What was he planning to spring tomorrow? He was tempted to deny the request, but realized it would seem arbitrary . . . "All right, Mr. Hammond, but I don't want the doctor waiting in court. He'll be on telephone alert tomorrow."

"Fine," Marc said.

Sturdivant recessed the court and Marc turned to Peter. "Get a good night's sleep," he said. "Don't worry too much. We'll get our chance to tell our story—and that jury is going to believe you." He hoped he sounded convincing.

Apparently not convincing enough, he thought, noting Peter's weak smile and slumped shoulders as he was escorted from the courtroom. Actually he'd been aware of Peter's lethargy and seeming disinterest in the proceedings for a while now, and it worried him. His eyes looked glazed, unfocused. He had been unnaturally quiet. These were signs of depression, and Marc worried that Peter might even be suicidal. When he left the courtroom Marc reported his fears to the Correction Department.

It had begun for Peter with his upset over seeing his mother dragged into this mess. Upset had reversed direction downward, to frustration, anger and feeling rock-bottom hopeless. He didn't have to be told the trial was going badly. Who the hell was the second man? Where was he? Marc Hammond put on a good front, but that's what it was . . . a front. When he looked at the faces of the jurors, it seemed to him they'd already convicted him. The cards were stacked. He was going to take the fall for someone else. Someone *important*, someone, he was sure, with a clean white collar, clean nails, and bloody hands. Fuck it.

He thought increasingly of Hank, of checking out the way Hank had. "They're afraid you're going to hang yourself up, Jorgensen," Correction Officer Kearney had told him, although a suicide watch was supposed to be done secretly. "Listen, you son-of-a-bitch, just don't do it on my watch."

Hank's suicide had been the third at Riker's that year and the media was pressuring the mayor about the correction department's lack of control. If Jorgensen died during his tour, Kearney knew he'd be in deep shit. So Kearney himself was keeping a constant eye on Peter. Peter couldn't take a leak without Kearney's surveillance.

But Kearney couldn't work around the clock. One day when Kearney was off Peter tried to rip portions off his sheet the way Hank had taught him. Kearney's stand-in caught him just in time and they took his sheets away from him.

Thanks to the Riker's grapevine, within a few hours every inmate in C-74 knew that Peter Jorgensen was being stopped from committing suicide. To entrepreneurs such as Big Bruno, the chief inmate of the quad, this was a golden opportunity. Bruno was six feet five, two-hundred-thirty pounds, a classic bully with the disposition of a tarantula who had a group of stooges that pimped for him, stole for him, kept him up to date on the grapevine. You paid Bruno or you served him or you were brutalized by him. Bruno now perceived that profit was to be made out of Peter Jorgensen and dispatched one of his toadies to bring Peter to him.

"You havin' trouble killin' yourself?" Bruno asked Peter.

"Maybe . . . not for long . . ."

Bruno shook his head. "They all guardin' their asses 'cause you'd be the fourth this year. Hank brought on the heat. You do it and all their asses are in a sling. You can't hang yourself up. They took your sheets. You got no way. They won't give you no belt. They won't even let you have shoelaces. You got no way, sucker. But I do."

Peter said nothing:

"Yeah, I got a way. How much is it worth to you, sucker? Don't answer, you ain't got shit. When's momma comin'?"

"I don't know, I'm in court every day."

"Tell her to come tomorrow and leave things for you so you can look nice in court. Your lawyer told you. You dig? Tell her you want some nice new shirts, and a nice new watch so you can tell how much more time you got left. Call momma and tell her to leave it all here tomorrow. Do it and I'll give you what you want. You'll go nice and quiet."

Peter went back to his cot, thought briefly about Bruno's offer, and called his mother, who when she got through crying agreed to do anything he asked. She bought the six shirts and a watch and promptly delivered them to the prison. Bruno was satisfied with what he saw. "Good man, that's good. I'm gonna make it easy for you." He looked to the left and right. "Shake my hand, man."

Peter did and felt a small wad of tissue paper transferred into his palm.

"That will do it, man. You got three pills there. One gets you high, two gets you sick, maybe you die, maybe you don't. Three, you're a goner. By the way, you won't need that cross anymore. Hand it over."

Peter resisted at first, then removed a silver crucifix and its chain from his neck and handed it to Bruno. He turned and went to the water fountain, filled his mouth with water. Back at his cot, he palmed the pills, quickly put them in his mouth, swallowed them and lay down, waiting.

The pills took effect shortly, but he wasn't high or hallucinating. Instead he felt his tensions and cares and suffering leave his body. This wasn't bad. He saw a rainbow, bright and vivid that faded into nothing, and then he fell into a jet-black soundless void . . .

Through the darkness he heard a voice, then a jeering laugh, then felt the sharp sting of a hand slapping his face. He woke up to the laughter of Officer Kearney and a group of inmates.

"You're some fuck-up, Jorgensen," Kearney said. "You can't do anything right."

Peter was drowsy, still under the effect of whatever drug he had taken. It took him a full minute to realize that he hadn't died and gone to hell, but that he had returned to the hell of the living. He looked at Kearney.

"What a line of shit Bruno sold you. You did what you did for *three lousy sleeping pills*. Now what are you going to do, sue him?"

And then Kearney's tone changed. "Now listen to me, you little shit. Don't try this again. Bruno is going to help me see to it that you don't. If you think it's bad now, see what happens if you try it again."

Things finally came into focus for Peter. Kearney had bought Bruno's cooperation in preventing a suicide attempt.

He had let Bruno rip him off. He had known about it from the beginning.

Peter faced the wall, still groggy from the pills. He was oblivious to the jeering chants—"Sleep–y, Sleepy–y, Sleepy–y"—from all over the quad. He closed his eyes with only one thought. "They can't watch me forever."

___ CHAPTER 26 ___

AS SOON AS court was recessed Marc Hammond placed a call to New York Hospital. "May I speak to Louella Martindale in Otolaryngology, please."

"Say again?" the operator said.

He could hardly say it the first time.

"Ear, nose and throat."

His attempt at humor did not register with the hospital operator. A special breed. "Dr. Martindale . . . yes . . . hold, please."

The phone buzzed. "Dr. Martindale speaking."

"Hello, doctor."

She knew who it was. Three years had passed since they had spoken to each other, but she would never fail to recognize his voice. "Marc. What ill wind brings this phone call?"

Marc hoped it wouldn't be an ill wind. Louella was a good friend. They'd been close at Yale before they went their separate ways. Louella was black, her background and his had nothing in common, which she pointed out to him more than once when he was trying for more than friendship. What they shared, though, in addition to good chemistry, were brains and drive. Louella, in fact, was the most determined person Hammond had ever met. He admired her. She had risen from the ghetto. All Louella Martindale ever needed was her foot in the door and she took care of the rest. She had gone through Yale University and Cornell Medical School on scholarships. Her talents as a doctor had been recognized after ten years of internship and residency and study for her specialty, and at the age of thirty-four she was named assistant chief of the Otolaryngology Department of New York Hospital.

They arranged to meet at her office in an hour. When Marc saw her, he was reminded of all the old feelings for her. She was still the strong, tall, graceful woman, with the slight frown; Louella seldom smiled, but she did when she saw Marc.

After the amenities and a minimum of chitchat, she told him she had a full schedule but would help him if she could. "You do want some help, right, Counselor? It's not memories of golden nights that bring you here." She smiled again.

"Half right," he said, and told her about the Jorgensen case and about Dr. Myron Lee's testimony and about the part that had bothered him and now did more than ever. She told him she thought he was right, and she told him why. Now he had to get her to court.

"Louella, I need you."

"Sounds like a proposition."

"Be careful, I might say yes . . . look, I need your testimony tomorrow. Need it bad."

"Tomorrow? Marc, I've got a killer schedule tomorrow—"

"It may save an innocent man's life."

Louella's eyes twinkled. "Marc, I truly love you, but

231

you've got some con in you—you always had. I'm not a forensic pathologist. I've never testified in court as a medical expert. I don't have the years of experience or the court appearances or the qualifications of a Myron Lee. My opinion won't be worth that much after the jury learns how short a time I've practiced my specialty. But I also think I smell a rat. Tell me, sweetheart, how many blacks do you have on the jury?"

He never could fool her. "Five. Three women and two men."

"And I'm going to be your token black for the benefit of my brothers and sisters on that jury?"

He shook his head. "A token black would be obvious. But someone who comes across as you will . . . well, the possible effect on the jury did cross my mind."

Louella did not appreciate the idea of being used, but she would not forget that when she was at her financial low and had told Marc she was about to quit Yale, he had said, "Don't you dare. How much do you need?"

She had been too proud to accept his offer, had scratched around and gotten it elsewhere, but his belief in her sealed their friendship.

"I have an eleven o'clock meeting that I can't get out of in the morning. I can be covered until then. Now hear this, Marc Hammond. I'll walk right off that witness stand if I'm delayed."

At 9:35 A.M. Marc addressed Judge Sturdivant. "Your Honor, I won't need Dr. Lee's further testimony. I have my own medical expert. I ask now for Mr. McCarthy's consent to my calling this defense witness now, even though he hasn't finished putting in his case."

"Any objections, Mr. McCarthy?" Sturdivant asked.

McCarthy wasn't too happy about a defense witness testifying before he finished his case, but he also felt he couldn't very well appear ungracious before the jury, especially in view of Hammond's accommodation of Dr. Lee. "No objection," he said.

Louella was a striking figure as she stood for the oath, slim and tall in a tailored burgundy suit.

"Dr. Martindale," Marc began, "where are you employed?"

"New York Hospital."

"And what is your position?"

"I'm assistant head of the department of otolaryngology."

"That refers to diseases of the ear, nose, and throat?"

"Yes."

"Would you please state your educational background?"

"I graduated from Yale with a bachelor of science degree, then Cornell Medical School at New York Hospital. I interned and had my residency and further study for my specialty at New York Hospital."

"Are you now a board-certified otolaryngologist?"

"Yes."

"I offer this witness as an expert, Your Honor, for the purpose of this trial."

Sturdivant turned toward McCarthy, who considered challenging her expertise. He would have certainly been able to establish that she had no forensic experience and was not a pathologist, but McCarthy was no fool. He had watched the black jurors' reactions when Dr. Martindale was testifying about her credentials. Their faces had shown an unmistakable pride.

"I have no objection, Your Honor."

Marc had cleared an important hurdle. The judge would tell the jury that Louella, because she qualified as an expert witness, could give her opinion based on hearsay. More important, the jury could give her testimony the same weight as Dr. Lee's. Marc began by asking Louella to repeat the general medical definitions Dr. Lee had testified to. His purpose was to display Louella's specific expertise. She was impressive, and he made sure that his questions allowed her answers to be more precise than Lee's had been. But he also made sure that her testimony did not contradict Dr. Lee's, just supplemented it. He used this approach to get to his point. He repeated Dr. Lee's testimony about the hyoid bone and then, as if an after-thought, asked, "By the way, Dr. Martindale, would you describe its shape."

"It's horseshoe shaped—over here." She pointed to her throat. "The larynx is here. It stabilizes the larynx."

"So the hyoid is above the larynx."

"Yes."

"Dr. Martindale, in the course of your training and present duties have you ever had personal medical experience with cases of death by manual strangulation?"

"Yes, I've performed several autopsies where death by manual strangulation was the cause."

"Isn't it a fact that a certain degree—a minimum de-gree—of strength would be required in the fingers or in the hands of the strangler in order to fracture the hyoid?"

"Yes, that's true. There would have to be a significant amount of pressure applied before the hyoid would be frac-tured."

"Dr. Martindale, if an individual's hands and fingers were not large enough to encircle the neck of his victim would he be able to exert the same degree of strength of force as a person whose hands could encircle the neck?"

"Probably not. That's why manual strangulation normally won't result in a fracture of the hyoid, as opposed to ligature strangulation, which will."

"What is the reason for that?"

"Leverage. The twisting of a scarf or a towel or a rope around the neck will fracture the hyoid bone easily because the pressure is supplied by the twisting object, not the fingers. A person of average strength can't exert the same pressure."

"Yet it is possible for one to fracture the hyoid through use of hands and fingers?"

"Yes, but the person applying the pressure would need to have more than average strength in his hands."

"And according to your testimony, Dr. Martindale, to accomplish that his fingers would have to encircle the neck, is that correct?"

"It would be extremely difficult to exert sufficient pressure otherwise. Unless, of course, there was no resistance."

"Mr. McCarthy," Marc asked, "may I please have People's Exhibit D in evidence?"

McCarthy handed the paper to Marc with a flourish, as if happy to accommodate him.

"Dr. Martindale," Marc said, "I show you People's Exhibit D, the autopsy report, prepared by Dr. Myron Lee after he personally conducted the autopsy. I direct your attention to the line I have marked in pencil. Will you please read what is written there?"

"Circumference of the neck: twenty-six centimeters."

"Dr. Lee has testified to the deceased's weight and height. I have marked those proportions in red pencil. Would you tell us if twenty-six centimeters neck circumference would be normal."

"I would say greater than normal. In my opinion the average neck circumference of a female with those proportions would range from twenty to twenty-five centimeters."

Marc motioned to Peter at the counsel table. "Mr. Jorgensen, would you please hold out your hands, fingers extended?" Peter, looking confused, did what Marc asked. Marc turned to Judge Sturdivant. "Your Honor, may I request that Dr. Martindale approach the counsel table in order to examine the defendant's hands?"

Sturdivant nodded, understanding too well what Marc was up to. Peter stood up. Louella left the witness stand, carefully examined Peter's hand and fingers and returned.

"Your Honor," Marc said, "will the district attorney stipulate that the defendant stands approximately six feet and weighs approximately one-hundred-sixty pounds?"

McCarthy moved quickly into the opening. "I will stipulate that he weighs approximately one-hundred-sixty pounds now. We don't know what he weighed at the time of the murder."

"Objection." McCarthy could indeed fight dirty. He had just, in effect, said that Peter was the killer. "Your Honor, that remark by the district attorney is so prejudicial and unfair that I am constrained to ask for a mistrial."

"Denied." Actually, he would have been grateful to have it over. But he could not give in to such a motion and he knew Hammond knew it.

"Then I ask Your Honor to instruct the jury to disregard Mr. McCarthy's remark."

Hammond was trying to take over his role . . . trying to push him . . . his palms were sweating again . . . "I will instruct the jury that the district attorney has stipulated that the defendant stands approximately six feet and now weighs approximately one-hundred-sixty pounds. Now let's get on with it, Mr. Hammond."

Marc shook his head, making sure that the jury saw his gesture. "Dr. Martindale, after having examined the defendant, how would you describe the size of his hands in terms of his body proportions?"

"I would say that his hands are smaller than normal for his proportions."

"That being so, would it be fair to say that the defendant's hands are not large enough to encircle a throat twenty-six centimeters in circumference in the area of the hyoid."

"Yes. His fingers are short, and his hands are small. I don't believe he could encircle a neck that size."

"Would it also be fair to say that the leverage required to exert necessary force would not be present."

"If there was any resistance, in my opinion the defendant could not have exerted enough pressure in manual strangulation to fracture the hyoid."

Hammond moved back of the counsel table. He aimed the question at Louella while looking at the jury. "But a person other than the defendant—with large hands, strong enough to exert the required leverage, and with fingers large enough to encircle the neck—that person could exert enough pressure to fracture the hyoid?"

"Yes," Louella said, "such a person could."

Allen Sturdivant, listening intently as any spectator, felt nothing. He knew what he had done, but, finally, had no memory of it. He was, he decided, splitting in two. "I have no further questions of this witness . . ." Marc's words brought him back to the dear familiar prosaic. He almost smiled his gratitude.

McCarthy now faced Louella. "Dr. Martindale, your response to counsel's question concerning the ability to fracture the hyoid were all based on the assumption that there was resistance by the deceased, isn't that true?"

"Yes."

"Let's assume otherwise. Let's assume that at some point the deceased became unconscious. Could this defendant then, with his relatively small hands and short fingers, have fractured the hyoid bone?"

"I don't think the question is clear."

"My fault, Dr. Martindale. Let me try to clarify it. A person can lose consciousness, but not necessarily die, as a result of being manually strangled, isn't that correct?"

"Yes. If the trachea is compressed, loss of consciousness could result."

"And naturally, if a person becomes unconscious, resistance ceases."

"Of course."

"And if the defendant managed to render her unconscious by merely compressing the trachea, and she lost consciousness, and could no longer resist, he could then strengthen his hold and fracture the hyoid."

"Yes," Louella said, "under those circumstances he could."

McCarthy smiled, but was careful not to gloat. Hammond's face fell. Both their reactions were premature. She hadn't finished her answer.

"But why would he want to?" she said quietly.

"I beg your pardon?"

"I said why would he want to? Asphyxiation by strangulation is not caused exclusively by fracture of the hyoid. If the trachea is compressed by outside pressure, under the hyoid, it could, as I said, result in loss of consciousness. But sustained compression will cut off oxygen flow to the brain and the body will stop functioning. If he did render her unconscious by compressing her trachea, and he didn't release his grip, she would have been just as dead. There would be no point then to change his grip and attempt to fracture the hyoid."

Marc Hammond wanted to jump up and cheer. Louella had delivered, God, had she delivered. The point was made that a strong man with strong hands, large fingers might have killed Andrea Blanchard . . . at least the seed of that thought had been implanted in the jury's minds, and that seed *could* flower into reasonable doubt.

McCarthy had had enough of Louella. He knew when to cut his potential losses. "I have no further questions," he said.

All in all, so far, Marc thought, a pretty good defense. For a change. But, Marc warned himself, hardly a life-saver.

CHAPTER 27

Brian McCarthy finished up the People's case by
calling two detectives from the homicide division, who described what they had found at the murder site. They were
effective witnesses for the prosecution in terms of shock
value, and Marc saw no percentage in lengthy cross-examination so that they could repeat the gory details to the
jury.

Now it was the defense's turn.

Nick Jenner, Peter Jorgensen's employer, had agreed to
testify on Peter's behalf. "Anything I can do for that kid,
I'll do," he had said to Marc Hammond. "I feel sorry for
him. I visited him at Riker's. He swears he didn't do it and
I believe him. It's not in his character and what's more, I'm
going to get you three more of my people to come to court
to testify, even though it means I'll be murdered for the
day."

Sounded good, Marc thought, but character witnesses
could take you just so far. Jenner was a round fat man who

looked like a casting director's idea of a southern sheriff. He was sworn at the opening of the afternoon session.

"Mr. Jenner," Marc began, "what is your occupation?"

"I own the Jenner garage—on West Seventy-second Street."

"Do you know the defendant, Peter Jorgensen?"

"Yes, I certainly do."

"How do you know him?"

"I employ him."

"How long has he been employed by you, Mr. Jenner?"

"Let's see, about three years now."

"What are his duties?"

"He's a mechanic—he works on engines, transmissions, ignition systems, carburetors, anything a car mechanic would be required to do."

"How many employees do you have?"

"Thirteen."

"Have you ever had the opportunity to discuss his reputation for honesty and reliability with your other employees, or with anyone else?"

"Yes, I have."

"What is that reputation?"

"Excellent. Everyone who's had any dealings with Pete— the fellas he works with, the customers—all come back to me with the same story. He's a good guy. Wouldn't take a dime that wasn't his. Once a customer left a wallet in the seat of a car he was working on. Must have fallen out of his pocket. It had over four hundred bucks in it. Pete turned it in to the customer when he came to pick up the car." Jenner pointed to Peter who was sitting with his head bowed. "He's a terrific kid. And you can be sure he didn't kill anyone."

Hammond had prepared Nick Jenner, as he would any witness, but Jenner insisted on giving his testimony in his own way. It wasn't bad.

"Thank you, Mr. Jenner. I have no further questions."

"I do, Mr. Jenner," McCarthy said, getting up.

Marc knew it was going too well.

"Mr. Jenner, what specific services does your garage provide?"

"Well, we park cars—daily and on a monthly basis—and we fix cars. Foreign or domestic—there are no better mechanics in the city."

"No doubt, and I'll bet you started as a mechanic yourself?"

"Sure did."

"And how many years have you worked as a mechanic?"

"More than thirty."

"It's hard work, isn't it, Mr. Jenner?"

"It's not easy."

"May I see your hands, Mr. Jenner?" McCarthy asked.

Marc's spirits continued to sag as he saw where McCarthy was heading. "Objection, Your Honor, this is not proper cross-examination of a character witness."

"Objection overruled."

Jenner extended his hands tentatively.

"Mr. Jenner, are these the hands of a man who has used wrenches and pliers and calibrators and all the other tools a mechanic needs for over thirty years?"

"Yes, sir."

"Would you say that to use these tools properly one would need a certain amount of strength in his hands?"

"Sure do. You need strong hands. You're turning and twisting couplings and bolts. A car comes in and if it's not lubricated for a long time the coupling or the connecting bolt is frozen and you have to apply a lot of pressure—"

"So a weak man—at least a man with weak hands—could not do that particular job well, could he?"

"Well, the tools can't do it themselves, can they?"

"Did you ever find that Peter Jorgensen did not have the hand strength to do the job?"

"No, sir, he could always handle it."

Terrific, Peter muttered to himself.

"And he's been doing this for three years while in your employ?"

"Yes."

"Thank you, Mr. Jenner. I have no further questions of this witness."

Jenner, before he exited, looked back at Peter, who nodded and even managed to smile in acknowledgment. Peter understood that Jenner's testimony tended to undercut Louella Martindale's, but there was still the fact that his employer, a stranger really, at least thought enough of him to sacrifice his time to come to try and help him. He felt good about that, while he felt rotten about the circumstances that required it.

Marc realized there was no point in calling the three co-workers of Peter who were waiting outside the courtroom to testify. Memory of the damaging testimony McCarthy had developed from Jenner would only be reinforced by McCarthy no matter if the workers said Peter was the greatest thing since Jesus Christ.

"I have no further witnesses available today, Your Honor," Marc said.

McCarthy allowed himself a half-smile . . . he had seen the others waiting in the hallway. He had no objection to the recess. Let the jury think on Jenner's testimony for a while. Dr. Louella Martindale's testimony may have temporarily hurt, but what he'd gotten from Jenner had repaired the damage.

Sturdivant declared a recess until the following day . . .

Jenner had left the stand and was waiting outside now with the other men. "How'd I do?" he said when he saw Hammond walk through the door.

243

"Fine," Marc said. "So good that I don't want to gild the lily. I've decided not to call your other guys."

"I don't understand, I thought you said the more the merrier."

"Sometimes yes, sometimes no. You were fine, Mr. Jenner. Let's leave it at that."

"Well, shit, I wish I'd known that before. You know what I lost by keeping those guys out of the shop today?"

"I'm sorry, Mr. Jenner—"

"We had an expression in the navy that I've used all my life, Mr. Hammond. 'Sorry don't feed the admiral's cat.'"

"You've got a point, Mr. Jenner," and to himself, In more ways than one.

You lose some, you win some, Marc told himself, trying to buck himself up, hoping to change his luck, *Peter's* luck, the following day. He needed to get the jury back on track— the pointing to someone else as the murderer. He had one more witness he could call before he called Peter. A reluctant witness.

Originally, Marc had not intended to call Andrea's neighbor, Irma Goldstein, who had told him about seeing Peter at a party in Andrea's apartment. That much alone seemed hardly helpful to Peter. But after thinking on it, he was convinced that the risk was worth it . . . in fact, given the way things were going, it was a risk he had to take. Irma Goldstein was a gossip, had, therefore, a gossip's inclination to mind other people's business and so could be a source of information about Andrea Blanchard's life and the people in it.

With little time to arrange for her to testify, the power of subpoena was a godsend, he thought as he drove directly to the Monte Carlo Apartments, walked into the lobby and waved to the doorman like he belonged there. The doorman waved back. Marc didn't know the Goldstein apartment

244

number but he knew its location, having been there before. He went up and rang the bell.

"Just a minute," he heard from inside. "Who is it?"

"Mrs. Goldstein?"

"Yes."

"I have something for you."

"I'm not dressed. What is it?"

"A subpoena."

"A what?"

"A subpoena. You're being called to testify at the Peter Jorgensen trial."

"Oh, my God. Well, I'm *not* letting you in."

"I'm sliding the subpoena under the door, Mrs. Goldstein. If you don't appear tomorrow at nine-thirty at the place indicated on the subpoena you will be subject to arrest for contempt."

Silence, then, "Oh, my *God*," followed by a subdued "wait a minute."

The door opened. Irma Goldstein stood in her glory, hair in the obligatory curlers, wearing a bathrobe that accentuated her bulk. "Come in," she said grudgingly.

The invitation extended only to the foyer, where she stood like a boulder before Marc, making it clear that the rest of her apartment was off-limits.

"I don't know anything," she said. "What do you want from my life?"

"Only the truth, Mrs. Goldstein."

"I've told you all I know. I once went to her apartment to give her ice. Period."

"But you saw other people go into her apartment at different times."

"I never said that."

"But you did and I can prove you did. If you lie when you take that stand tomorrow you will be subject to prosecution for perjury."

245

Marc felt no guilt. Sometimes, at least up to a point, the ends justified the means. Embarrassing and pressuring Mrs. Goldstein was the least of his worries. He understood her reluctance . . . she didn't want revealed to the world what a *yenta* she was. He handed her the subpoena.

"My husband will kill me . . ." Her voice sounded like chalk on a blackboard. It could make a strong man wince.

Marc tried to calm her. "No, he won't. After you testify tomorrow I'll talk to him—"

"Big deal. I'll be all over the papers and television by then. Oh, he's going to kill me . . ."

Marc would have liked to talk to her some about her testimony, but she was too upset. He had to continue the pressure, though. "Be prompt tomorrow, Mrs. Goldstein," he said. "Meet me in court at nine A.M. tomorrow. I'll want to talk to you before you testify."

She arrived in court on the dot of nine dressed all in black as if in mourning. Marc took her into a small room that was provided for counsel. After only a few minutes he was pleased to discover that his hunch about her had been right.

He put her on the stand as soon as the jury was seated, noting that she appeared calmer than the previous day. She was going to be able to do what came naturally . . . talk about other people.

"Where do you live, Mrs. Goldstein?"

"In the Monte Carlo Apartments, Sixty-third Street and Central Park West."

"What apartment?"

"Eleven-H."

"Where is that apartment with relation to the deceased's apartment?"

"Right across the hall."

"Mrs. Goldstein, were you home last Christmas?"

"No, I was in Fort Lauderdale. We always go down there from the twenty-first until the fifth of January."

"Was anyone occupying your apartment on Christmas Eve?"

"No. The whole family, my husband and children, were with me in Florida."

Marc wanted to establish quickly that Mrs. Goldstein was not being called for the purpose of eyewitness testimony to anything that occurred on the night of the murder. He then proceeded to take her back in time and have her tell what she had seen at Andrea Blanchard's party. He had nothing to lose. He had already decided that Peter was going to have to testify, and in that testimony Peter was going to reveal his lengthy association with Andrea and his frequent presence in her home.

Now he came to his point: "Mrs. Goldstein, did you ever see the defendant, Peter Jorgensen, enter Andrea Blanchard's apartment?"

"Yes, I did. Several times."

"Did you witness these visits during the day or the evening?"

"The evening . . . I mean late at night . . . that's why I looked—"

"Looked? What do you mean?"

"Last year there were some burglaries in the building. I don't go to bed early—usually after midnight. When I hear noises in the hall at that hour . . . well, I check to see who it is. That's only natural."

"Yes . . . and how do you do that? How do you check to see who it is?"

"Sometimes by opening the door and sometimes by looking through the peephole."

Marc put himself in front of the jury, directing his question at the witness but facing the jurors.

"Mrs. Goldstein, during such times did you ever see any

men other than the defendant enter Andrea Blanchard's apartment at various times after midnight?"

"Yes—several times."

"How many such men did you see?"

"At least three."

"Did you recognize any of them?"

"Yes—one, I recognized."

The courtroom suddenly hushed. Marc let it build. All eyes were on the witness, which was the only relief for Allen Sturdivant.

"Before we get to him, Mrs. Goldstein, will you tell this jury how you saw these men. I mean, did you see their faces?"

"No, only their backs. Andrea would open the door and they would go in and she would close the door. One was tall, broad-shouldered. I saw him several times. He always wore a hat, summer or winter, and always with the brim turned down."

Sturdivant sat frozen. No emotion showed, except a slight flush that he felt instantly branded him to the whole courtroom.

"You said you saw this tall broad-shouldered man with the hat several times. How many is several?"

"I don't know . . . maybe ten."

"But you never saw his face?"

"No, I told you I didn't."

"All right, now tell us about the second man?"

"The one I recognized?"

"No, we'll get to him in a moment."

"Well, the second man, I only saw him visit her once. He was very short, and thin. He looked like a jockey."

"And now we come to the third man, the man you recognized. How could you recognize him if you didn't see his face?"

"Because I've seen this man at least once a week for the past two years. I recognized him from his hair and his build."

"And who was that man?"

"The superintendent of our building, Julio Benitez."

A reporter scribbled a lead for his story: "Peephole Lady Fingers Super . . ."

Marc let it all sink in with the jury before he continued. "His visits also were after midnight?"

"Yes."

"And when he visited Andrea Blanchard was he dressed in workclothes?"

"No, he was always dressed in a regular suit."

"So," Marc said, "would it be fair to say that he wasn't visiting her on official business?"

Marc waited for McCarthy's objection to the obviously improper question. He was calling for speculation, yet McCarthy let it go.

"Yes, I think so," Mrs. Goldstein said.

"Thank you. Your witness, Mr. McCarthy."

McCarthy had let the speculation question go because he wasn't going to dignify even the possibility of another suspect by a technical challenge. He was going after Irma Goldstein.

"Mrs. Goldstein, you testified that you were aware of burglaries occurring in your building?"

"Yes, sir."

"How many?"

"What?"

"How many burglaries were you aware of?"

She stared into space. "I don't know the exact number."

"Do you know the names of the people who were burglarized?"

"No."

"Do you know the location of the apartments that were burglarized?"

"Yes—one of them."

"One of them . . . was it on your floor?"

"No."

McCarthy paused. "Isn't it a fact, Mrs. Goldstein, that the threat of burglary was not the reason that you looked through the peephole to spy on Andrea Blanchard?"

"Objection." Marc was on his feet. "There was no testimony that she spied on anyone. Those are the district attorney's words."

"Overruled. The witness may answer the question."

"No," she said, "I was nervous. It was late at night. I don't spy."

"From your own testimony you looked through that peephole after midnight—let's see, ten, thirteen, fifteen times, if not more. Always after midnight. *Always* looking for burglars? Is that what you want us to believe, Mrs. Goldstein?"

"But it's *true*," she said, her voice rising.

"I remind you that you are testifying under oath, Mrs. Goldstein."

"What do you *want* from me? I didn't want to come here in the first place." She pointed at Marc. *"He* served me with a summons—"

"Mr. Hammond served you personally with a subpoena?"

"Yes."

"When did he serve you?"

"Last night."

"And did you talk about your testimony when he served you?"

"No."

"Did you see and speak to him before taking the witness stand?"

"No."

Marc was boiling. He had told her at least twice how to answer . . . that she had indeed discussed her testimony

250

with him before she took the stand. It would have been the most natural thing for her to say, especially when it was the plain truth. But clearly she had panicked.

"Well," McCarthy said, "I'm sure the jury believes that to the same extent as the rest of your gossip-ridden testimony." He looked at her, shook his head. "I have no further questions of this witness."

Marc tried to assess the possible damage. McCarthy's cross-examination had raised the question of Irma Goldstein's credibility. Still, he didn't believe that her being a busybody would make the jurors disbelieve her testimony about late night visitors. And if they believed that, then they could also believe, at least speculate, that one of those visitors could have murdered Andrea Blanchard. He didn't need twelve jurors to have the thought. One who would not give in to the rest could be enough.

There was no point in any redirect. He let Irma Goldstein go. She had served her purpose. She had given a name as a possible suspect. Which was the most he'd hoped for.

"Your Honor," he said, "I request that the Court issue a subpoena to Julio Benitez, the person named by the previous witness. I wish to call him as the next defense witness. If he can be served I plan to call him tomorrow morning."

"And if Mr. Hammond doesn't call him, Your Honor, I will," McCarthy said.

Sturdivant nodded, signed Marc's subpoena and recessed for the day.

He should, he thought, be grateful to Julio Benitez. He was not. Strange . . .

CHAPTER 28

THE NEXT DAY the court was advised that a flu bug had felled a juror but that doctors said he would be able to return to duty in twenty-four hours. After being so informed by the clerk, Judge Sturdivant assembled the rest of the jury and excused them, at the same time instructing them not to discuss the case and to appear at nine sharp the following morning. The attorneys welcomed the news. Like most trial lawyers they appreciated a break in the action, an opportunity to regroup, think through what had happened to date, to prepare for new witnesses.

For Allen Sturdivant the delay was pluperfect hell—to use a favorite phrase of his old Latin teacher at Choate when doing a critique on one of his student's more execrable renderings of *The Aeneid*. He felt like a man on a perpetual roller-coaster—one moment up when testimony moved away from any possible uncovering of him, the next minute plummeting when the obverse happened. Yet it wasn't really that simple, not anymore. The previous day's witness . . . he couldn't remember her name . . . identifying the superintendent of Andrea's building by name . . . that he *did* remember . . . Julio Benitez . . . should have been a relief, speaking to his original desire to see the innocent Peter Jorgensen get off on the basis of reasonable doubt that he did it, that somebody else might well have, and at the same time not being compromised himself. He remembered his sense of not feeling anything resembling pleasure or relief at the end of the testimony naming Benitez, and wondered why. He still did. Was it that he now wanted Jorgensen to be found guilty? Or this Benitez, or anybody else? No, certainly not. Lord, he hadn't deteriorated that far, sunk that low . . .

Low, yes, that's where he felt. Low, the lowest depths. The emotion was no longer an ache or a regret or missing Andrea or any such copable with sentiments. It was a burning in the pit of his stomach. An ulcer? No, it was too sudden, and besides he'd once had the beginning of an ulcer and it was cured and altogether under control. But the burning . . . an interesting word, conjuring up the most primitive notions hardly in the lexicon—intellectual or emotional—of a Harvard-educated man. Burning . . . fire and brimstone . . . more appropriate for a Baptist minister than someone whose tree was quintessential WASP, who was an elder in his Episcopalian church, where no backwoods howlings or popish trappings were conceivable.

He was beginning to sweat again, another outré reaction that was nowhere in his background. In his circles one kept one's cool. No matter what. In his circle . . . some joke . . . the circles of hell, Dante's version, of course . . . God, he had to have some relief. To stop the thoughts, to stop the *feelings*. He'd never been much at showing feelings, not even to his daughters, whom he deeply loved. Nor to Andrea, who in his fashion he also cared about more than he could show. Loren was no problem; she demanded nothing in this area, which for years he'd thought was an advantage. It was Andrea who had shown him something about letting himself go, if only in the sexual act. He was grateful for her practiced techniques, and badly missed them now. At times she could be cruel, provoking and taunting, but at least it had also served to arouse him, to allow him to *show* some feelings.

He remembered the card that a friend, Elliot Hastings, had once insisted he take—a card on which Elliot had written the telephone number of the most exclusive callgirl ring in America, catering to top executives, professional men, politicians. A California judge and a United States senator were, Elliot said, among its clientele. Discretion and confidentiality were its hallmarks. On the card Elliot had written, "King Arthur at the castle. Red Rose." If Allen called the number that was all he needed to say. It meant that he was referred by Elliot and that the meeting would be at the New York Hilton. A red rose in the lapel would identify him to the young lady, who would meet him in the open lounge.

Sturdivant took the card out of his drawer, dialed the number.

"Good morning," a cheery voice answered.

"This is . . . King Arthur at the castle . . . Red Rose."

"What time, please?"

"Three P.M.?"

"The messenger will be at the castle at precisely three P.M., King Arthur. Have a nice day."

He unlocked the bottom drawer of his cabinet and took out the gray fedora and dark-tinted glasses he had used when he visited Andrea. He placed them in his briefcase, cashed a check for five hundred dollars at his bank, bought a red rose and attached it to his lapel. Wearing his dark glasses, he arrived at the Hilton at two-thirty. He put on the fedora in a stall in the men's room, checked in at the desk under

254

the name of Gordon, was given a room key and waited in the lounge.

She arrived precisely at three. She was a beautiful redhead, much younger than he'd expected, and was carrying a briefcase. She smiled pleasantly, one board member to another, as it were. Without thinking, he got up and shook her hand, feeling instantly foolish, ridiculous.

They walked, she slightly in the lead, toward the elevator, carrying their briefcases, two executives ascending to do business. From the time they met until they entered the room not a word passed between them. It had rained earlier in the day and she was carrying a raincoat, which she now placed on a chair and stood there, waiting for his pleasure, or pain.

"Hello," she said. Then walked to him and kissed him gently on the lips. "You're tense. Don't be. For the short time we're here, forget the world outside. Do whatever you want to do. I'm here to help you. And don't be shy. There will be no shame here. We've left that outside too."

Nicely rendered, but clearly a set speech. At least Andrea had meant what she said . . . but this wasn't Andrea, and this wasn't escape. This was ridiculous. He might welcome or at least deal with self-disgust, or guilt, but to feel ridiculous . . . that cut too deep. Quickly, he took out the five hundred dollars, placed it on the bed, left the room and the hotel at a near run.

Back at the suite in the Carlyle, he felt relief only at not finding Loren there. He slumped down in a chair, knowing that if there was to be any escape for him, it did not lie in such outlandish places as a callgirl's smile. Then where? And how? Sleep saved him from seeking answers to the unanswerable.

When court resumed the next day, Julio Benitez entered accompanied by the dean of the Puerto Rican bar, Alfredo

Gomez. Gomez always wore a fresh white carnation and was always impeccably dressed. His charm and prowess with the ladies was well known. He hinted as to Castilian ancestors and to birth in Cadiz, though those who remembered him from his East Harlem youth had some trouble with that. No matter, under all the show and pretense he was one smart lawyer.

Gomez's client, Julio Benitez, had left Cuba in 1980 in the Mariel boat lift. He had been about to receive a degree in mechanical engineering from the University of Havana and would have graduated had he not fallen from grace and gone to a jail for a year because he succumbed to his habit of finding things before other people lost them. Nevertheless, he was good with his hands, he was handsome and he was bright. He applied his education well and was given the job at the Monte Carlo because the owner felt he could handle it. And he did. The only problem was that little things—like little diamond rings—began to be missed by various tenants. Julio, charmer that he was, escaped suspicion. Other employees did not and were fired.

Nonetheless, it could be said for Julio Benitez that adultery was not ordinarily his style. He was a family man, devoted to his wife and children. But Andrea Blanchard was something else, a woman to turn the staunchest man's head, and after his second visit to her apartment in the line of duty, one thing led . . . with her leading . . . to another. Subsequent visits by Julio were a combination of pleasure with an indulgence of his weakness. If his activities had been limited to his dalliance with a tenant, Benitez would have been concerned only with possible embarrassment. But the service of the subpoena triggered concern that someone would discover that he was also stealing her blind. And so he contacted Alfredo Gomez, who explained to him the benefits of the American Constitution, especially the Fifth Amendment—and assured his client that he would never spend a day in jail *if* he followed orders.

When the trial resumed and Julio Benitez was sworn, Alfredo Gomez took the floor like a Latin Olivier. "Your Honor—my name is Alfredo Gomez. I represent this witness, Julio Benitez. I have advised him that unless Your Honor confers immunity that he is not to answer any questions put to him on the grounds that his answers may tend to incriminate him, all in derogation of his rights granted him under the Fifth Amendment of the Constitution of the United States."

Benitez was under subpoena and thereby compelled to testify. But by invoking the Fifth he could refuse to answer unless directed to by the judge, and if the judge did order him to answer he could not be prosecuted for anything he would admit to on the witness stand, even something leading to proof of a criminal act. If he refused he was subject to punishment for contempt; if he lied, he could be prosecuted for perjury.

Marc Hammond was pleased. This request for immunity would tend to strike the jury as a cover-up. He also had to appear to want the jury to hear Benitez's testimony, although leaving them with a sense of a cover-up of Benitez would insure that the jury be suspicious of him, and at least further doubt Peter's guilt; if Benitez's testimony proved harmless, Peter was not served.

"Your Honor, I request that you grant immunity to this witness so that we may hear evidence vital to this trial."

McCarthy was stronger about it. "Judge, I join in this request. It's important that this jury be not left with the wrong impression as to why Mr. Benitez has invoked the Fifth Amendment."

Which confirmed Marc's concern now about Benitez's testimony.

"We'll discuss this in the robing room," Sturdivant said.

When the lawyers and Sturdivant were alone, the door closed, Sturdivant turned on them, fire in his eyes—more animation, it occurred to Marc, than the judge had shown in some time.

"What is this? What are you trying to make of this trial? A cheap shabby sideshow for the tabloids—?"

"But, Judge," McCarthy said, "it's important that the jury hear all the facts about this man so they're not misled about him as a suspect—"

"Important? What seems important here is to destroy the name of an individual who is not here to defend herself. That, Mr. McCarthy, and you too, Mr. Hammond, is bad practice. It also is cheap and a travesty of justice. You both ought to be ashamed of yourselves, as I am . . ."

Both attorneys were too surprised to protest further, and quickly left to take up their places at their respective counsel tables.

Left alone, Allen Sturdivant swallowed two antacid pills that were weak palliatives for the burning that flared in his stomach. He shook his head at his own words about protecting the reputation of "an individual" who wasn't there. He knew he was not the first with Andrea but she was being painted here in one dimension. The ease and warmth she gave him at the best of their times could not be told or understood, but it had been real . . . except was it Andrea that he had been talking about? Or was he really talking about himself? And he was here, although not able to defend himself. Of course, when he returned to the legal situation, he realized he had to grant immunity to Benitez. Both the prosecution and the defense had requested it, there was no logical reason for denying it. He knew that it might also bring testimony that might further divert attention from him . . . but that seemed not to matter. Not now, not anymore.

He took a deep breath, stood and walked into the court-room, resumed his chair and faced the jury. "In view of the joint requests of counsel, I am granting immunity to this witness." He then faced Benitez, whose face was creased with worry as he listened to the judge. "Mr. Benitez, any-thing that you testify to now may not be used as evidence against you. You may not be prosecuted for anything that may be revealed by your testimony, either concerning what you have said or what you have done. Do you understand?"

"Yes, sir."

"Having told you that, I now direct you to answer all questions put to you unless I rule otherwise. If you refuse to answer after being so directed you will be in contempt of the court, subject to a sentence of thirty days and a fine of five hundred dollars. Do you understand that too?"

"Yes, sir."

"I also advise you that if you have answered falsely to any questions put to you, you will be subject to prosecution for perjury, a Class D felony under the penal law, and if convicted you may be sentenced to imprisonment for a term up to seven years. Do you understand that?"

"Yes, yes sir."

Gomez, eager to register his presence on the press, now spoke up. "Your Honor, forgive the intrusion, but I believe my client wishes to converse with me. May I approach the witness stand?"

Sturdivant nodded. Gomez walked to the stand and he and Benitez spoke in Spanish . . . "What do I say if they ask me if I ever took anything from her apartment?" "Tell the *truth*, for God's sake. They can't prosecute you for it. And it's better to get exposed as a thief than be convicted as a killer, which you're not." "But I'll lose my job—" "So you'll get another job." "But if I tell them about the times I was with the woman I'll lose my wife." "So you'll get another wife. Look, Benitez, you paid me to keep you out of jail. That's what I'm doing. All the rest is bullshit." "And what if I lie?" "Then you can kiss your ass good-by—you, your job, *and* your wife."

Gomez smiled, patted Benitez on the shoulder, fingered his carnation and left the witness stand. "Thank you, Your Honor," he said in his most courtly manner. "I'm satisfied that my client fully understands your instructions."

Benitez was sworn in and Marc gazed at him silently. The lean Cuban was sweating profusely. That was good, a signal to the jury that Benitez was afraid. Of what, was left to speculation.

"Mr. Benitez, you are the superintendent of the Monte Carlo Apartments, is that correct?"

"Yes, sir."

"How long have you held that job?"

"Two years."

"Did you know the deceased, Andrea Blanchard?"

"Yes, sir."

"Did you ever have occasion to be present in her apartment?"

"Yes."

"How many times would you say you were in her apartment in the past two years?"

"Several times."

"What's several? More than five?"

"Yes."

"More than ten?"

"Yes."

"More than thirty?"

"About thirty, I would say. I'm not sure."

"And will you tell this Court and the jury, please, why you visited her apartment so many times?"

The air conditioner in the courtroom was working well, but Julio Benitez was still sweating a lake. As far as he was concerned, jail was jail, and the American jail couldn't be much better than the Cuban fort they had locked him in. Once was enough. He would have to tell the truth.

"Sometimes to fix things in her apartment."

"What about the other times?"

Benitez squirmed in the witness chair. "Sometimes to . . . to make love?" Benitez's voice was a whisper.

"Please speak up, Mr. Benitez, so His Honor and the jury can hear your answers."

"We made love."

"You had sexual relations with Andrea Blanchard?"

"Yes."

"How many times?"

"Eight, nine?"

"Tell us, Mr. Benitez, the circumstances of the first time you had sexual relations with Andrea Blanchard."

"Well, she called me to fix a leaking pipe."

"When?"

"I think it was in May."

"About a year ago?"

"Yes."

"Go ahead."

"All my men were busy, so I took the call personally. The bathroom was up the stairs, next to her bedroom. She let me in and I opened the pipe and saw that the trouble was the washer. I didn't have that size washer with me. I had a few more calls to make and I told her I'd be back in an hour. When I came back, the front door was open. I walked upstairs to her bedroom. You had to go through the bedroom to get to the bathroom. When I opened the door to the bedroom she was lying on the bed. She had a glass in her hand. She didn't have any clothes on—" Benitez stopped, squirming in his seat.

"Why have you stopped, Mr. Benitez?"

"Do I have to tell all of it?"

"I'm afraid so."

261

"Well, I think she'd had a lot to drink and . . . she asked me to have sex with her."

"She asked you?"

"Yes. I didn't want to. I had my wife, my children, in our apartment downstairs. I didn't need that. But she was a beautiful woman and—well, we did it."

"And you visited her seven or eight more times and you had relations with her at those times."

"Yes."

"At night?"

"Yes, after that first time."

"How did she let you know when she wanted you to come to her?"

"She'd leave a note in a plain envelope. There is a special box in the lobby for tenants to leave me messages to tell me what their problems are and when they will be home."

"What did you tell your wife when you left your apartment those evenings?"

"I told her I was going to a union meeting."

Smiles from the spectators . . . God, how Sturdivant wanted to wipe the smiles off those faces . . . to wipe away this whole awful display, this trial . . . all of it . . .

Hammond bore down. "Mr. Benitez, did there come a time when these sexual encounters ended?"

"Yes."

"How were they ended?"

"She stopped writing me."

"That bothered you, didn't it?"

"No, I was glad it stopped—"

"You had eight or nine such meetings with this woman you have called beautiful, who was obviously irresistible to you, who also caused guilty feelings in you for betraying your wife, and suddenly she cuts you off, no longer wants you, and you're asking this Court to believe you were *glad*, that you felt no anger toward her?"

"That's *right*. I was glad it was over. It was eating me up, what I was doing."

Marc looked to the jury, then back to Benitez. "When was the last time that you had relations with Andrea Blanchard?"

"Last October."

"Have you seen her at all since then?"

"Only in the lobby."

"And when you saw her in the lobby, after she stopped calling you, after your relationship had ended so abruptly, what did you say to her?"

"Hello."

Laughter. Marc did not like the answer. It was too guileless. He would have to press harder. "Isn't it a fact that when the sex stopped you contacted her and when she turned you down you were enraged—?"

"Objection. None of this is in evidence. Purely the work of Mr. Hammond's vivid imagination."

"Sustained." Sturdivant was pleased with his ruling. It was the right one, never mind who it helped or hurt.

"All right," Marc said, having made his point, "I'll withdraw the question and ask you this. Mr. Benitez, will you tell the Court and the jury where you were on Christmas Eve?"

"At a party in my apartment."

"Who was present?"

"My family—my wife, my daughters and my sons-in-law, my sisters, my brother-in-law, my nieces and nephews."

"Quite a group. Your apartment is on the first floor of the Monte Carlo, is that right?"

"Yes."

"And is the service elevator next to your apartment?"

"Yes."

"And if you wanted to, it would only have been a matter

263

of minutes for you to leave your apartment, take the empty freight elevator to the eleventh floor, strangle Andrea Blanchard and return to the party. With all these people, they wouldn't even know you were gone."

"No, that's a *lie,*" and simultaneous with the denial came an objection from McCarthy, accusing Marc of concocting fairytales.

But Marc had developed his red herring. More, he believed in it. "I withdraw the question, Your Honor. I'm done with the witness."

McCarthy from the start had felt that Benitez was trying to hide something, and that it was not Andrea Blanchard's murder. He was too credible in his testimony about how he felt when the relationship ended. He was nervous, all right, and he was afraid he'd incriminate himself about something from the first, but what . . . ? Well, what do building personnel usually get themselves in trouble over? Stealing from the tenants, that's what. Could be this Latin lover had a guilty conscience about more than a few quickies with Andrea Blanchard. "Mr. Benitez, did you appear in court today in response to a subpoena?"

Benitez was using his red handkerchief. "Yes."

"And after you were served with that subpoena, you called your lawyer, Mr. Gomez, is that correct?"

"Yes."

"And did he tell you that after immunity is given on you, you must answer truthfully?"

"Yes."

"Did you ever leave your apartment that evening?"

"*No,* not for a minute."

"And your whole family and relatives are able to testify to that?"

"Yes. We were together all evening."

"Mr. Benitez, I believe you. But I must ask you a question . . . did you ever remove articles from Andrea Blanchard's apartment not given to you as presents?"

"Absolutely *not*. I've never stolen anything in my life. I am an honest man." Benitez's lie, the first in his testimony, was an automatic reflex. It was a lie he'd needed to use more than once in the past.

McCarthy was pleased. He had made his point. Benitez's reaction was unnatural, a change of face and tone from his previous answers. He was not a good liar, even if a chronic one. He was convincing, McCarthy felt, about not having gone to Andrea Blanchard's apartment that night. What he did obviously fear was being exposed as a thief. The looks on the faces of some of the jurors were enough for McCarthy. He didn't need to go further. Benitez wasn't on trial, although Hammond had tried to make it seem so.

Nonetheless, to Julio Benitez's way of thinking it had been a bad day indeed. He had blown a grand to Gomez and faced a living hell with Mrs. Benitez. He also realized, as he sped back to the Monte Carlo, that he needed to dispose of the loot in the metal box in his dresser drawer. That damn lawyer had been too close for comfort.

As for Marc Hammond, and his client Peter, it had been a day of ups and downs. At first it had seemed that Benitez might make a plausible suspect, thereby drawing steam out of McCarthy's case against Peter. And in the heat of the courtroom, Marc had convinced himself that Benitez might well have been guilty. But after some calmer reflection in the few minutes from the end of court for the day to joining Peter in the detention area next to the courthouse, he had pretty much come to the same conclusion that McCarthy obviously had, that Benitez was more convincing as a likely petty thief than a murderer. All of which made the day end on a downer. Now, though, he had the obligation of finding something, and trying to believe it, to tell Peter to keep his hopes from going through the floor again.

"Things are looking better, Peter," he said, and then, with a serious face, "but I won't deny that I'd hoped for something more for our side from Benitez. We're not out of the woods, and I'd be kidding you if I said otherwise, but I can tell you that we're better off than before. Benitez may not have been the man, but as an acknowledged ex-lover of Andrea Blanchard he's created for the jury an immediate sense of her behavior, and more important, behavior that can convince them there were others with motives to kill her. And that helps throw doubt on your guilt. Tomorrow you're going to testify. We've gone over your testimony, but the thing to remember is that you must answer the district attorney's cross-examination calmly and honestly. Try not to show, not even to feel, fear. A jury can smell fear like a dog does, and it can prejudice them. When I question you, listen to me, but look at the jury when you answer. You don't need to convince me, you need to convince them. Try especially to make eye contact with the three I mentioned to you."

"Two, seven and nine," Peter said automatically.

"Right. Don't ignore anyone, but concentrate on them." Marc could only pray that he had read the expressions of doubt on those three jurors accurately. "And remember above everything else, tell the truth. There are a lot of wiseguys in this business who don't think the truth counts. I'm not one of them. Our job is to make the jury believe the truth."

He allowed himself a smile of encouragement and gave Peter a pat on the back. "Hang in, Peter, see you tomorrow," and then he joined Helen Jorgensen outside in the hall.

"See him tonight, Mrs. Jorgensen. I think he's built up a little confidence, at least hope, and your visit will be important. Tell him what I've been trying to get across—

that we do have a shot. I believe that. There are at least some questions raised in the past few days that are bothering some of the jurors. Okay?"

Helen Jorgensen nodded, but had thoughts of her own about what she needed most of all to say to her son.

Peter walked into the visitor's room at C-74 on Riker's smiling for his mother's benefit.

It didn't work. All the emotion that Helen had suppressed through the ordeal of the trial burst through. She wept openly as she embraced her son, which brought tears from him too. No words were needed for that moment, both understood how much they needed each other, and how much they hurt each other.

But Helen had a larger cross. She had to unburden herself to her son now, before tomorrow, before the next crisis in their lives. They sat at the wooden table, looking at each other. Then she spoke. "I'm so sorry, Peter, I hope you will forgive me. I pray that God will forgive me—"

"Forgive you? What for?"

"At the beginning . . . the stories in the press . . . your saying that you were there . . . and then when I found your keys—oh, God, forgive me, but I thought you . . . " She couldn't finish the awful sentence.

Peter said quickly, "If I didn't know the truth, the way things looked I'd have believed it too."

"But when your lawyer convinced me that you were innocent I still—" Helen turned away.

Peter squeezed her hand, encouraging her to go on or stop, it was all right.

"Andrea had complained to me about . . . things missing. I didn't know about the super. After they arrested you I thought, God forgive me, that you stole those things. Julio

267

was lying today. He's the thief. And it breaks my heart that I could think that you were."

The tears and her misery took over, and Peter tried to console her as he embraced her. "Don't worry, Ma. Everything will be all right."

And for the moment he almost believed it.

CHAPTER 29

Loren Sturdivant had hoped the crisis of resolve in her husband had been taken care of the night of the dinner at the Waldorf, when she had earlier confronted him in their hotel room and forced him to get back on their preordained track to the governor's mansion. That night he had seemed to have his old glow, aura of leadership once again, but the respite was temporary. He was becoming, it seemed, more irresolute each day. When they were together he rarely spoke, would not go out, went to bed early. He was a man going through the motions, not really there. Some candidate . . . Charlie Sweeney had mentioned it in passing, and although he was concerned he did not seem aware of the extent of the problem. "Once he starts hitting the stump," Sweeney had said, "he'll be fine. When he needs it, he'll have it."

Loren had nodded, but knew better. It seemed the Jorgensen case was nearing an end, and unless something were done, and done fast, Allen would be in no condition to take over the campaign from her and other stand-ins.

She called her husband from Buffalo, where she had been meeting with some of the state leaders, and arranged to join him for a quiet dinner at the Carlyle suite. They had not had much time together since Loren had taken up her duties as surrogate candidate, and even that little time had precious little communication.

When Allen arrived at six-thirty he looked considerably more drawn and pale than when she had last seen him only five days earlier. What especially came through to her was his withdrawal, his seeming distraction. He began sentences, left them hanging, either didn't seem to hear her when she talked or, if he did, answered her in evasive non sequiturs.

Dinner was silence. When they finished Loren took Allen's hand in hers, a rare show of affection. "We have to discuss the campaign," she said quietly. "This afternoon's papers say the Jorgensen trial will be over in a week. Is that true?"

He didn't answer. He looked straight ahead, past her. She put her hand to his face, and for a moment, a rare moment, she felt a tenderness toward him, something long buried in the effluvia of the years. But Loren realized that what she felt for Allen was more pity than tenderness. She removed her hand from his face.

"Allen, did you hear me? Will the trial—?"

"Yes, the trial. It will be over soon . . . a week, yes, about a week . . . I can tell you that justice will be done . . ." And he meant it, but had no idea how justice was to be served when the judge— He cut off the thoughts, retreated into himself once again, even smiling at his wife, a not frequent event.

Loren handed him a list of his scheduled campaign appearances, looked closely at him. "Allen, we need to go over these."

Allen absently let the papers drop to the table, stood

270

up and walked around the room, running his hands through his thick hair, then returned to his chair, sitting there, saying nothing, a sick smile lingering. It was, Loren realized finally, impossible to reach him. He just wasn't there.

She patted his hand. "It's all right, Allen. I think you ought to go into the bedroom and rest. Maybe, after the trial ends, we'll take a few days in Palm Beach, a few days down there and you'll be a new person, ready to campaign."

"Yes," he said, "I can't remember ever being this tired." He smiled and walked off to the bedroom.

Loren, watching her once vigorous husband, decided he was far beyond the reach of the sort of leverage she had been able to apply before. It gave her no pleasure, she assured herself, but it was clear that he could not possibly be a viable candidate. This man could hardly be expected to rouse the voters. His speech at the Waldorf had been his last hurrah. Even if he got no worse, the press, always sensitive to these things, would pounce on his appearance and remoteness like the wolves they were. Loren would be like a sacrificial lamb, and she couldn't allow *that*.

She walked to the window and stared out at the shimmering New York skyline. Now once again she had to make the hard decision—just a few weeks before she had forced Allen to stay in the race. It shouldn't require nearly as much effort to get him to pull out. And it had to be done. Allen could not win, and his losing would destroy . . . everything.

There was no time to waste. She knew what she had to do.

Like Loren, Jon Klyk was a star attraction on the campaign circuit. As candidate for lieutenant governor he covered the upstate rallies while Loren handled New York City, presumably until her husband was free of his judicial duties to take over.

Klyk was resting in a Rochester hotel room before addressing a local party function when he received the phone call from Loren. On the one hand he should have hated her guts. She had, after all, blackmailed him out of the race, thereby accomplishing what no one else had the balls even to try. Yet after working together on the few occasions that their paths crossed on the campaign trail, he felt a surprising closeness developing between them. It was not just that their sexual encounter had been a ten. There was more to his feeling for her, although he hadn't as yet been able to pinpoint it. In any case, when she told him that she wanted to meet with him, he found himself eagerly looking forward to it. The next evening he was scheduled to address the party faithful at a dinner in Albany, while Loren had a meeting in Manhattan at about the same time. The forty-five minute flight was no problem. She arranged to take the early morning flight and return to the city in the late afternoon.

Klyk met her at the airport. The reporters were staked out at his hotel. "No story, fellas," Klyk told them. "Judge Sturdivant will be free and in action next week. We'll all have plenty to say then. Now we're just having agenda talks. See ya, folks," and nudged them gently but firmly out of the suite.

Alone now, Klyk eyed Loren and liked what he saw. She had lost a little weight, which was flattering. In spite of, or maybe because of her punishing schedule, she looked especially vibrant, alive. Yes, this woman was *alive*, all over.

He pulled her to him and kissed her.

She responded, then pulled away. "We've got some talking to do—first." She smiled and sat down. He lit her cigarette, which she had taken from a gold case. He had never seen her smoke before. Apparently the tensions of the campaign were getting even to her some, which showed that the Iron Lady was human after all. He liked that.

"I don't know whether I should talk to you," he said. "Our last serious talk cost me the nomination."

"You never had it to lose," Loren said. "But maybe our little talk now will get it for you."

He saw that she was dead serious, waited for the other shoe to drop.

"Jon, something has happened to Allen. Something serious. I'm not sure whether it's physical or psychological, and we don't have time to find out. To put it as directly as possible, I feel almost certain that he'll withdraw from the race, possibly within the week."

Klyk tried to mask the shock of her announcement. "Withdraw? With a little push from you?"

"Yes. I'll suggest it to him." Just as she had "suggested" he'd better stay in it or else his darling daughters would read all about him in the papers. He was obviously past that stage of vulnerability now. Sad to say, Allen Sturdivant, once a good man and formidable candidate, had become a mere husk of himself. Too bad, but when an investment went sour, you didn't stay with it. You sold. Her father had taught her that.

"Loren, I know what the word 'suggest' means to you," Jon was saying. "As a recent victim, I ought to. Now, I wonder what's going on in that beautiful head—"

"I do have something in mind," she said quickly. . . . "Is there a procedure for the party to designate you the candidate when Allen withdraws?"

"You mean *if*."

"No. I'm telling you his withdrawal is a certainty. Please answer my question, Jon."

273

"Well, yes," said Klyk, "there is such a procedure."

"Is it complicated?"

"No. It's relatively easy, could be done through a meeting of the state committee. But I'm not interested—"

"Why not?"

"Because I would be second choice, and that's not my style. I couldn't win. Beale would tear us apart. Allen's withdrawal and my integrity would always be questioned. It won't work."

"Will you let me try to convince you that it can?"

"Do I have a choice?"

"First off, I'll have all the medical substantiation I need about Allen's deteriorating heart condition. A man with a bad heart can't run for governor. The public will understand that, and sympathize with it."

"What heart condition?"

Loren simply looked at him, then shrugged.

Klyk shook his head. "You, pretty lady, never cease to amaze me."

"And as for your being able to carry the state," she went on, "it can be done, I assure you. I've been quoted a hundred and fifty thousand dollars for a thirty-second spot on Sixty Minutes. I have a tentative commitment for five consecutive thirty-second spots in primetime leaders. We'll match contributions from Mickey Goldman's political action committee dollar for dollar. We'll have telephone banks manned seven days a week, but only after intensive surveys on receptivity. We'll have all the street money we need to stroke party volunteers. I understand that they must be kept happy."

Klyk continued to watch her, transfixed, and in the process changing from nonbeliever to skeptic to almost convinced. Loren Sturdivant was a special breed—beautiful, brilliant and instinctively a street fighter. Clearly she had done her homework.

Her voice gained in intensity as she continued . . . "Besides the media we'll spend as much as we
have to on polling. I tell you now, the pollsters I hire will
give us the numbers we need for our purposes. The results
of our polls will shape the press coverage of the campaign.
The issues aren't that important. What *is* important is a
bandwagon effect that we need to create. You're already
something of a myth. We'll build on that to a point where
reality and myth will blend together and the public won't
know where one begins and the other leaves off. Not only
will I help you do it—we'll run together."

Klyk took hold of her arm. "Hold it. You're racing. Are
you saying what I think you're saying?"

"Yes, the ticket will be Klyk–Sturdivant. Just a reversal
of the names. I intend to ask Sweeney to have the party
designate me as your running mate."

Klyk shook his head, not because he thought it wouldn't
work but because, at that moment, he was beginning to feel
it *could* work. "Do you have any idea of how much this is
going to cost?"

"Yes, and I've allotted more than enough—fifteen million."

Klyk whistled. Fifteen million. No one had ever spent
that much on a gubernatorial election.

She looked at him quizzically. "Does the money bother
you, Jon? Don't let it. After all, it's my money."

"I just don't know . . ."

She stood and put her arms around him, then kissed him.
"Jon," she whispered into his neck, "we'll do it together.
We'll come at Beale and he won't know what hit him. I've
got the feel of this thing, of the way people react . . . the
feeling you've known for years. And I like it. We've got
to take advantage of this moment, Jon. We can be winners.
Both of us."

Her eyes were sparkling now, she kissed him again and

he broke away. "Listen, I think we better be honest with each other . . . I get the distinct feeling that I'm being used." He was half-smiling but he meant it.

"Used? I'm putting fifteen million on the line. You should be used like that all your life, Jon Klyk."

He had to admit it was a tantalizing prospect, and that while she would receive a secondary benefit, he would, after all, be the chief beneficiary. It just could work out, and not only on account of the unlimited funds. Her drive, combined with his long-time savvy and know-how, would be a tough combination to beat. They were both aggressive, ambitious and charismatic. Together they could do it . . . the blueprint for victory was there . . . "How do we convince Charlie to go along?"

"Does he really have a choice at this point? Allen doesn't pull out unless I say so. If he stays in, Beale wins. And I tell you, and I'll convince Charlie, Allen can't campaign."

"So your price for Allen pulling out is lieutenant governor."

"And you, my darling, get the nomination for governor. We'll see Sweeney together—and you'll recommend this. You'll endorse it."

"I will?"

"Yes, you will. Because you *know* it will work."

He sat down on the couch. "Fifteen million is a hell of a lot of money even if you say it fast. But even that much won't get the job done if it's not spent right. I won't go into this unless I have total control, and that means *I* say how the money is allotted."

"Agreed. The money will be deposited in any form and under any names you wish."

"And total control over everything else?"

"I am your obedient servant."

276

"Bullshit."

"I thank you for that."

And so it was done. He pulled her down to the couch.

"Have we time to seal this historic agreement?"

"I've got an hour," she answered almost coquettishly.

"An hour is plenty. I'm not as young as I used to be."

CHAPTER 30

MARC FELT HE had presented his defense—what there was of it—as well and as carefully as he knew how. But he also knew if he relied only on what he had Peter Jorgensen stood to be convicted of a crime he didn't commit. Too much hung on that damn first confession. He needed, at the least, something to convince the jury that Peter had been *forced* to make his first false statement. If he could show that it was Lawrence who was covering up the truth the idea would be planted in the jury's mind that somewhere under the carpet there was dirt. And, he reminded himself, he only needed to plant a permanent seed of doubt in only one juror's mind—

Dave Darby. Yes . . . McCarthy had not called Dave Darby. Not at the Huntely hearing, not at the trial. Why not? If McCarthy really believed Joe Lawrence's testimony wouldn't he have called Darby to corroborate and reinforce Lawrence's version of the events of that night? Didn't, then, McCarthy have his own doubts about Lawrence's testimony, and if so, he was too smart to gild a flawed lily.

All right, Marc told himself, he should have thought of it earlier, but like the man said, nobody's perfect, especially in the heat of a murder trial, and better late than never and so forth . . .

He had to call Darby to testify, but such a move also had its risks. It would break the cardinal rule of never calling a witness unless you know in advance what his testimony would be, but the desperate situation called for desperate measures.

He needed to get Darby into court before he could rehearse his testimony with Lawrence. The trial was to resume the following morning. He had to act now. He made his phone call.

"Twentieth precinct, Sergeant Paulson."

"Yes, I'm a friend of Officer Darby. I'd like to contact him. It's important."

Marc waited at the phone. He heard the sergeant call out, "Anybody know where Darby's workin'?" Then Paulson was back on the phone. "He's off today. He'll be doing an eight to four tomorrow."

"Thank you, sergeant."

God bless you, sergeant. Finally, at long last, a break. At eight o'clock in the morning Hammond could serve the subpoena while Darby was at rollcall before beginning his tour.

Marc knew police procedure. During the trial Lawrence had been signed out to McCarthy, which meant that during the trial he waited in the D.A.'s office. Although he had already testified, his presence was required for consultation and for possible rebuttal testimony which could not be given until the defense's case had concluded. Lawrence and Darby's separate assignments during the trial would not make it easy for them to communicate in the few hours between the service of the subpoena on Darby and his testimony.

Marc looked all over the courthouse for Judge Sturdivant,

but he could not be found to sign the subpoena. Apparently he had left for the day. However, any other judge sitting in the criminal term of the supreme court could sign it for him. Marc headed for Judge Victor Pierce's chambers.

"What's this for?" Pierce asked, looking at the paper Marc had asked him to sign.

"It's a judicial subpoena. Judge Sturdivant won't be available until tomorrow. It's important to the defense that this be served immediately."

Pierce, as with everything, would only act if he felt it were advantageous to him. "I would prefer to have Judge Sturdivant sign it."

Marc knew Pierce—and his weakness. "Judge, can I level with you?"

"Go ahead . . ."

"This testimony is crucial to my case. I'm asking that you not only sign it but authorize me to forward your direction to the police department that Darby specifically not discuss the case with a sworn witness who may be still called on rebuttal—his partner. And, if you permit me, I intend to make a full statement in open court about how, in the interests of justice, you took such steps to insure the integrity of the trial. My statement will no doubt be reported by the press . . ."

Pierce nodded and signed the subpoena. "And it *is* my order that he is not to discuss this case with his partner or with anyone else."

Marc thanked the judge, took the paper to the clerk and had the court seal affixed.

The next morning at the eight o'clock rollcall at the twentieth precinct Marc served the desk sergeant, who called Darby. By police department rules a police officer under subpoena, even if subpoenaed by the defense, was obliged to report to the D.A.'s office before testifying. Marc, aware

280

of that regulation, phoned McCarthy and put him on notice about Judge Pierce's specific orders.

McCarthy, of course, was furious. "What the hell right does Pierce have to interfere in this trial?"

"Brian, I'm sure you're not going to question his authority to issue an interest-of-justice order in the absence of the trial judge."

McCarthy knew he'd been had. The order was fair and he knew it. "All right, all right, I'll see to it that they don't talk to each other."

"And another thing, Brian . . . I know I don't have to say that the spirit of Pierce's order would be violated if *you* talked to Darby about Lawrence's testimony."

"I'll make believe I didn't hear that," McCarthy said as he slammed down the phone.

"Call your first witness, Mr. Hammond."

"The defense calls Officer David Darby."

Darby was sworn and waited uneasily for Marc Hammond's questions. He was upset and frustrated at not having been able to talk to Joe Lawrence. He had, in fact, forgotten the details—not what happened the night of the arrest—but what Lawrence and he had agreed had happened. That conversation between them had taken place almost a month earlier.

"Officer Darby, were you on duty on the midnight to eight A.M. shift on December twenty-fourth last?"

"Yes, sir."

"What was your assignment that evening?"

"R.M.P.—Radio Motor Patrol."

"Were you alone in the radio car?"

"No, I was with my partner, Officer Joseph Lawrence."

"And did you make an arrest during that tour?"

"Yes."

"Will you tell this Court and jury the circumstances of that arrest?"

"It was a little after we started the tour. We turned from Central Park West onto Sixty-third Street. Just after we turned we saw this individual—the defendant—fall from the top of a spiked fence."

"If I may interrupt, Officer—*you* saw him fall?"

"Oh, yes, I saw it."

"How did he land?"

"On his left foot."

"Did you take any action?"

"Yes, sir. My partner, Officer Lawrence, used the bull-horn and told the defendant not to move and that he was under arrest."

"Did he obey the order?"

Darby could not remember what he and Lawrence had agreed on. He began to sweat. *Better tell them he tried to escape*, he thought. *That at least was the truth . . .*

"No, sir, at least not at first. He got up and tried to run. But he hurt his foot so bad in that fall that he just collapsed."

Marc looked at the jury, meaningfully, he hoped, after Darby's answer, then went on: "Are you telling this jury that the defendant tried to run after you told him not to move?"

"He did, Counselor. And if he hadn't broken his foot, we would have had to chase him."

The courtroom rustled. Marc saw what every defense counsel looks for—signs of skepticism on the juror's faces.

"Did you and Officer Lawrence get out of the car?"

"Officer Lawrence did. I remained in the patrol car."

"And did your partner, Officer Lawrence, order the defendant to stand?"

"I think I just told you, counselor, that his ankle was busted. All he did was squirm on the ground."

"Nevertheless, there came a time when he was searched, a normal procedure after making an arrest?"

"Yes, he was."

"How was that done?"

"Lawrence spread-eagled him over the hood of the car."

"Please describe to the jury what you mean by spread-eagled."

"Legs spread apart, arms apart, resting on the hood."

"Well, how did he get into that position if he couldn't stand?"

"Officer Lawrence helped him off the ground."

"Are you sure of that?"

"Yes, sure."

"He didn't get up on his own power after Officer Lawrence asked him to?"

"No way. If he hadn't lifted him off that ground he would have froze to death. He just plain couldn't move."

Another ripple in the courtroom, followed by more facial reaction from the jurors. It seemed that they, at least, were beginning to remember the specifics of Joe Lawrence's testimony.

"May I have a moment, Your Honor?" Marc asked.

Sturdivant nodded.

Hammond perused his notes, but he wasn't reading them. This was just a time-out to think. He had a decision to make. Should he go any further? He had made his point. Lawrence had lied and the jury knew it. In this one, for now, the defense was ahead, and Marc was conscious of every lawyer's fear of the "one more question syndrome" that could undo all that had been accomplished. Darby certainly would not go on to admit that Peter gave his statement under painful duress. Darby had thought he was helping the prosecutor by emphasizing what he thought was a plus for them—Peter's attempted escape. Chances were that from here on his testimony would conform to Lawrence's. There was no point in going any further with it.

"I have no more questions of this witness," Marc finally said.

McCarthy stood up slowly and looked at Darby. Darby looked back, smiling and expecting friendly questions. McCarthy sat down. "I have no cross-examination of this witness, Your Honor."

Marc squeezed Peter's hand and said *sotto voce*, "This was our round, Peter."

But not entirely.

"Your Honor," Marc said, "I move to strike the testimony of the first statement given to Officer Lawrence at the time of his original arrest for burglary on the ground that it was involuntarily made."

"Motion denied."

"As an alternative I ask Your Honor to instruct the jury that if they find that the statement was obtained through duress or otherwise involuntarily acquired that they may disregard it entirely."

"Motion denied." The judge's voice was flat. His ruling seemed to have come by rote.

Denied? Even though Sturdivant had decided at the pre-trial hearing that the statement would not be suppressed and that the jury could hear it, it was considered basic that the defendant got two bites of the apple. After hearing the statement, the jury could still find as a matter of fact that it had been involuntarily obtained and if so could disregard it when considering the evidence.

"I will instruct the jury that they may only consider the truth or falsity of the statement," Sturdivant said, still in that peculiarly flat, toneless voice.

What neither Marc, nor McCarthy nor anyone else in that courtroom, perhaps including Sturdivant himself, could know was that Judge Allen Sturdivant could only with the greatest effort bring himself to concentrate on the trial and the defendant before him . . . he was too concentrated on another—himself—and on conducting *that* trial.

CHAPTER 31

THE NEXT DAY the intoning of Judge Sturdivant's denial of Marc's motion that, based on Joe Lawrence's testimony, Peter's first confession be suppressed as evidence was like a dire melody—a dirge?—in Marc's head as he resumed his seat in the courtroom. Well, perhaps he was exaggerating. He had, after all, brought out evidence in testimony that certainly indicated Peter's so-called confession after he was first arrested had been extracted from him while he was in pain. All right, it didn't prove he was innocent, or that the confession was phony, but it at least could indicate that to one or more jurors. He had to believe that . . . Still, the judge refusing to declare the testimony as inadmissible no doubt raised feelings in the jury that would tend to counter these doubts of guilt . . . Such as, if it was gotten under duress, why did the judge allow it? . . . It was the old pattern of the trial repeating itself—one step forward, a step backward. Maybe a step and a half.

He looked now at the jury, nothing but impassive faces, no longer betraying anything responsive to his case, as he had hoped he had seen earlier, for example, among the three jurors he'd selected out to Peter for special attention when testifying. He scanned the courtroom, as he occasionally had done earlier in the trial, looking for reactions, or taking a break, or both. This time it was a near-aimless gesture, something to do as he asked himself if he had raised enough reasonable doubt in any juror's mind to get Peter acquitted. He had done everything he could. The trial was nearly over. Had he done his job? . . .

As he looked about the courtroom Marc could not be aware of the intense young man sitting in the spectators' section, a young man who had been in court every day since the trial had begun. Nor, of course, could he have been aware of the young man's extreme agitation, which had been building for several days, but had now reached an all but uncontrollable peak. Indeed, Vito Mondo's upset had begun early in the trial, when he looked on the man whom he, like most of the spectators, presumed was guilty of killing in cold blood the lovely Andrea Blanchard that he remembered so vividly from that day several summers ago in the passport division of the U.S. Consulate in Milan. He realized that this was hardly a lawyerlike attitude, that he had learned that in American jurisprudence a man was innocent until proved guilty beyond the reasonable doubt of a jury of his peers. Still, books and theory collided in his viscera with his memories. And when he listened to those grisly details in the testimony about Andrea's body, listened to how she was strangled, he took it all as a personal affront . . . realizing as he did so that it was presumptuous of him, not to mention unprofessional. But as the trial went on, and the defense counsel, Mr. Hammond, began to bring out testimony that left the door open for doubts about this Peter Jorgensen's guilt, and what's more the possibility that another man might have done it, he realized things were not so simple as he might have wished. At first he had

287

resisted the notion of Andrea . . . who over the years had assumed the proportions of a fantasy lady, not of this world but perfect and beyond human weakness . . . being very much of this world, a woman who apparently had had numerous lovers. It was a cold slap in the face to a worshipper such as himself—almost like a betrayal. Well, from now on he would concentrate more on the trial, on the evidence. He would leave his mind open to the possibility that another, as Mr. Hammond had repeatedly tried to bring out, had done the deed—another lover who for reasons unknown wanted Andrea Blanchard, the not so divine Andrea Blanchard, dead. And as Vito, self-acknowledged tyro in the law, watched and listened to the proceeding and its players, he became increasingly aware of the judge, wondering at times at the judge's rulings, then dismissing his doubts as due to his lack of experience and knowledge. After all, he had not yet even begun to practice. He had come here to learn. How could he presume to question a distinguished American judge, a man, he had read in the papers, soon to be a candidate for the governorship of New York State.

But if Vito remonstrated with himself over his still virgin status in the law, he could not altogether ignore his own intelligence and talent for reasoning, both of which had been honed considerably during his stint at the Bologna law school. He still thought certain of the judge's rulings were a bit strange, and more . . . as he allowed himself to listen to and observe the judge, he began to have the feeling that he had seen the eminent Judge Allen Sturdivant somewhere before. At first he dismissed this thought, just as he had all notions of a man other than the defendant being guilty of Andrea Blanchard's murder. But it was a feeling that would not go away, would not be dismissed. Where, though? Vito Mondo did not, after all, move in the circles that a personage such as Judge Sturdivant did. When the lady who lived across the hall from Andrea Blanchard mentioned a man calling on her who was tall and large and built more solidly than the defendant, he had tried to dismiss this testimony from his mind, still wanting Peter Jorgensen to be found guilty. But now, as the trial seemed to be coming to an end, he recalled that testimony, or rather it surfaced, almost against his will. And as it did so he found himself staring at the judge, and thinking back to the Andrea Blanchard of that magical day in late July, and thinking too for the first time of the man who had been with her. True, he had not paid much attention to the man at the time . . . other than to envy him his good fortune of being with this American goddess, but he did see his face, and, God help him, as he sat now in this American courtroom, at the trial of the killer of his fantasy lady, it occurred to him that the judge . . . no, not possible . . . but *yes*, possible . . . the judge, the distinguished and important Judge Allen Sturdivant, was also the man he had seen with Andrea Blanchard that day in Milan. And if that were so, if the judge was one of the male friends of Andrea Blanchard that Mr. Hammond had called "the other man," could it not be . . . ?

Vito sat for several moments as though paralyzed in his seat. Court was about to adjourn for the day. The case against the defendant was still in the balance, thanks to the dedication and skill of the defense attorney Mr. Marc Hammond, but who knew how it would come out? If he, Vito Mondo, as a man of the law, a man who revered not only the law but in particular American jurisprudence, failed to come forward with possibly important evidence simply because he might be wrong or embarrassed, how could he live with himself? He shook his head, trying to summon up the courage of his convictions, then abruptly got up from the front-row spectator seat just behind the press area and hurried after Marc Hammond, who was disappearing into the corridor outside the courtroom.

"Mr. Hammond, I am very sorry to disturb you, but I

289

feel I must talk to you. My name is Vito Mondo, you do not know me but I believe it is important that we talk. Can you spare me, sir, a few minutes . . . ?"

Marc, wanting nothing more than to get away from the court and to see Randy, looked at this carefully dressed young man, resisted the impulse to tell him to get lost, and said impatiently, "What can I do for you Mr.—Mondo? I am rather busy and have an appointment—"

"Sir, it has to do with the case . . . I mean, with the judge and the murdered lady. I know it sounds strange to you but—"

"Who the hell *are* you?" Marc said not too graciously, but after Vito Mondo quickly told him that he was a graduate lawyer just arrived in the country before the trial and had been following the trial every day, Marc decided he had better listen to the man, even if he might turn out to be a total crank. He could hardly afford to turn away anything, anybody who might help his case, help make it stronger.

He took Vito to Sally's, a popular watering hole near the courthouse for trial lawyers and a judge or two to relax after a stressful day in court. After they were seated in a quiet corner, Marc looked closely at the man across from him. "All right, Mr.—I'm sorry, what was it again?"

"Mondo, Vito Mondo . . . Mr. Hammond . . ." And Vito then proceeded to fill Marc in on how he met Andrea Blanchard in Milan as a clerk in the passport division of the U.S. Consulate, on how she had affected him, and he told Marc about the well-built distinguished looking man who had been with her, and how he remembered envying him so much, and how . . . he hesitated here, forced himself to go on . . . how he had gradually during the trial begun to lose his early prejudice against the defendant, thanks to Marc's witnesses and handling of testimony, especially the idea that there was another man who might have had a good reason for wanting Andrea Blanchard dead, an important man who could have felt threatened by his association with her, and as he became freed-up from his longstanding idolatry of Andrea Blanchard, and prejudice against Marc's client, he had begun to watch closely all the players in the trial, including the judge . . . and as he did so began to have the strong feeling, and it would not go away, that he had seen the judge somewhere before, and now, at last, that the somewhere had been with Andrea Blanchard that day in Milan. . . . "I could be crazy, Mr. Hammond, I probably am, but the idea of the other man, my doubt about your client's guilt because of what you have brought out at the trial, all put together with Andrea Blanchard and the judge who I believe is going to be a candidate for your important position of governor of the State of New York . . . well, sir, I thought I had at least to tell you these things. Justice, I have been taught, is supposed to exclude nobody . . ."

Listening to this remarkable spiel, Marc found himself at first annoyed, then at once increasingly furious and excited. The idea of Judge Allen Sturdivant being involved in a crime . . . Sturdivant above all people . . . on the face of it seemed preposterous, indeed, crazy. Except what kind of prejudice in reverse was that? Who said judges, and other exalted types, were never guilty of crimes? What goddamn inhibiting conventional wisdom was that? And then his mind raced over the times when the judge's rulings seemed so strange to him, and how he had rationalized them for himself . . . never, of course, for a moment suspecting that the man sitting in judgment should perhaps be in the place of the man sweating at the defense table. But he still needed to check this more. There still was no *proof* . . . only a remarkable series of circumstances that *might* add up to . . .

"I'm sorry, Mr Hammond, you look upset. Perhaps I should not have bothered you with this story, I made a mistake—"

291

"No . . . no, you didn't, you were right to tell me this. I thank you. Look, order yourself another drink, tell the bartender it's on me, and thank you . . ."

He hurried out of Sally's, actually ran to his office, where he pulled out the bulging case file. One swatch of testimony including comment from Judge Sturdivant particularly needed to be checked. It had surfaced in his mind as Vito Mondo gave his remarkable recital, which in turn sparked remembrances of the times during the trial when he had been especially startled or surprised by the judge's words. It took him too long in his impatience to find the testimony, but at last there it was, in his questioning of Helen Jorgensen.

By Mr. Hammond:

Q: "You have testified that you saw a turned-over ashtray on the floor beside the body of the deceased. That ashtray would normally have been on the cocktail table near the couch, is that correct?"

A: "Yes . . ."

Q: "Was there anything else that belonged on the cocktail table that you saw on the floor?"

A: "No, not that I remember."

Q: "Where was the telephone, the one you used to call nine-one-one?"

A: "It was on the end table—"

Q: "Are you sure it wasn't on the floor beside the body?"

Mr. McCarthy: "Objection. This has been asked and answered."

The Court: "Sustained. The witness has testified that the only object she saw on the floor was the whisky glass—"

Mr. Hammond: "Maybe I heard her incorrectly, Your Honor. I thought she said ashtray."

The Court: "I stand corrected, Mr. Hammond. I was the one who misheard. Please continue."

The witness: "Wait a minute. I think there was a whisky glass on the floor. I didn't remember until now. I'm sorry."

Mr. Hammond: "Are you saying that His Honor's mistaken reference to a whisky glass caused you to remember it?" . . .

Marc reread it, reread it again, before letting the transcript fall from his fingers to the desk. "Mistaken reference," he had said. Like hell, "mistaken." Without knowing it he had been defense counsel for more than Peter Jorgensen. At that moment, as he had privately at other times in his rationalizations, he was unwittingly explaining, defending the *judge* . . . because who else could have known about that whisky glass except somebody who was *there*. . . . His mind had rejected even the possibility that the other man could have been the judge. It still did, with the evidence staring him in the face. It was mind boggling, and yet it fitted with so much that had seemed to make little sense earlier. Yes, God help him, and Judge Allen Sturdivant, it *fitted*. And Vito Mondo's story put the lock on it.

He was still shaking his head in disbelief at what he now had to believe, and reconstructed for himself some of what must have happened that night . . . After Sturdivant had killed Andrea Blanchard he no doubt inventoried all the objects in the room, wiped his prints off everything he had touched then made his way down the stairs before Peter could see him clearly enough to identify him. He had been plain lucky in that last . . .

But now what? He had evidence, but no proof. None at all. And the evidence was supposition, speculation. Besides, the notion of a trial lawyer walking into a judge's chambers and accusing him of murder was about as crazy as anything ever dreamed up by the hottest hotshot lawyer in a courtroom. And he was not, he hoped, a hotshot lawyer. What he was was a lawyer with the most godawful dilemma imaginable, and he had to decide what to do about it between now and the next morning before court convened.

He phoned Randy, told her he was sorry but that the trial had taken an unexpected turn, that he'd be lousy company.

"I've just got to sleep on this thing, honey."

"I understand," she said. "But while you're sleeping on it, can't a girl get in the act? So to speak?"

"Okay, you've got yourself a deal. I hope you don't regret it."

She didn't.

By nine A.M. the next morning Marc had made up his mind. He really never had any option, he decided, as he nodded to the court officer sitting behind the desk in the reception area and said he wanted to see the judge. Marc knew Sturdivant would be in . . . it was common knowledge around the courthouse that he was an early bird among the judges, especially during a trial. The officer dialed the judge's extension, told his law secretary, Tony Fortuna, that Mr. Hammond was waiting to see him. Minutes passed, then Fortuna appeared and told Marc that the judge did not want to see him *ex parte* but that if he contacted Brian McCarthy the judge would see both in the robing room before the trial resumed.

Marc led Fortuna aside, spoke quietly to be sure he was not overheard. "Tony, I get his point, but please tell the judge that we'll be discussing a very personal matter. If necessary I'll fill in McCarthy after our conversation."

Fortuna shrugged. "I'll tell him but I don't promise anything."

Fortuna walked down the hall and into the chambers. Five minutes later the court officer at the desk picked up the phone.

"Yes, sir," he said, "I'll send him right in. The judge will see you now, Mr. Hammond."

As Marc was escorted by Fortuna into the judge's spacious outer office and then into the inner sanctum, he felt like a condemned man about to pull the switch on himself. The judge sat behind his desk, his face gray, eyes puffed. During the trial both Marc and McCarthy had noticed the change in the judge's appearance, and had attributed it to the pressure of his impending candidacy compounded by the normal tensions generated by a highly publicized murder trial. Now Marc knew better.

"Yes, Marc?" A faint smile seemed to play on the judge's mouth, and for the moment Marc went blank, unable to think of anything except that this was the first time the judge had ever called him by his first name. The brief silence that followed seemed a physical thing between them.

"Judge, I want to thank you for seeing me this way. I've got something to say, I have to say it on behalf of my client. I realize that you—"

The judge seemed almost visibly to relax, which surprised Marc. "Come on, Marc, let's get on with it. What's on your mind . . . ?"

"Well, sir . . ." And Marc proceeded to make what he realized was like a summary to a jury, except this one was halting, embarrassed, the worst delivery he'd ever made. But he forced himself on, feeling at times almost foolish, until he reminded himself that an innocent man was his client, and a guilty one was sitting there in front of him. A judge. A *judge*. When he had finished, linking the relationship with Andrea Blanchard described by Vito Mondo with the inadvertent comment about the whisky glass, and with the at times peculiar rulings, he told the judge that he realized none of this was proof, that he understood that it would be his word and a wet-behind-the-ears Italian law school graduate against the eminent jurist Allen Sturdivant, but the judge stopped him with an impatient wave of the hand. This is it, he thought, Good-by Marc Hammond, promising attorney.

"Mr. Hammond"—no more Marc—"I've heard enough.

I will see you in court. Please close the door on your way out."

Allen Sturdivant leaned back in his chair, closed his eyes. Thanks to Marc Hammond . . . peculiar notion, giving thanks to the man who was the instrument of his destruction . . . except of course the real instrument was himself . . . More accurately, the feeling that came over him now was, if not gratitude toward Hammond, he wasn't that perverse, but a profound sense of relief, the relief that he had been looking for during that ridiculous abortive rendezvous with the prostitute, the relief that had been there during the best moments with Andrea . . . No question, it was Hammond's handling of the case, his guts in confronting him just now when he knew perfectly well that it could have been the end of his career, that was helping to push him to what he'd been moving toward as more and more evidence came out and as his own behavior in reaction to Hammond's conduct of the defense led him further and further to the edge, to judging himself rather than Peter Jorgensen. Hammond, of course, couldn't have known this . . . he hadn't realized it himself during most of the trial, but it was true—the trial he had conducted parallel with the official one was the trial of the judge. And the judge now stood convicted. All that was left was for the judge to pronounce sentence.

He got up and adjusted his robes, proceeded out of his chambers into the hall and the brief walk to the courtroom entrance. As he did so he thought of how he'd once tried to tell himself that there were two Allen Sturdivants, or rather only one, the good and decent man that he'd always thought he was, or at least tried to be . . . that this aberration who shared his skin could not take over his better self. Well, that mind game was no longer possible. He was and always had been the man who had strangled to death

296

another human being, indeed, a human being that at one time he had cared deeply about. No, he was not a split-personality . . . he was what he was, and for all the good in him, what he was was a man who had committed murder, and for reasons of ambition and frustration. Was this the man to be governor one day, maybe even president? If Andrea's death had served any purpose, at least it had kept that prospect from ever becoming a reality. And don't, he quickly instructed himself, start feeling too noble about that . . .

"Hear ye, hear ye, hear ye. All those who have business before this court give your attention and ye shall be heard. The Honorable Allen Sturdivant, Justice of the Supreme Court presiding. Please be seated and maintain silence."

The court clerk spoke his litany in loud deep tones, and although he enjoyed his moment in the sun he was surprised at the opportunity, since few judges still requested that formality. It was the first time Judge Sturdivant had requested it. He would soon learn why, if not soon get over the shock of it.

The courtroom was still. Marc waited for the blade to fall. He could not look at the judge, or at Peter.

"I want to make a statement," the judge was saying, in a firm voice. "This trial has been a fraud perpetrated by myself. I am responsible for the death of Andrea Blanchard. Details will be released in a separate written statement, which will be turned over to the district attorney. I will wait in my chambers to surrender to his office. I now dismiss the indictment of Peter Jorgensen, which is my last official act as a justice of the supreme court."

He then quickly got up and left the courtroom, and in his wake a stunned courtroom remained in their seats for several moments, not quite believing what they had just heard, surely not able to take it in. Brian McCarthy could only

297

shake his head in disbelief. Marc, instead of feeling a huge relief, felt he himself had colluded in some sort of killing. Which, of course, in a way he had. Peter Jorgensen was numb, not moving. It would be many hours before he could accept that he was free and out of this awful nightmare, and much longer to understand that the *judge* was the condemned man.

CHAPTER 32

THE CELL DOOR clanged shut behind him. Sturdivant sat on his cot, staring at the wall. He was placed in protective custody, and in his case that order of protection was scrupulously obeyed, the Commissioner of Correction himself having directed that around-the-clock personnel be assigned to watch him.

They would have preferred to avoid this headache, but Sturdivant wasn't making it easy for them. Marc Hammond had visited him the first day he was placed in detention at Rikers, and while he was friendly he refused to allow Marc to make an application for bail, which would have been granted.

"Judge," Marc had said, "this just does *not* make sense."

"Perhaps not," Sturdivant said, "except to me. I want no bail—I want no freedom—I want the punishment I deserve."

And as the days passed in C-74, Sturdivant fought the protective custody order and threatened the Commissioner with a Federal civil rights suit if they persisted in segregating him from the rest of the prison population. They tried to reason with him, pointing out the obvious dangers to an ex-judge whose job it was to send criminals there. He refused to listen, and finally they threw up their hands. After he signed a form stipulating that he had refused the City's protection and releasing the Correction Department from all liability, he was moved to the dorm, mixed in with the general population. The special protection detail was called off, and Sturdivant was on his own, mingling with the other inmates at meal time and at work periods. Nevertheless, over his continued objection, he was placed in a single cell in C-74. They were not about to invite trouble by assigning him a cot on the dorm floor.

His exposure to the other inmates gave him adequate opportunity to pick up the prison grapevine. In less than forty-eight hours in C-74 Sturdivant knew that Correction Officer Kearney was on the take, that he and Big Bruno were partners in their own corrupt network within the walls of the Quad, and that through that alliance anything was possible—drugs, forcible sex, extortion—all commodities that could be purchased through the combined influence of Bruno and Kearney. The bad apples in the Correction Department might be the exception, but because of the way the Quad was set up it took only one to spoil the barrel. The rip-off of Peter Jorgensen with the fake suicide pills was only one example of how Kearney and Bruno worked together, and how freely Bruno could maneuver with Kearney's protection.

Big Bruno, head honcho and boss of the prison population in the Quad, had been sentenced by Judge Sturdivant to state's prison when he was sixteen years of age. Sturdivant remembered Bruno. Normally a first-offender, especially a youth, would not receive the four years he had given him. But this was an especially vicious act . . . Bruno had

300

knocked on the door of an apartment and when the frail eighty-year-old woman opened the door he was not satisfied with terrorizing her by tying her to a chair and ransacking the place and taking her pitifully few possessions. No, just for kicks he also pushed her over and, by her testimony, laughed while she struggled on the floor. She suffered cracked ribs, a deep concussion and a broken pelvis, and it was a medical miracle that she had survived.

Sturdivant remembered Bruno to be an arrogant, vicious, altogether unrepentant kid. Nonetheless, the parole board, in its wisdom, let him out after eighteen months, a lapse of judgment that soon paid off when eight months after he was released, Bruno was arrested for assault. His lawyer had plea-bargained to a year and, once out, Bruno again was convicted, this time on a robbery charge, and sentenced to imprisonment in Rikers, a three-time loser.

Bruno seemed to feed off of his own cruelty. He was proud of his status as the big bad dude who took on the system, and his brutality blossomed in the prison environment. Six-feet-three, 230 pounds, he was an awesome and frightening figure. No one who wanted to go on living would even think of reporting him to an official of the Correction Department—not even anonymously. The inmates soon discovered that anonymous informants didn't remain anonymous very long.

Within an hour after Sturdivant was released to the general prison population, Bruno spread the word that he was going to take care of the judge who had sentenced him. According to Bruno's code, it would have been a blow to his prestige not to take vengeance on the man who had sentenced him to four years for his first offense. Indeed, it violated Bruno's sensitivities that a young lad such as himself who had never been arrested before—more to the point had not been caught—should receive any sentence stiffer than probation.

Sturdivant, of course, heard about the threats, and felt

remarkably calm . . . matters were proceeding as planned. Instead of avoiding Bruno, he sought him out.

It was a week later, it had been raining all day. Tempers got especially raw on such days when there was no chance to exercise outdoors. Men felt even more penned up. When two of the inmates went to take showers before the designated time, they knew they were risking special punishment and would lose some privileges but didn't give a damn. When they approached the shower area, they weren't too surprised to hear one of the showers running . . . it seemed some of the other inmates had the same idea. They felt differently when they got into the shower area and spotted the colored water gurgling down the drain. The color was red. It was coming from the nude body of the late Judge Allen Sturdivant, crumpled in a fetal position beneath the shower, his throat cut, his mouth gagged, hands and feet securely tied.

Outstanding Bestsellers!